Not My Time

Not My Time

Riverpeak Heroes Book 01

Jessica Salina

4 Horsemen
Publications, Inc.

Not My Time
Copyright © 2023 Jessica Salina. All rights reserved.

4 Horsemen
Publications, Inc.

4 Horsemen Publications, Inc.
1497 Main St. Suite 169
Dunedin, FL 34698
4horsemenpublications.com
info@4horsemenpublications.com

Cover by J. Kotick
Typeset by S. Wilder
Editor Blair Parke

All rights to the work within are reserved to the author and publisher. No part of this publication may be reproduced, stored in a retrieval system, or transmitted in any form or by any means, electronic, mechanical, photocopying, recording, scanning, or otherwise, except as permitted under Section 107 or 108 of the 1976 International Copyright Act, without prior written permission except in brief quotations embodied in critical articles and reviews. Please contact either the Publisher or Author to gain permission.

This is a work of fiction. All characters, organizations, and events portrayed in this novel are either products of the author's imagination or are used fictitiously.

Library of Congress Control Number: 2022945571

Print ISBN: 979-8-8232-0051-6
Hardcover ISBN: 978-1-64450-723-0
Audio ISBN: 979-8-8232-0049-3
EBook ISBN: 979-8-8232-0050-9

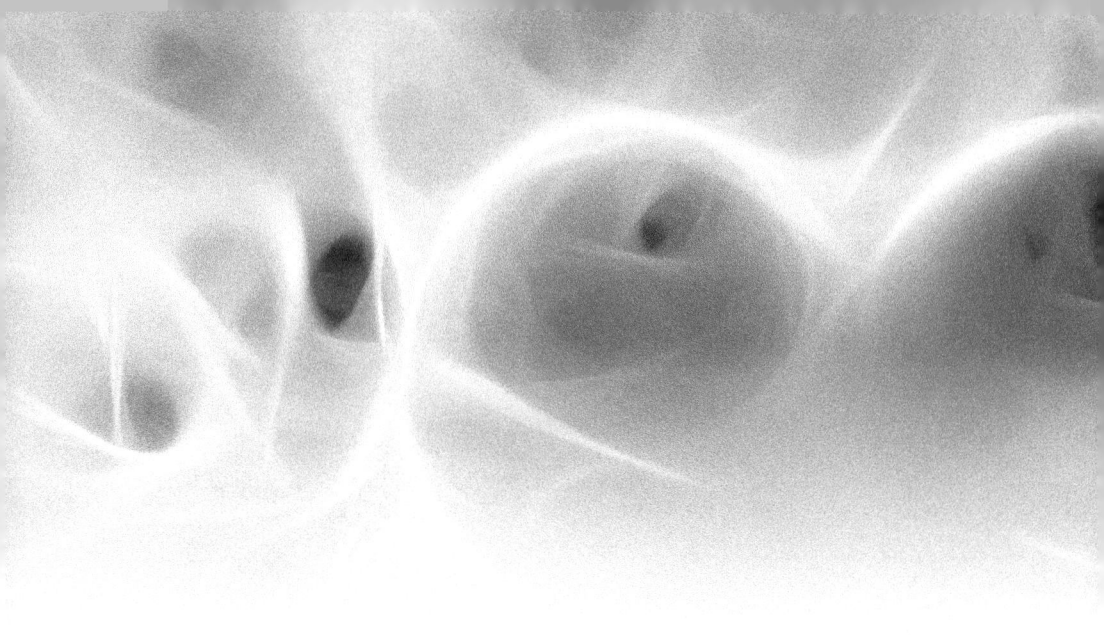

DEDICATION

To my husband, Anthony, who has acted as both my biggest cheerleader and fight scene coordinator.
And to my best friend, Michele, for all of your support and helping me find Kane Kelly lookalikes on TikTok.

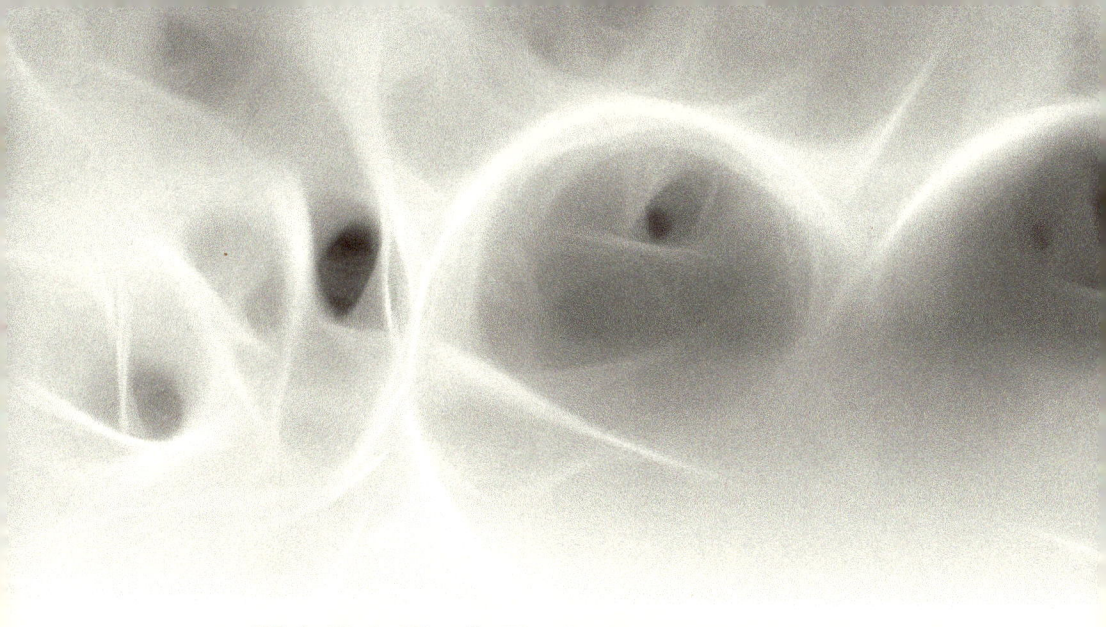

TABLE OF CONTENTS

Chapter One 1
Chapter Two 15
Chapter Three 25
Chapter Four 33
Chapter Five 43
Chapter Six 54
Chapter Seven 66
Chapter Eight 75
Chapter Nine 87
Chapter Ten 96
Chapter Eleven 107
Chapter Twelve 119
Chapter Thirteen 131
Chapter Fourteen 143
Chapter Fifteen 152
Chapter Sixteen 164
Chapter Seventeen 175

Chapter Eighteen 187
Chapter Nineteen 198
Chapter Twenty 209

Book Club Questions 221
Author Bio 223

CHAPTER ONE

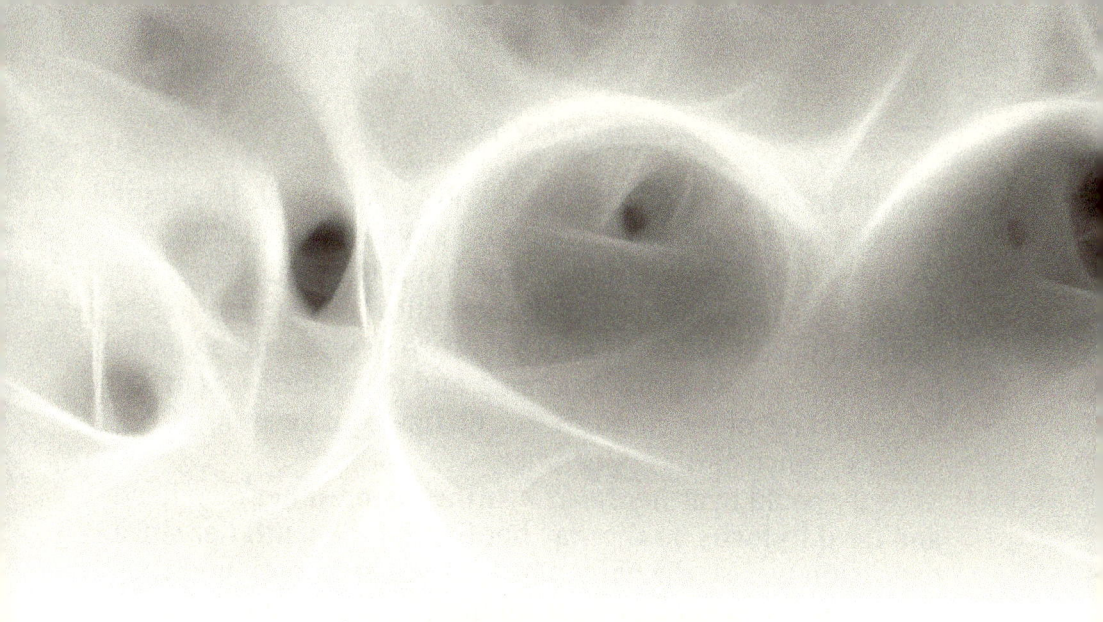

Rory Miller all but jumped when she heard a whistle from the shadows. Her breath quickened as she glanced around campus, looking for the source of the sound. In the dark, it was hard to tell. Some of the streetlights that normally illuminated the sidewalk were out, making it harder than usual to see on their way back to her friend Naomi's dorm from the library. Her friend Naomi, who was with Rory, reached for the keys in her purse, in case she'd need the pink tube of pepper spray attached to them.

A male voice called, "Haven't seen you in a while."

Rory's anxiety hadn't been for nothing, despite the university police's claim that she was just being overdramatic about her classmate-turned-stalker. Her stomach sank further and further into her body, along with any courage she might have had left. She wanted to find those officers and scream, "I told you so!" in their faces, but it was too late now.

"Why haven't you been showing up to class? I've been looking forward to seeing you, you know," the familiar voice said.

The answer to that question was that their professor let Rory finish the course online, but Daniel didn't need to know that. In fact, their professor was the only person, other than

NOT MY TIME

Naomi and her friends, who took Rory seriously. The light Daniel now stood beneath cast a long shadow, making his already towering stature that much more intimidating. His baggy T-shirt made his lean frame billow out, appearing as though he were wider. His casual attire helped him blend in as he followed her around campus, and if anything was in the large pockets of his cargo shorts, no one could ever tell from a quick glance of his appearance.

Rory could hear her heart beating faster in her own head and tried to focus on the way her feet felt beneath her since her vision was so dizzying. She glanced at Naomi, and they both took steps back away from him, inch by inch, in hopes of not alerting him. Naomi nodded at her, her silent way of saying they needed to be ready to run and stick together. Being alone was dangerous for both of them right now, but especially for Rory.

With her hand still in her purse, Naomi opened her phone's voice recording app she kept handy for her journalism classes. She made sure it was on and then held onto Rory's hand to comfort her friend.

Before they could think of a response, another voice—gruff and muffled—rang through the night. It almost sounded electronic, as if a modifier was changing the man's voice. "Do you know him, miss?"

Rory looked at the sound of the new person. A man wearing black and dark blue came from what seemed like nowhere. A mask covered his entire face, except for his eyes, and a scarf and cowl that wrapped around him a few times covered his mouth, neck, and the top of his head. His shoulders were narrower than Daniel's, and the stranger was significantly less stocky, so Rory wasn't sure what to think just yet of any potential odds.

"Unfortunately," Rory answered. She wasn't sure if she should be afraid of the presence of this new man, but something in her gut told her he was there to help them. She hoped she was right about the newcomer. Her gut was right about Daniel following her around campus, trying to find her alone

CHAPTER ONE

late at night after their classes wrapped, and sending cryptic text messages hinting at her location.

"Aw, Rory, don't be like that," Daniel said. He took a few slow steps toward her, and his pasty skin seemed to shine beneath the streetlight he was now under, almost making him glow. "I don't know why you don't talk to me."

"Don't even fucking think about it, pal," the mystery man said, as he held a hand up. Without looking away from him, the man asked, "Rory, was it? Is he bothering you?"

Rory nodded. She felt a lump in her throat where she once felt her heartbeat, but she wasn't entirely convinced she was even breathing at that point. She wanted to speak, but her voice was frozen in fear.

"He's been stalking her since the start of the semester," Naomi said. She held her head up high, making the two braids in her black hair look even longer. "Campus police haven't exactly been helpful. His name is Daniel Sanders."

"Oh, shut up," Daniel retorted, wasting no time defending himself. "I am not stalking her. That's just being extreme."

The guy in the mask scoffed. "Then what the hell do you call this?"

"Can't a guy get out there and pursue a woman? I thought chicks liked that," Daniel said.

"Oh my God, ew," Naomi reflexively said under her breath. Rory had been too stunned to say anything at all, feeling quite like a deer in the headlights. She glanced around, hoping someone else might show up to intervene and scare Daniel away—a teacher, an administrator, anyone who might show some authority. The man in the mask wasn't scaring him; she wondered if anything would.

"Choose your next words wisely," the masked man replied. "Or else we'll have a problem."

Daniel rolled his eyes and reached for the large side pocket of his cargo shorts. Before he could grab whatever was in there, the man in the mask was on him in a second. Rory jumped at the sudden movement. Naomi stayed grounded and gripped her hand tighter. Suddenly, the man in black and blue had Daniel pinned down and unable to move. Daniel reached for his pocket again once he was on the ground, but the other man beat him to it as he pulled out a handgun.

"What are you doing with a gun, buddy?"

The masked figure whacked Daniel across the face with the handgun, hard enough to knock him out. Naomi held her friend close to her side after the sound of the man hitting Daniel made her jump again, but the fight was over before it even began.

The masked man kneeled over Daniel and examined him for a moment to make sure that he was, in fact, unconscious. Once he determined Daniel was out and would be for a while, he stood, taking the gun with him. He kicked Daniel again for good measure, this time in the shoulder, in a surprisingly casual way.

The stranger held his hands up as he slowly approached the women so they could see where the gun was with his finger away from the trigger. Naomi noticed that Rory's trembling had slowed down, but Rory's breathing was still labored and her eyes were wider than Naomi had ever seen.

When the masked man was closer to them, he nodded his head toward the hand holding the gun. "I'm going to take this apart now, okay? I promise I won't hurt you. No funny business."

Rory nodded. He gradually lowered his hands and then detached the slide from the top of the gun and tossed it. The slide clattered across the ground until it landed right at Rory's feet. She stared at it for a moment and then looked up at the masked man, trying to say something but bursting into sobs instead. Naomi took a hold of the slide as Rory's body caved in on itself.

"Hey, hey," the man whispered at Rory's crying. His voice was still gruff and hard to make out, but his tone was gentler. He reached for his cowl and tore off a small piece of fabric. "I, uh, don't have any tissues or a handkerchief or anything. So, I hope this will work."

Rory smiled at him as she cried, attempting to say her thanks and hoped that it would be a sufficient means of

CHAPTER ONE

communication to him. She accepted the second offering from him and wiped her face with the tattered fabric.

"That pathetic asshole won't bother you anymore," the man said. "I'll personally see to it. Okay?"

Through her tears, Rory asked, "Who are you?"

"I don't have a name. But some people call me Hematite."

The name was familiar; she had heard of him on the news, but she wasn't sure if he really existed. Hematite was as good as a local cryptid, the local vigilante superhero that no one ever got a good look at but everyone seemed to have a story about. Rory's breathing had been heavy and labored; however, she finally found her voice again. But before she could even say thank you, he was gone without a trace.

While Naomi called the police on her cell phone, Rory just stared at the spot where Hematite had been standing. She glanced around, trying to see where he hid in the shadows or how he disappeared like lightning, but there was no trace of her savior.

Rory pulled her car into park and gasped as she realized where she was. She looked around and saw that she reached her destination, a parking lot of the small plaza in Denver where the rooftops only partially blocked her view of the Rocky Mountains. She wondered how long she had been lost in her thoughts. The flashback from eight years ago felt as real as the car she was sitting in; she guessed driving out here for her first therapy appointment triggered it. She cursed to herself as she unbuckled her seatbelt and hoped she hadn't run a red light without realizing it.

The snowfall was delicate, like it wasn't in any rush to leave the skies. It left thick flakes on her windshield that were piling up now that the wiper was turned off. She took a deep breath, hesitant to abandon the warmth of her car to venture into the therapist's office. She reached for her scarf in the passenger seat and put it back on to brace herself, both emotionally and physically, for heading out into the cold for a moment and into her first therapy appointment. Despite the light snow, the sky was still clear enough to get a decent view of the white-tipped mountains and rolling pines. Even though Rory preferred the summer, she always loved the way they looked like larger-than-life paintings in the winter, especially as the afternoon sun sparkled across the snow.

At her appointment, Rory wasn't sure where to begin once she sat on the sofa in the therapist's office. As she looked around, she felt uncomfortable trying to gauge the environment and ground herself. She reminded herself that she drove here all the way from Riverpeak, about a ninety-minute drive, and only had an hour with Dr. Marissa Thornton. As nervous as she was, she hated the thought of wasting precious time.

Dr. Thornton was a straight-haired brunette with a warm smile. Tattoos covered both of her arms, and her white dress shirt failed to hide them; the designs were still visible through the sheer sleeves. The lack of frills or stiffness helped Rory feel more at ease. Her office was pleasantly warm with plenty of plants and books on a mahogany shelf, but Rory's overall discomfort came from within.

"So, let's dive right into it. What brings you in today?" Dr. Thornton asked. The steam from her fresh mug of coffee billowed over her face in wisps as she drank, but Rory found the aroma soothing.

"I've been putting off therapy for a while now," Rory confessed. "At first, I thought I was managing just fine. But after a few years, my friends and I have noticed I've been getting progressively more paranoid and nervous."

Rory knew that her feelings never went away but had just been buried. However, she wasn't sure how to articulate that in a way that made sense. Her eyes darted over to glance out the window for a second until she snapped her gaze back to the office and tried to put what she was feeling into words.

"Sorry, I'm new to this," Rory said. "This is surprisingly difficult for me."

"It's okay," Dr. Thornton said. "It can be nerve-wracking at first."

CHAPTER ONE

Rory swallowed a lump in her throat. She cracked her knuckles a few times as she nodded.

"Why don't you tell me how you've been feeling to start?"

Rory liked that; having to verbalize what happened to her felt like too much right off the bat.

"Have you been sleeping?"

"I couldn't tell you the last time I got a full night's sleep," Rory said with a nervous laugh. "I'm pretty much fine during the day; it helps that I keep busy. But once I'm alone at night and lay down to sleep, the anxiety or flashbacks come rolling in. I take melatonin to force myself along, or I'll play a game on my phone to keep myself distracted until I pass out, but it still sucks. I told myself that this year would be my year for healing."

"What does that mean?" Dr. Thornton asked. There was no judgment in her voice.

Rory took a second to think about it. "I... I guess I've been hiding from what happened in the past instead of allowing myself to feel it." She rolled her shoulders back. "I guess I'm finally ready to feel normal again."

"Are you experiencing any other symptoms?" So far, Dr. Thornton's style seemed straightforward as she probed Rory for more information. Rory appreciated that.

"I'm very jumpy. Can't even stand to be jump-scared on Halloween," Rory said. "If I watch a horror movie with friends, I have to be cuddled up to one of them and have a blanket handy for comfort. But we avoid those."

Dr. Thornton wrote something down on the notepad resting on her lap. "Sounds like your fight-or-flight is always turned on."

"Oh yeah. A few months ago, I started boxing classes to feel powerful again. I was, uh, stalked in college," Rory said. "Probably should have started with that so this made more sense. I don't think I ever got over it."

"I'm sorry to hear that happened to you," Dr. Thornton said. Rory could tell from the softness in her voice that she meant it.

"Thanks, I guess." Rory shrugged. "You know, I didn't even know the guy," she recalled. "Some random dude from one of my Gen Ed classes. He was obsessed with me, and I couldn't even say why."

The therapist frowned. "That sounds like cause for post-traumatic stress disorder."

"That's sort of what I suspected."

"Does he still live in Denver?"

"No, no. He's long gone," Rory said. She brushed some of her tight, highlighted curls back with her fingers to push them out of her face. "He, uh, got arrested. He followed me and my friend Naomi home one night. Had a gun on him and everything." Rory paused and took a deep breath. Even just recalling the memory had her feeling tense and her heart rate increasing.

"You're okay," Dr. Thornton reminded her.

"Have you heard of Hematite?" Rory asked as she felt some warmth return to her face.

"The vigilante?"

"Yeah."

"I have. He's been working in the Denver area for a long time now, hasn't he?"

Rory nodded. "He saved me. Hard to believe, I know. I tried getting help before it escalated to that point, but the cops on campus didn't take me seriously." Rory exhaled after recalling what happened to Dr. Thornton. Her knee was bouncing subconsciously. "I wish I could thank him, but I don't think that's going to happen, given there's no way of knowing who he is. So now we're here."

"Maybe try writing a letter to him, even if he never sees it. It can even be a simple message in your phone's notes app or a Google doc. That may help you find some closure."

"I don't even know what I'd say. That's the funny part," Rory admitted. "Like, I feel like there's so much I'd want to tell him. But if I ever came face to face, I'd fall flat."

"Writing your feelings down may help you start," Dr. Thornton said. "Start small. Maybe a feelings journal or one of those daily mood log apps you can get for your phone."

Rory nodded again. "Not a bad idea."

CHAPTER ONE

Dr. Thornton then asked, "Where was your family during all this?"

"They, uh... they physically were here but weren't emotionally. Some of my friends were there for me. My friend Naomi, the one who was with me? She and her now-fiancé, Brad, were super helpful. So was my friend Kane. He and Naomi pretty much took turns that whole year making sure I was never alone."

Rory smiled at the memory of waking up the following morning to Kane in her dorm room. Naomi had let him in after Rory had gone to sleep, so Kane was sitting in a chair by her bedside. Before Naomi woke up, he must have fallen asleep, as she found him slumped over with his head resting on Naomi's knee.

However, as Rory continued answering Dr. Thornton's questions, her smile turned back into a frown. "But my family sort of suggested to me it was my fault for attracting the attention," she said. "Which is weird because, like I said, I don't even know why this guy picked me of all people. They helped me through the motions, but part of why they moved to Riverpeak when I was born was because it's safe. Maybe they were just too shocked to process it. I dunno."

Rory was certain that Riverpeak wasn't even on the maps, but after her college experience in the city, she didn't mind returning to her roots. Everyone from Riverpeak somehow stayed in Riverpeak. Even if they left for university, the residents always found their way back to the tiny mountain town. The familiarity of a small town that no one had ever heard of was comforting to Rory and helped her feel secure in times of distress. Rather than feeling stuck, she felt at home there.

"There are crappy people everywhere; it's not your fault," Dr. Thornton said. "Do you believe me when I say that?"

Rory didn't have an answer.

Dr. Thornton's words rang through Rory's head with each hit of the punching bag that afternoon. She couldn't hear her boxing gloves making an impact, but the meeting with her new therapist replayed with every punch or jab.

Rory made a mental note to never go to boxing class after therapy again. Now that she had a name for her feelings, and some first steps to proper healing, she thought she might burst because coming to grips with her emotions was too much for her to handle.

Rory kept asking herself if she believed it when Dr. Thornton told her she was safe and what happened to her wasn't her fault. However, at that moment, she didn't have an answer, and as much as she wished it would come with each hit of the bag, it never did.

She hoped her workout would have cleared her mind, as it often did, but her head still felt like it was spinning. She did nothing all those years ago to warrant what happened to her with Daniel, but Rory still had those doubts that plagued her from time to time. Every time she hit the punching bag that day, she imagined it was Daniel. Rory remembered the tension in her body that night as she inevitably waited for something to happen and remembered the way her jaw felt stuck when he whistled at her from the darkness. Had it not been for Hematite, she didn't know what might have happened—and she was too frightened to think about what that alternate reality might have looked like. She didn't snap out of it until the class switched to some ab workouts to end the class, where she was forced to focus on nothing but keeping herself steady during long planks.

Rory put some music on once she returned to her single-family home. She lived in a modest one-bedroom in the suburbs of their small town, not much larger than a studio. Rory didn't want to be alone with her thoughts anymore, so whipping up dinner would serve as a pleasant distraction. Her mind usually wandered, often in directions she didn't like for it to go, so at least she could focus on her meal and the lyrics of the song playing. Background noise meant she wasn't alone with her thoughts; it didn't matter what it was to her, so long as it kept her mind occupied.

CHAPTER ONE

When she stared at herself in the mirror as she brushed her teeth later that night, she saw more than just her reflection of olive skin and curls, but a culmination of life experiences. Looking into her own eyes snapped her out of her nightly disassociation, so she tried not to stare in the mirror for too long.

After she finished in the bathroom, Rory frowned at the stack of papers still facing her. On a normal day, she was on top of grading her high school students' work, but she had been putting off grading their history assignments for the last few weeks. It wasn't her intention, but she'd been zoning out more and more frequently. She wasn't sure why now, of all times, she was thinking about her stalker, as it had been years since he tried anything; having to get bailed out of jail was enough to spook him out of Colorado entirely. The New Year meant she was even closer to approaching a decade since the attack, but it seemed as if everything was coming out of the shadows of her mind where she had tucked it all away for safekeeping.

The days were starting to all blend into one in Rory's head. Her rhythm of waking up, picking up Kane, teaching at school, and then going home to drown herself in busy work was making her lose all track of time. The only things keeping Rory aware of the day of the week were her lesson plans and school holidays. As much as she hated being alone with her own thoughts, the idea of letting the time pass around her and doing nothing about it didn't sit quite right with her either.

This isn't fair to the students, Rory thought. *They deserve a teacher who is always present.*

Thankfully, her disassociation presented itself as part of her routine that night. She'd check the answer key, grade a quiz, and then take a swig of hot tea. The routine was easy to fall into, and before she could even realize what she was doing, she was in a rhythm that kept her out of her own head and grading her papers. She wished every night could come with such ease.

When Kane texted her around 10:30 that night, she'd been so in the zone that she was caught off guard. Kane Kelly was one of her closest friends that she met through Brad and Naomi. Kane had a full ride at the university, thanks to scholarships and grants for low-income, first-generation students. He played the part of a carefree party boy well, but Rory knew the moment she met him, he was a lot smarter than he'd ever give himself credit for. Since then, Kane hadn't changed much. His weekend routine comprised of spending time with his friend Shawn Jameson at the bars downtown and drinking away like they were still 21, not 27. He rarely texted her while he was out, so she wasn't sure if she should be excited or worried.

[Kane: You home?]

Its shortness was unlike Kane's, and the cryptic words had Rory concerned.

[Rory: I am, what's up?]

She tried to continue grading the last of the quizzes while she waited for Kane to answer, but she could feel her anxiety spiking in the way her knee bounced up and down again.

[Kane: Ok good. I'm out with Jameson. We heard some gunshots nearby. Just making sure you're safe.]

Rory sighed as she texted him back.

[Rory: Are you guys okay?!]

[Kane: Yeah, we're fine. I'll see you tomorrow!]

Rory groaned. She knew Kane well enough to tell that something was off, but she wasn't sure what. On any given day, Kane was an open book with Rory, so the uncertainty of his text had her a bit on edge. She chalked it up to Kane likely being under the influence of alcohol, but she turned the news on to see what may be happening.

"Breaking news," the anchor kicked off. "At least one person is dead after shots were fired in downtown Riverpeak. We have not confirmed his identity, but the victim appears to be the local masked vigilante Hematite."

Rory dropped her remote in shock and suddenly snapped out of her dissociative state. She felt a lump in her throat when she tried to swallow a sip of chamomile tea, her hand shaking as she set the mug down.

"Police tell us that the victim's description is in line with Hematite, a street fighter who has remained a mystery to

CHAPTER ONE

Riverpeak for more than a decade," the other anchor said. "The suspected shooter is now in custody. Police say he claims another anonymous figure hired him."

"They tell us the suspect blamed a man named Stone Breaker. We have a crew on their way to the scene now for more updates."

"What?" Rory asked herself. She wasn't sure why a stranger would want to kill Hematite, never mind hurt him. And with a name like Stone Breaker, she thought this had to be a targeted attack.

Rory rushed to grab her phone, desperate for more information. It was hard for her to accept that Hematite was dead, and she had never heard of anyone going by the name Stone Breaker, so she felt too shocked to process what was happening right away. She went to Twitter, hoping for live reports from bystanders and found the video of the suspected shooter being arrested with little hassle.

"This was for Stone Breaker! There's more of us!" the suspect shouted. Despite the suspect's anger, he didn't seem as he was inebriated or tweaking out. In fact, it was a sort of calm rage—the type that scared Rory the most.

"What the hell kind of name is Stone Breaker?" she muttered to herself with disgust as she Googled the name on her phone. She found a new YouTube channel belonging to someone of the same name and tapped into it, afraid of what she might find.

There was only one video, a trailer for his channel. Stone Breaker's video opened up with a tacky lightning bolt transition and sound effect. He too was masked, wearing what looked like a 3D-printed face shield that hid his identity. However, Rory could see the pale color of his neck, showing that he wasn't wearing anything beneath his face covering. A bright yellow lightning bolt was painted across the stone-gray mask, but the outline of the lightning bolt looked messy as though they tried to patch it up with a marker.

"Masked vigilantes are ruining our city," he began. The monotone, deep sound of his voice hinted that Stone Breaker was using a voice modifier to disguise himself. "If you agree, then you're in the right place. It's about high time we let the thin blue line do their work rather than take matters into our own hands. It's time we stop people like Hematite once and for all."

Rory couldn't believe what she was hearing. While she understood that vigilantism wasn't everyone's cup of tea, she thought all of Riverpeak considered Hematite a hometown hero, especially considering it was the community who named him.

"Hematite claims to protect this city," Stone Breaker continued. "But I think that he's just getting in the way and inciting crime."

Rory couldn't bear to watch it anymore, even though there were still three minutes left in the video. She closed out of the YouTube app and tossed her phone onto her couch. She decided instead to focus on the news, hoping for word that Hematite wasn't dead and that there was some huge misunderstanding. When the local news channels were on a commercial break, she grabbed her phone again and opted for panic-scrolling through social media.

The night felt like a blur to Rory. The hours felt like they were moving in slow motion, but when she looked at the time on the corner of her phone screen, she saw it was already three in the morning. She realized the news she was hoping for would never come and accepted that his death was true. Filled with grief, Rory opened her jewelry box in her bedroom and removed a small, torn piece of dark fabric from it. She held it with care in her fingers, letting the softness soothe her.

Rory clutched the fabric to her chest and, for the first time in years, let herself weep. Her sobs racked her body to the point of sharpness in her lungs.

So much for a year of healing, she thought.

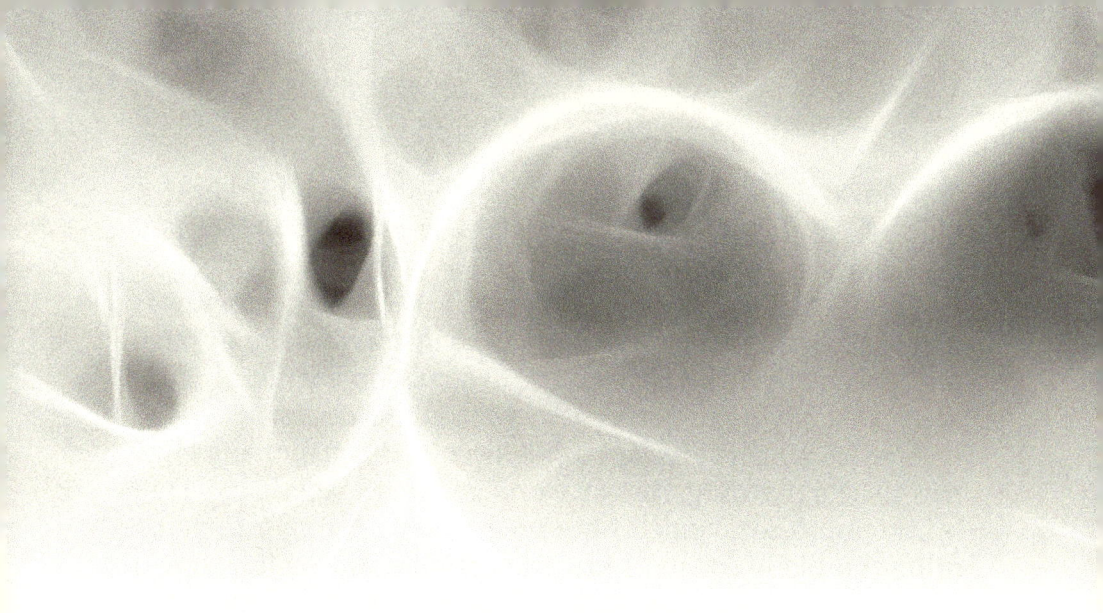

CHAPTER TWO

Kane Kelly woke up with the worst headache of his life on Monday morning, already feeling the effects of Sunday night's events. He could tell that he was getting closer to thirty; he was still young, but not as quick to recoup from a night of drinking as he used to be ten years ago. He rubbed his temples, sighed, and grimaced as he got out of bed. His entire body ached, but he'd have to just pop some painkillers and carry on with his day to conceal his current state.

He made the short trek from his bed to his bathroom in his studio apartment, finding the cold of the fake hardwood floor beneath his feet soothing. There wasn't much on the walls of the small apartment, but he didn't mind. The few things that were there were old housewarming gifts or recycled from his college dorm, which he thought made the space a little more special. Because he had little to decorate with, the studio felt anything but cramped. Rory liked to call his studio apartment minimalist, but he just called it being poor.

Kane tried to remember the events of the night before, but it was hazy. He remembered getting in a fight, and then it all came flooding back when he looked at himself in his bathroom mirror after washing his face. A fresh, round scar rested on his ribcage. He pushed back his long blonde hair, turned around, and craned his neck so he could check his back. It didn't take long to find the scar's twin as the pink popped against his ivory skin.

Of all the ways Kane had been attacked, getting shot was one of his least favorite. *At least the bullet went clean through this time*, he thought. He'd had to fish out some bullets before and hated having to get some help from his doctor.

Immortality had its perks, but he considered moments like this to be a real drag. He had worked with a specialist at a lab on the more rural side of town who was helping him determine the likely cause of his immortality. But so far, they'd only been able to guess that it had to do with his mother's drug addiction; the dealers were putting something in the methamphetamines, but he still hadn't found out what. Kane used HIPAA laws to his advantage to make sure they were sworn to secrecy over what they found.

The knocking on his door startled him. He looked at his watch; Rory was there thirty minutes before her usual time. He didn't even bother to put the rest of his clothes on and answered the door while he continued brushing his teeth. She was holding a bag from the local cafe and two cups of coffee.

Rory looked ever the academic, as per usual. Her curls were down today with only a few pieces tied back to stay out of her face, and she kept her makeup simple. Some liner rested on her lids to distract from bloodshot eyes, and she had some foundation on, but Kane could tell the flush on her cheeks was natural, not from whatever blush she used. She was the social studies teacher at Riverpeak High and someone could tell that just by looking at her with her wide-leg black trousers and brown button-up blouse tucked into it. Kane always teased her that she looked like she belonged in a gender-swapped remake of an *Indiana Jones* movie. He never told her this part, but he thought it suited her well.

Kane noticed Rory was wearing her glasses today; on a normal day, she would opt for contacts.

"Don't hate me for being super early," Rory said as Kane let her through the door. She looked Kane up and down before she concluded, "And you're as good as naked. Shit, Kane, did

CHAPTER TWO

I..." Rory dropped her voice to a whisper. "Did I fuck up? Is someone—?"

Kane's laugh was stifled by his toothbrush. "No, no one's here. I never score. You know that. Come on in; I don't give a shit," he said with a shrug.

"I come bearing breakfast," she said. "So, I hope that makes up for my being early."

Rory and Kane both worked at Riverpeak High School; his apartment complex was on her way there, so she was always his ride. Kane had made his old Honda Prelude functional and he took pride in it, but Rory insisted they just carpool to prevent his work of art from falling to pieces in the street.

Kane just patted her shoulder in response before he walked back to the bathroom. Despite having known each other for years, Rory had never seen Kane shirtless before. She took the opportunity to check him out as she sat down on a barstool in his kitchenette. Rory only got a quick glance before he moved into the other room, but seeing his strong back, he was more muscular than she thought he'd be. Beneath his clothes, he looked fairly scrawny, but she realized she was mistaken.

"Don't hate me for not having any pants on. In my defense, you're super early," Kane replied once he spit out his toothpaste. *He sounds extra exhausted*, Rory noted.

"You're lucky you're cute," she retorted. "Everything alright, Kay?"

"Yeah, yeah." He walked over to his bureau to get dressed. "Rough night last night. The usual."

He couldn't see it as he reached for some pants and an undershirt, but Rory frowned at his confession. "Well, I got your favorite coffee and sandwich. That should help you out, I hope."

"Always does. You're the best. I might ask you to marry me if some other guy doesn't snatch you up before we're thirty." He winked as he joined her at the counter. Kane brushed his blonde hair, which reached halfway down his neck, out of his face. "I'd be a terrible husband, so you better be careful."

Rory laughed; Kane had been telling her that for years, but she often wondered if he meant it about being a bad husband.

Had it been anyone else, the behavior would have annoyed Rory. She rarely associated with flirts who cracked sex jokes often and were unafraid of dirty talk being part of casual conversation. But Kane was Kane, and his delivery always toed the line between charming and over the top. Rory couldn't remember a day where Kane didn't make her laugh at least once.

"I can never tell when you're flirting with me for real anymore."

"Eh, I can't either." Kane shrugged and took a sip of coffee. "Why breakfast today? You always cook at home."

"I wanted a pleasant start to the day and figured I'd treat myself."

Kane noticed her brief pause as he chewed his breakfast. Rory then asked, "Did you watch the news last night?"

Kane shook his head. "No, you know I don't have cable."

"I mean, me neither, Kay, but it's all over the local channels. Facebook, TikTok, everywhere. They found Hematite dead last night. I think I cried myself to sleep. I took a *lot* of melatonin gummies to help the process along, though."

That would explain why she is wearing glasses instead of her usual contact lenses, Kane thought. *Rory never wears her contacts after a good cry.*

"Oh, shit," Kane said. "I'm sorry, Rory. I know he meant a lot to you." Kane took a bite of the breakfast sandwich that Rory brought him and took his time chewing it. He felt his heartbeat speed up and struggled to look into her dark eyes, which only appeared darker with her mood.

Now he remembered every detail of last night. He also remembered texting Rory in his dying stupor last night and mentally scrambled to recall what he may have sent her. She wasn't saying anything out of the ordinary, so he allowed himself to relax. *Clearly*, he thought, *I didn't out myself.*

"Yeah. The cops found him after someone reported some gunshots downtown. It was breaking at eleven. They think it was someone working with that Stone Breaker prick, whoever that is. What a stupid fucking name."

CHAPTER TWO

"Yeah, that guy sounds like a real piece of shit." Kane took another bite. He did everything in his power to pretend that he did not know what Rory was talking about. He found that eating and drinking his coffee was helping him mask his expressions.

"God only knows the cops in this town are totally useless, so." Rory sighed, then sipped her coffee. "It's weird, though. When I was driving here, the radio station was talking about it, and they said his body actually went missing. They think someone broke in overnight to steal it. I'll have to see if Naomi has any info that they aren't sharing yet."

"Maybe he's not really dead." Kane hoped the suggestion would cheer her up.

"I dunno. The news said he got shot in the lungs. I'm not sure how anyone could come back from that."

Kane had so much he wanted to say to comfort her, but he knew he couldn't. He wanted to explain to Rory that Hematite was fine, and his outfit was in the dryer, waiting to be hung up. He wanted to say that he simply woke up in the coroner's office and was the one to bust a window—no body snatchers involved. Hematite was, in fact, very much alive, and he wanted nothing more than to tell her that with the utmost confidence.

But Kane couldn't explain last night to Rory. He would much rather she think his behavior this morning was from a hangover instead of getting the shit kicked out of him because Rory did not know that Kane was actually Hematite, and Kane would prefer it stay that way.

Kane didn't even know what else to say at that moment. He was always so afraid he would slip up or say something that gave away too much. If he wasn't careful, one misplaced word would be all it took to clue Rory into his secret identity, but he prioritized her safety over anything else—even if it meant lying to her for the last eight years. Rory was one of the wittiest people he knew, though, so it hadn't been a easy task.

He was relieved when Rory continued the conversation. "When I heard the news, I thought I was gonna puke. I've spent almost a decade on and off trying to find him again, hoping

I'd see him. I never got to thank him for the night he saved me, and that's all I've wanted to do. Now I can't. I should have taken this more seriously while I could have."

Kane moved his hand to her back to rub small circles to comfort her. Every time he touched her, he felt his heart swell, but he tried to just push his feelings down like he had since day one. Their friendship and her safety both meant too much to him to risk stating his feelings for her.

"I'm sure he doesn't need your thanks. That's not why heroes do it, you know."

Rory's smile was a sad one. "Yeah, I guess you're right."

When they arrived at Riverpeak High School, they hadn't even started the homeroom period before an assembly was called. All students and faculty were to report to the gymnasium right away.

Rory took attendance as her class made their way back out their doors and led her students through the halls. It was a small school, only one two-story building for classrooms, since it was such a small town wedged between the mountains. The gymnasium was detached and was separated by the football field on campus.

One of Rory's students walked alongside her. "Hey, Miss Miller! Long time, no see. Do you know what the assembly is about?" Jordan asked. "It seems kind of random. They've never done one right after winter break before."

Jordan was a normal teenager, not quite nerdy enough to hang out with the bookworms and not quite trendy enough to be invited into the popular cliques since her parents kept her busy at their local cafe. Jordan always wore her dark hair in twin braids in a way that reminded Rory of her friend Naomi, except Jordan's hair was naturally curly whereas Naomi's was silky and straight.

"Your guess is as good as mine, if I'm being honest. If they told us anything, I missed the memo." As they walked, Rory made a note of Jordan's attendance, not wanting to forget later.

CHAPTER TWO

"Hey." Rory turned to her left and saw that Kane caught up to her. "So, uh, what's this assembly? Did they tell us, and I just missed the email or something?" he asked.

"I dunno either." She shook her head. "Glad it's not just me."

Kane turned as he walked to look at his English students behind him. "Sorry, guys. The smart one doesn't know either." He looked back at Rory, patted her shoulder, and shot her a wink before returning to his class to make sure no one snuck off. "I'll see you inside."

A few of her students whispered, but Rory ignored it. A lot of the kids theorized that she and Kane were dating over the years, but it was amusing at this point. She separated from her class once they reached the gymnasium to join Kane and the rest of the faculty. They sat together as they always did, not helping their case against any dating rumors that their students were spreading.

The gymnasium hardly looked any different from when Rory and Kane were students there; despite both growing up in Riverpeak, they never had classes together until college where they met through Naomi and bonded over their undergraduate teacher program. The bleachers showed their age and even though the floor was freshly waxed over winter break, Rory could still see years of scuff marks and scratches from basketball games. A few banners hung up on the wall behind them, highlighting basketball championships they won over the years. Their success had been the only thing to put them on the local maps.

A man with balding brown hair and blue eyes was standing at the podium, accompanied by the school principal, who looked like his polar opposite with her tight, voluminous blonde curls.

Rory recognized him from a few stories Naomi had covered for Channel 10: Councilman Tom Stevens, best known for a few scandals that were mostly forgotten about by the public. His green shirt was about half a size too small for him with his white tie hiding the buttons threatening to pop open.

"Good morning, Riverpeak High School." The principal's tone lacked any of the enthusiasm one would expect from her words. "We have a special guest today. Please give a warm welcome to Tom Stevens from our town council."

The students partook in a polite golf clap. Rory and Kane did not.

"Thank you for sharing your time with me this morning." His voice boomed with overconfidence already. "I come here on behalf of the city council to talk to you about some concerning trends in our town."

He paused as he straightened out his papers on the podium and then continued. "As many of you may have heard, the masked vigilante Hematite is dead." He sounded like a perfect, polished politician who kept his emotions in check, but Rory could see the slight upturn of his lips.

This news caused a few students to whisper, which resulted in a gentle shushing from the principal. Her mouth was stuck in a thin line as if she wasn't happy about the situation at hand but that she had no choice and had to go along with it.

"We do not want to see this trend of vigilante violence rise. Our police force does a wonderful job keeping Riverpeak safe. Vigilantes do not help our city; rather, they inspire and incite violence."

Rory's mind flashed to what Stone Breaker said on YouTube; the word choice couldn't have been a coincidence. Before she could get too angry, she felt Kane's hand on her leg. Kane gave her knee a gentle squeeze.

"Should any of you be interested in pursuing a path of law enforcement, I have partnered with the University of Colorado's criminal justice program and our local police department to spread awareness of how you can help keep Riverpeak safe. We'll be by the cafeteria all day today to answer any questions you may have. Thank you."

They played a short video advertising the university's criminal justice program to finish out the assembly. Rory couldn't bring herself to watch it. From what she heard, though, it wasn't even pretending to be anything but the propaganda that it was.

"You okay?" Kane whispered. Even if he hadn't known her, it was obvious she was in anguish just from looking at her. Her jaw was tight, and her shoulders hunched inward.

CHAPTER TWO

Rory almost nodded but remembered she was trying to heal after everything that happened to her. *She couldn't move on if she didn't face her feelings*, she thought, so she shook her head and hoped she didn't draw any attention to her and Kane.

"We know the truth." Kane felt like such a liar for saying it to Rory, so he tried to remind himself of the context to feel less like a hypocrite. *Juggling my costume changes is about to become a lot more difficult*, he thought. "Don't worry. I'm here."

"Thanks, Kay." Her voice almost cracked.

Kane pondered his next move as the video played and paid no attention to it; he knew from experience how much of a joke the Riverpeak Police Department was. If they were half-competent, he wouldn't be searching for answers about how he got his powers and why he was getting shot at in the process.

There was a reason Kane couldn't die from the shooting last night beyond just pure luck at birth, and he was determined to figure out why. He couldn't put his finger on it, but he felt like Stevens was part of that answer.

After the assembly ended, Rory returned to her classroom with a smile on her face, but nothing about it was genuine. She adjusted her glasses on her nose before she said, "Alright, time for current events, though I could probably guess what most of you have picked." She placed her hands on her hips as she asked, "Show of hands, who picked Hematite's death as their topic for the day?"

Two-thirds of the class raised their hands. Rory allowed her smile to drop at that and exhaled as she looked out at the sea of hands before her.

"Alright, let's handle this a little differently today. You guys can lower your hands," she said. "How many people here have been personally affected by Hematite or know someone who has been? Close your eyes and then raise your hands."

Rory already felt like she had taken a knife to the heart with the news, but it cut even deeper when she saw every single hand raise up.

"Okay, open your eyes before you lower your hands. Look around."

Her class was silent as everyone glanced around them, seeing every single hand in the air. Rory sat on the top of her desk as she thought of what to say next. She had never seen them all so quiet as they all brought their hands back to their sides.

"I don't want to spend the entire class talking about Hematite. But it's clear that he's had quite the impact on all of us, myself included. If anyone needs to talk, my door is always open, okay?"

A few voices chimed together, "Thanks, Miss Miller."

Jordan raised her hand.

"Yes, Jordan?"

"Why would anyone want to kill Hematite? He stopped some guys from mugging my dad when he closed up the café one night last year, and people are *still* coming in to offer to pay for Hematite's drinks. Not that he ever comes in."

Rory bit the inside of her lip. "Well, I'd bet that Hematite gained a few enemies by doing what he does. But I don't know what might have sparked it now."

"My mom says that crime's gonna get worse here."

"It might," Rory said with a shrug. "I won't lie to you guys. We can't be sure. But you all are safe here, okay?"

Rory swallowed after she said it, hoping that it was true. She wasn't even sure of it herself, but as she looked at the crowd of concerned teenage faces before her, she knew she had to be strong for them.

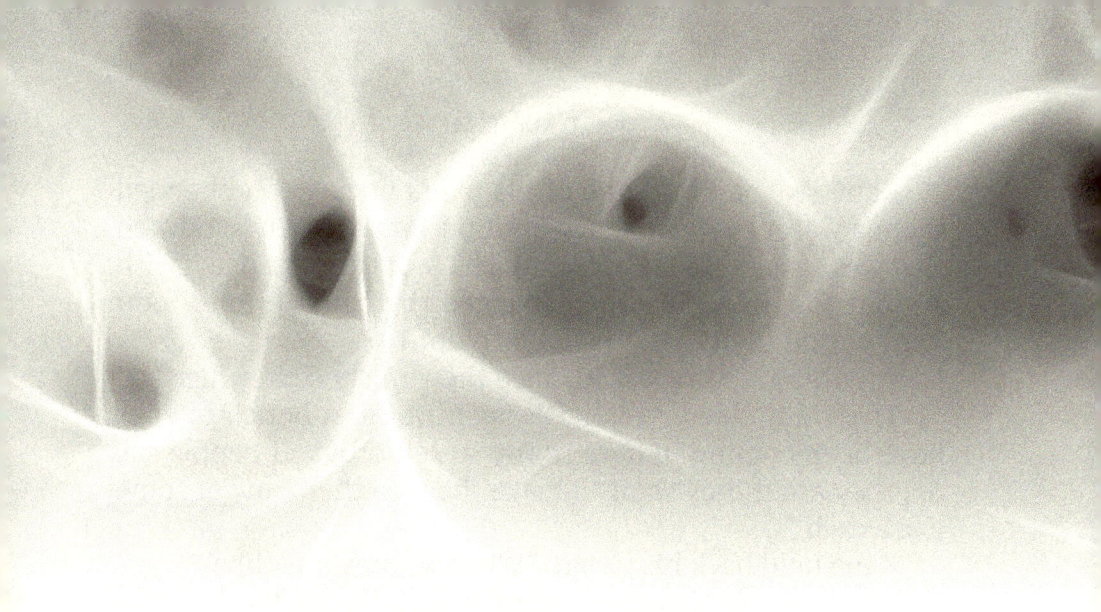

CHAPTER THREE

Kane, dressed as Hematite, dropped a stack of blankets by the front door and then wandered through the halls of the long-abandoned two-story office building on the east side of the city. Some company once considered moving their headquarters here, but their office was overrun by a handful of the unhoused people that used to pop their tents up over the lot. The city never stopped them, and they weren't why Kane was there—he was just glad they had a roof over their heads in the winter, even if it wasn't ideal.

Kane sauntered the halls, trying to not alert anyone to his presence until he reached a cubicle in the back corner. He ghosted his knuckles over the cubicle wall and knocked to see if the person he was looking for was inside.

"Hematite?" Their head popped up from beneath the desk. "Holy shit, you're alive?"

"Shh." Kane put his finger to his mouth, though no one could see his mouth beneath his many layers. He crouched down to be eye level with them. The teenager had blonde hair like Kane's, but longer and more unruly. They reminded Kane of himself, and he realized just now that he didn't know their name.

Kane reached into one of his pants pockets and handed them a water bottle and a peanut butter-and-jelly sandwich that was covered in plastic wrap. The teenager grasped it with a quiet thanks before they snagged their first bite of food. They closed their eyes in contentment.

"Anything?" Kane asked, once they finished chewing.

The kid nodded. "Yeah, it's been weird. A bunch of guys have been coming in here trying to sell drugs. If people say no, they ask if they want to make them so they can get some extra cash."

Kane held back his groan. "What do they look like?"

"The one that's here the most is really tall. Clearly works out and has short brown hair. What day is it?"

"Wednesday."

"You might see him; it's his day today. Be careful, okay?"

"You too, kid. Your parents doing alright?"

He nodded. "Their withdrawals have been something wicked, but they're managing. They're sleeping two floors up. My mom said she feels way less productive, but I think she knows it's for the best."

Kane smiled beneath his mask. "Good. Thanks again, bud."

Kane made his way back to the front of the office, careful to stay away from the windows to stay in the dark. He heard a few whispers as he walked through but paid them no mind. After all these years, he was bound to get caught dead somewhere; he just hated the aftermath of it.

When Kane reached the door, he came face to face with the man his teenage friend warned him about.

"Well, I'll be damned," the man said with a smirk. "I thought Stone Breaker had Shatterstone and his buddies take care of you."

"Yeah, I think they thought that too." He held his arms out. "But here I am."

As the man approached, Kane put his hands up to cover his face. The man was taller and bulkier than Kane was, so Kane knew what was coming next; these types usually assumed they'd have the upper hand. Just as Kane predicted, the man swung first, trying to get a punch in, but Kane bobbed and

CHAPTER THREE

weaved away just in time. He shifted his footing to switch positions with the man, wanting to lead him away from the office building. Kane mentally thanked God that it worked, as his attacker took some steps toward him, throwing punches but missing because of poor, sloppy technique. Kane's long pants and hoodie helped him blend in with the night, which only helped his case as they moved away from the building and close to the shadows.

Just as Kane let his guard down, he flew back into a building after being kicked in the shoulder with a steel-toed boot. Kane felt his shoulder pop when he hit the wall with a force he hadn't expected. Kane groaned as he reached for his shoulder. He rushed to crack it, grateful that it wasn't dislocated, and then grabbed for one of the billy clubs clipped to his belt. Even with his boxing wraps and the black wool gloves that he wore over them, the metal was cold to the touch in the frigid January air. His adrenaline was pumping now, but he knew his back would hurt like hell in the morning.

As he swung at his attacker with the club, Kane thought about everything that culminated up to this moment. He thought of how he was getting pretty sick and tired of everything he put up with. After years of working to clean up his city, he had only scratched the surface; the long road ahead was far from encouraging.

The man's instinct was to protect his face after being whacked with the club, leaving his body wide open for Kane to hit. Kane sighed, thought of Rory and his sister Kayla for some much-needed motivation, and punched his attacker in the ribs with a left hook. Kane knew he could take the hits and make it out okay, a luxury most others didn't have, so he carried on with the fight. The man spat out blood, which stained the snow beneath their feet, and he popped a tooth out along with it. Kane whacked him again with the billy club, which finally knocked his attacker down.

His opponent was twice his weight and a few inches taller than him, so having the man on his knees would make his job easier. Kane grabbed him by the collar of his shirt.

"What do you want, man?" the attacker asked in pain.

"Who sent you?" Kane was already out of patience for this guy before the fight even began. "Who and why?"

"He'll fucking kill me, man." He seemed to have accepted his fate. If he was afraid, he didn't show it.

"Answer the question." Kane pulled the man's head back a bit to get a better look at him. "Who and why?"

"He's no different from you. He's just looking out for him and his own, you know?"

"Who, Stone Breaker?" Kane scoffed. Stone Breaker was new on the scene, having been around the east side of town for maybe a few months, but he'd been a major pain in Kane's ass since he arrived. "He's delusional if he thinks we are anything alike."

"Just knock me out. You won't kill me, right?" His voice shook now, and his lip started quivering. Kane would never tire of seeing how quickly they mentally broke. "That's not your style, I know that. But he *will* kill me, man. I'm serious."

Kane didn't see a point in asking any more questions; he got as much as he could. This wasn't the first junkie that Stone Breaker sent after him, and he was sure it wouldn't be the last. He hit the man one last time in the jaw, and it was enough to knock him out. He dropped him and called it a night.

"Stupid fucking name, anyway," Kane muttered to himself.

As he made his way to the closest fire escape to travel by rooftop through the east side, he paused on the street corner. Someone had spray-painted a memorial for Hematite, including a portrait of him in his disguise of black masks, scarves, and hoods that took up much of the brick wall. A few people laid flowers by it, and someone had lit a candle that had already burned out and melted down. Kane frowned at the sight as he moved on.

Kane scaled the fence of the storage facility to not be detected and made his way to his unit. It had been under a pseudonym, using his old fake ID from college so he could avoid raising any suspicions when renting the storage unit out. His unit was plain, only decorated by a few news articles on the wall that he had pieced together in hopes of finding answers to why he could not die. That question plagued him

CHAPTER THREE

the most, and the closer he got to figuring it out, the more criminals seemed to pop up to stop him from uncovering the truth.

When he was inside his storage unit, Kane sighed as he sat down in the metal folding chair. The chair had been as cold as the brick wall earlier, but the chill felt nice on his back after his fight. He glanced up at the camera he had set up in front of him and took a moment to compose himself.

Once he felt ready, Kane straightened his posture and confirmed that his voice modifier was on. He double-checked that he'd tucked his blonde locks into his balaclava before recording. He then lowered his hood farther over his face, making sure it cast a shadow over his eyes, and then he spoke. Being a public figure wasn't his thing, especially when he donned the Hematite getup. But he knew the people were mourning and if he didn't say something, things would only get worse at the hands of Stone Breaker.

Rory had the local news station on as she did her dishes to support Naomi; it was her friend's first time as an in-studio reporter, finally getting a cushier gig instead of being out in the field. Rory wouldn't miss it for the world. She dried her hands to grab a quick photo of Naomi, sharing it on her Instagram Stories with the text, "THAT'S MY GIIIIIRL!!!" and the heart eyes emoji over it.

"And breaking news," Naomi read from her spot, standing by the monitor with the station's logo flashing on it. Naomi looked sharp, her black hair curled and her makeup the perfect combination of glamorous and natural. Rory could detect focus and fierceness in Naomi's dark eyes, which was how she could tell this story was serious. "We have confirmed that Hematite is alive. This just came into our station within the last few minutes."

Rory dropped the sponge into the sink.

"We received this video from Hematite. Take a look."

Rory was frozen in place at her kitchen sink as she watched the video roll. Hematite was in a dark room, wearing the same clothing as always. He'd changed his voice in the video's post-production even more than it was in real life, but he included captioning. Rory didn't need the captions; she could make out every word.

"My name is Hematite," he said. His eyes weren't visible, but she could tell he was addressing the camera by his posture. "And I'm here to let you know that you can't kill me so easily. Corruption has allowed our town to house a dark underbelly for far too long." His tone was serious, even with the voice modifier, and Rory sensed this was acting as both a threat to whoever was after him and as reassurance to those who stood behind him. "The ones who hired my attempted killer are none other than Stone Breaker and his crew, who I believe are directly connected to our city government. Mark my words: I'm not going anywhere, so you can end your little propaganda tour."

The video cut to black, so the news switched back to Naomi in the studio. She said, "For those of you just joining us, Hematite is alive. There is no confirmation that this is the real Hematite, whose body went missing after he was found dead last week, or if it is a copycat vigilante. The video sent to us had a lot of security locks on it, so we couldn't confirm the validity of the sender's information. Either way, you can rely on us to keep you updated the second we can confirm."

Rory heard nothing the news anchors said after that. She was in a complete daze, shocked at the news report and video. She could tell from his voice and build that this was the same Hematite who saved her when she was in college; Rory felt it in her gut. Seeing him on the screen was enough to bring her back to that day on campus. The memories made her body tense up, starting at her jaw and shoulders and moving downward. She tried to just focus on the surrounding room instead, rattling off a few mental notes about her safety and her surroundings to try and ground herself at the moment. The last thing she wanted was to relive the scariest day of her life in vivid detail twice in one week.

CHAPTER THREE

She was in her apartment.

She was safe.

Hematite was alive.

After all those years of wishing she could have thanked him, Rory realized that now she was given her chance. She grabbed her phone with shaky hands she could not control and sent a simple text to Naomi, asking her to call her once she got off work. When Naomi did, Rory was quick to answer.

"Hey! Glad you called."

"Hey. Sorry, I didn't mean to hit FaceTime. My thumb must have slipped," Naomi said with a laugh.

"Eh, no biggie." From the video call, Rory could see that Naomi was still in her car and hadn't left the news station yet.

"I take it you saw the video?"

"Yeah. Good job, by the way. Listen … do you want to help me find out who Hematite is?"

Naomi grinned. "I would love to. I was wondering when you'd ask me that."

"It's about time I get some closure. I don't even know what I'll say when I find him, but I have to."

"Have you practiced at all?" Naomi asked.

"My therapist suggested writing him a letter, even if I never get to deliver it to him. The note in my phone that I set aside for it has been sitting blank," Rory revealed.

"I'm sure it'll come to you when you meet him again. He saved our lives, after all! Yours especially." Rory could hear the excitement in Naomi's voice when she said, "Can you imagine if we actually found him?" Naomi had that sparkle in her eyes that she got whenever she had something new to research. She was an investigative journalist through and through after all.

Rory closed her eyes and tried to envision meeting him again. She pictured herself standing before him, unsure of his face or unfiltered voice, but able to say thank you once and for all—but the words still felt trapped in her throat.

"What if we reveal him to the world by accident?" Rory asked.

Naomi sighed. "Don't tell me you're having second thoughts. Rory, you've wanted this forever!"

"And I don't want it at the expense of ruining his career. What if we mess this up for him?"

"I doubt we will. And if you're really unsure, why don't we start with Stone Breaker? It'll be a good test run of our sleuthing skills, and then there won't be any harm done if we reveal a secret identity. If anything, it'll help the cops get a guy wanted for an attempted murderer ... and help Hematite find the guy after him." Her smile hinted at her confidence, something Rory desperately wanted to borrow.

Rory nodded. She liked Naomi's idea, and though she could not care less about helping the police, who never helped her when she needed it, she wanted more than anything to help Hematite. Naomi knew that this compromise would appeal to Rory's need for closure after everything that happened to her in college.

"I'm in." Rory felt a sort of conviction she hadn't felt in a long time. "Hematite helped us. It's time we help him."

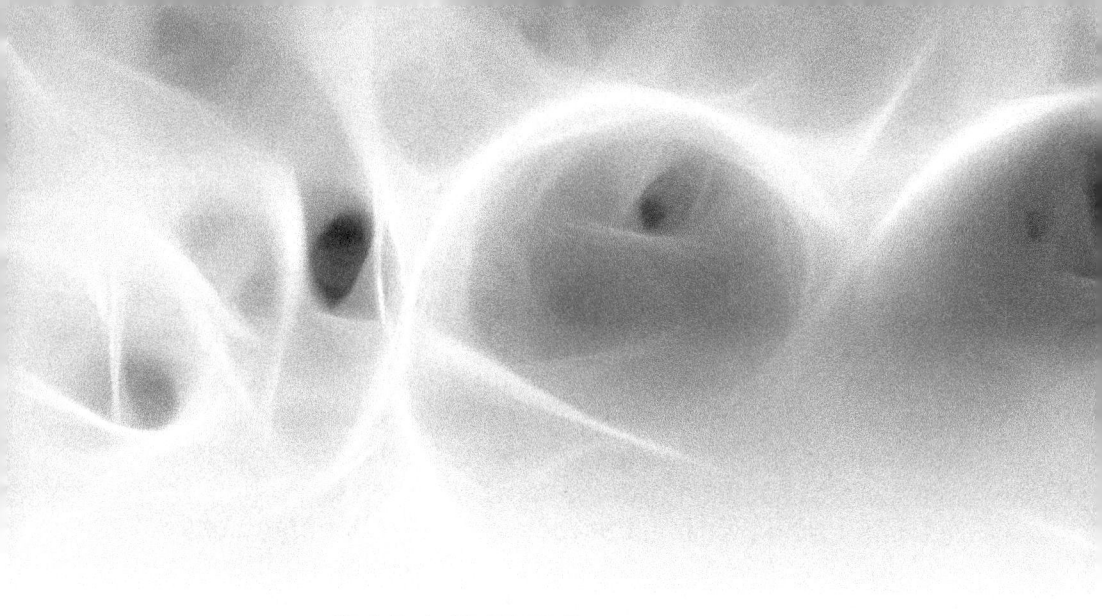

CHAPTER FOUR

Kane was sitting atop the local pharmacy with a peanut butter-and-jelly sandwich in his full Hematite regalia when Rory called. He shoved part of the sandwich in his mouth and, as he chewed faster than he ever had in his life, reached for the off switch on his voice-changer. He somehow picked up the call just before the last ring.

"Hey!" He still kept an eye below to continue his patrol. He normally went from town to town but had been focusing more on Riverpeak lately to hone in on Stone Breaker since he suspected he was close; all the attacks had been happening in Riverpeak. "What are you doing up this late?"

"I could ask you the same thing," Rory said. "Hey, listen, do you wanna help me and Naomi out with something? We could use all the help we could get."

"What's going on?"

"Well, there's a sort of vigilante video war going on. Have you seen it?"

"I mean, who hasn't?"

"Naomi and I want to figure out who Hematite and Stone Breaker are. You down?"

Kane had a feeling this would happen eventually, but he was still unprepared for it. He buried his nerves and kept his composure when he said, "Like, right now?"

"I mean, she and I are, at least. But you don't need to head over here or anything if you're busy."

"Yeah, I'm on my way to meet up with Jameson at the bar." Kane winced at himself; he hated lying to her, but it was a necessary evil. "He and his girlfriend are having some issues again, so I promised him I'd come out. You know how they get, can't stop fighting. But maybe some other night, okay?"

"Oh, okay." Rory sounded disappointed, and it killed him to hear her voice drop like that. "Have fun with Jameson. Call me if you need a ride home, alright?"

"Thanks, Mom," Kane teased. "Have a good night. Tell Naomi I said hi." He sighed as he hung the phone up. "Shit," he muttered to himself. He paused as he tried to think through his panic. He questioned how far Rory could actually go down the rabbit hole before reaching a dead end.

Kane knew Rory well enough to know that if anyone could figure his identity out, it was her. She was stubborn and resourceful enough, plus she never knew when to quit. With Naomi helping her too, their likelihood of discovering who Hematite was just skyrocketed. Kane thought that if Rory was going to uncover who Hematite was, he'd rather she heard it from him—and he wasn't ready to tell her just yet.

He opened the YouTube app on his phone and quickly found Stone Breaker's channel. There was a new upload from only a few minutes ago, so Kane clicked on it. The video opened with a lightning bolt sound effect; Kane thought it looked cheesy, especially since it matched the mask's haphazard paint job.

"This video is for Hematite," Stone Breaker said. He was sitting in what looked like an office. Kane could only see him from the chest up; Stone Breaker had darkened the room, but it looked like he wore a black hoodie and a light blue beanie to hide his hair from view. "I've about had it with you wreaking havoc on my town. You can talk about Riverpeak's underbelly all you want, but the people need the stability that we're providing them. Let's see how you like me when I don't hold back,

CHAPTER FOUR

Hematite—and let's see how many times it'll take for me to take you down. If I can't kill you, maybe I can unmask you."

"What a fucking asshole," Kane said with a roll of his eyes. He pocketed his phone and knew he only had one place to turn to right now. The last bite of his PB&J sat forgotten in his lap after answering his phone and watching the video, so he took one last bite of his sandwich, tossed the crumbs for the pigeons sitting on the other end of the roof, and left.

Elijah Baron did not expect to hear a knocking at his back door, of all places, at nearly midnight. He walked to his kitchen to peer out the back window, only to see Hematite standing there in his full regalia. If it weren't for the large hood, Elijah might have been able to see his eyes, but the shadow from the fabric covered them.

Elijah answered the door right away. His full lips curled up into a smile. "It's been a while since you've been here."

"Yeah, well, I need your help again," Hematite said. "Is now a good time?" He assumed the answer was yes, based on how Elijah was dressed. His loose auburn curls, usually tucked beneath a hat, were on full display, something that Kane had tried to tell Elijah would be beneficial to show in his search for a girlfriend after years of being single. Elijah was still wearing jeans and an anime T-shirt, officially off the clock but not going to bed soon. His five o'clock shadow made his typically light, golden skin take on a much paler hue, but his dark green eyes looked lively despite the late-night hour. Kane always ran the risk of running into their mutual friend and Elijah's roommate, Brad, when he showed up unannounced in need of tech support like this, but it was a risk he was willing to take.

"Sure, come on in. Brad is already asleep since he has an early shift at the clinic tomorrow, so it's just us." He closed the door behind him and was sure to lock it. "One second." He jogged to the front of the house to close the blinds that were still open. "Okay, you're good."

"Thanks. I have a few people who are trying to figure out who I am."

"Isn't that half of the Denver area?" Elijah ran a hand through his hair. "Especially after your video that you sent me to encrypt for the news stations?"

"I mean seriously trying to find out who I am and who can actually figure it out," Hematite stressed. "Can you let me know if that's possible? These people are equal parts determined and capable."

Elijah furrowed his thick brows. "And what if it is possible and I find out who you are in the process? Doesn't that go against our agreement?"

"Fuck the agreement," Hematite said without a second thought. "You've been helping me since we were kids, Elijah. I can trust you, and I don't think anyone knows that you've been helping me. You should be safe, even if you know. And I'll still hold up my end of the deal."

"Alright then. Suit yourself."

The agreement was something they established when Hematite first came on the scene. Elijah had been the most intelligent kid in their class since kindergarten and Kane recognized this. He considered Elijah one of his best friends, so he went to him whenever he needed help with anything tech-related—something that especially came in handy when he was first starting out as Hematite and didn't have his own computer, only an old flip phone.

In return, Elijah and his family had 24/7 access to Hematite in the event they needed help, so long as they asked no questions or tried to find out who he was. Elijah found value in the deal since his family was the only Jewish one in their backwoods mountain town. Their neighbors were accepting people, and the town was diverse enough, but he'd rather be safe than sorry against any antisemitism.

However, it had been twelve years since they made the deal, and a lot had changed since they were in high school.

Hematite cleared his throat and dropped the hood of his cowl. He yanked off his balaclava, messing up his blonde hair beneath it, and sighed. Elijah watched him turn off the voice

CHAPTER FOUR

changer beneath it, which rested by his neck. He then said, "It's me, dude."

Elijah's eyes widened. "Kane?"

"Yeah." Kane shrugged. "If you're gonna make sure no one knows … you've gotta know."

"Holy shit, man." Elijah took a moment to process the revelation. "Of all the people I would have guessed, it was not you."

Kane laughed. "That's kind of the idea."

"Come on, we can head to my office. Let me just check the blinds upstairs." Elijah felt shellshocked but knew they had work to do if people were trying to crack Kane's code. He ran upstairs, double-checking the blinds and making sure Brad was still asleep. After a moment, he came back down to let Kane know it was all clear.

Elijah's home office had more monitors in it than Kane knew what to do with. His desk was one of the large corner ones that took up considerable space in the room. Elijah's office always sent Kane down memory lane, what with the photos of them throughout the years and the different basketball and baseball trophies Elijah earned in high school.

"Alright, let me log in to my personal laptop here." Elijah grabbed a laptop on the edge of the desk that was connected to one of the many monitors, so it had a second screen effect. The laptop had two stickers on the back: one that he bought from one of the high school fundraisers featuring the school mascot, a mountain goat, and the other from an anime that Kane didn't recognize. "I have an extra chair in my bedroom if you want to bring it over so you can sit down. Let me get to work here."

"Yeah, thanks."

When Kane returned, Elijah asked, "So, who is trying to figure you out? That'll help me know where to start in our search. If I can try to trace their likely footsteps, I can see if it'll work."

"Stone Breaker is actively threatening me, for starters. He filmed a video and uploaded it on YouTube earlier tonight."

Elijah rolled his eyes. "He used YouTube? What an amateur. There's a way to dig out an IP out of just about anything online." He pulled up the website. "Who else?"

"Rory is getting serious. She's always been curious, but I think my temporary death the other night lit a flame under her ass."

He stopped in his tracks and turned to look at Kane. "Rory?"

Kane nodded as his lips formed a thin line. "Rory."

Elijah raised a brow. "Rory Miller? The Rory that you have been madly in love with since our freshman year of college?" Elijah sounded a bit annoyed, but he didn't bother to correct his tone. "*The* Rory that you work with at the high school?"

"Yeah. That Rory."

Elijah rubbed his temples as his expression dropped. "Why is it so awful if she finds you out, dude? I take it this," he said, as he vaguely gestured at Kane in the Hematite getup, "is why you haven't told her, right?"

"Can you imagine what would happen if word got out Hematite had a girlfriend?" Kane countered. "Especially now that I have someone actively trying to kill me at every turn?"

"Dude, you said it yourself. I've been helping you since we were in high school. No one has found us out and probably never will," Elijah said. His voice went monotone, the telltale sign he was getting aggravated. "Even with all this Stone Breaker stuff, I've been fine."

But Kane was standing firm. "I can't risk it, Elijah."

Elijah shook his head and said, "I think you should tell her either way. Regardless of if you date her, you know? You spend more time with her than you do with any of us anymore. Don't get me wrong; I'm not mad about it, especially since we're about to spend a lot of time together again with Brad's wedding coming up. I'm just sayin'."

"Us" referred to Elijah, Brad, Shawn, and Kane. The four of them had been tight-knit since grade school, and despite life taking them in different directions, the four of them were still in Riverpeak—as was everyone else in their high school—and thus they still had strong friendships. Their time together was briefer than it had been as children, but they all took comfort in knowing the others were there.

"But how do I just tell her that?" Kane asked. "I can't just say, 'Hi Rory, I genuinely care for you and want to be completely honest with you, so I thought I should tell you I'm a masked

CHAPTER FOUR

vigilante that goes by the nickname Hematite. You might have heard of him. Sorry that I've been lying to you for nearly a decade.'" He rolled his eyes. "Yeah, that would go over well."

Elijah sighed. "I mean, maybe you could try that, but just a little less blunt? Like, 'Hey, I have something I've been meaning to tell you for a while, just never really had the right moment. May come as a shock to you. Viewer discretion is advised,' sort of thing."

Kane groaned. Elijah had always been the type to be honest, so much so that it was often what got them in trouble as kids. Before Kane could object, Elijah changed the subject.

"Luckily for us, Stone Breaker is right beneath our noses. The IP address in the video is actually from here in Riverpeak. I was expecting him to be closer to Denver, but I guess he's here."

Elijah pulled the video up again and hit play. Stone Breaker's voice was, similarly to Kane's when he wore his Hematite disguise, modified from some form of electronics when he was in his uniform. It was hard to tell who it was by voice alone, but Elijah grabbed the URL and plugged it into a video downloader.

"He's filming these on Main Street," Elijah said. He took a screenshot of the video as he waited for it to download, opened Photoshop, and then brightened up the shadows. "This looks like the offices in City Hall."

"How can you tell?"

"If you zoom in, you can see a plaque of their logo behind him a bit." Elijah did exactly that and pointed it out to Kane. "See?"

"Can you tell whose office it is?"

"It's barely decorated. Let me see what else I can find. We're on the right track. Oh, good, this download is ready."

"What are you doing with it?"

"I'm going to try messing with the playback settings and see if we can get this voice to sound more natural. I have a feeling he's using an audio filter over this, though, besides whatever he's using to mess with his voice."

Kane watched closely as Elijah threw the video into editing software and adjusted the pitch. After a few different tries, Elijah sat back in triumph at the final result—a much more natural-sounding audio. It was significantly higher in pitch than the modification, but that didn't surprise Kane.

"Sound familiar to you?" Elijah asked. "I'd be willing to bet this is his actual voice."

"Unfortunately, no. I feel like this is a guy I've never met in my life." He sighed as he put his head in his hands. "I'm sure they're wrapped up in this drug ring. It's been driving me fucking crazy lately."

"You've gotten pretty deep, huh?"

Kane nodded. "That's an understatement. Some little twerp called Shatterstone killed me the other night, alongside some random junkies he brought to tag team it. He's working with Stone Breaker. The only reason I didn't kick his ass was that he brought a damn gun to a fistfight and then ran." Kane was grateful that Elijah already knew about his immortality; it was one less thing he had to explain tonight.

"What a coward," Elijah said. "It didn't sound like him?"

"No, and I don't think he was changing his voice. It looked like his outfit was kinda half-assed. Pretty sure he grabbed whatever he could at Goodwill and ran with it."

"Hmm. Weird." Elijah's brows furrowed and his nose scrunched up subconsciously as he worked. "Okay, this could be helpful. Here's a full list of everyone who works out of City Hall. I'll keep this open so we can see who is old enough to have a son around our age. Maybe younger?"

Kane shook his head. "They're runts, but they're close in age to us."

"Good to know," Elijah said. "Every bit helps. But first, time to do some research on you, my friend."

Kane thought his eyes would go crossed if he tried to follow what Elijah was doing closely, so he just let him get to work.

"Nope, nothing on the internet connecting you to Hematite," Elijah said. "Now let's see what happens when I look up your identity…" Kane waited with bated breath before Elijah announced, "Nope, you're good. I think if anyone will find out, it's Rory, since she knows you. But if I'm some guy's dickhead son who doesn't know you from a hole in the wall, I won't know what to look for."

CHAPTER FOUR

"Wait, what's that supposed to mean?"

"It means that I wouldn't put anything past Rory. You two are best friends, dude. Have been for years. There's nothing here, so you don't have to worry about that. I've been doing my job well for you," he said with a chuckle. "But Rory's... well, she's Rory."

"Yeah. That's for sure."

Rory felt less unnerved heading back into Dr. Thornton's office. She wasn't still feeling completely vulnerable since her last visit two weeks ago, but Dr. Thornton was slowly yet surely earning her trust.

"How's everything been the last few weeks?" Dr. Thornton asked.

"I just feel really weak, mentally and physically," Rory confessed. "Everything's been catching up to me. My boxing classes are helping with the physical aspect but not as much of the mental as I was hoping."

"You're a lot stronger than you think, Rory," Dr. Thornton said. "After all, you're here. This takes a lot of courage."

"I guess so," Rory said. "I tried writing a letter to Hematite; it didn't exactly work. But I have been logging a feelings journal every night! I got an app on my phone like you suggested."

"That's great," she said. "Why don't you think the letter to Hematite worked?"

"I dunno," Rory said. "I think it's hard for me to envision him like he's real, you know? It's so hard when I don't know who he is, and I have no idea how he'd take it. It's not like Kane or Naomi, where I know them and can guess how they'd respond. I don't really like not knowing what to expect."

"Are you afraid of being alone again after your family wasn't emotionally there when you needed them?" Dr. Thornton asked.

Rory released a deep breath that she didn't realize she was holding in. "Probably. I just didn't know how to put the words to it. But the thing is, I don't even care what Hematite is like behind the mask. I just know I'm grateful, you know?"

"That makes sense, yes." Dr. Thornton jotted down some notes. "This is the second time you've mentioned Kane. What's your relationship again, exactly?"

"He's one of my best friends. He was there for me through it all. We're still super close." Rory wrestled with her feelings, and then she said, "If he'd just settle down for five minutes, I might ask him on a date."

Dr. Thornton smiled. "Why don't you try writing a letter to him, then, instead of Hematite? You mentioned Naomi, too, yeah? Write one for each of them. You don't have to send it to them if you're too embarrassed."

"Sure, yeah," Rory said. "I'll try. That might be easier."

"And you said the feelings journal has been working out for you?"

"So far. It's become easier to identify what's making me jumpy or paranoid." That was true. She realized it was little things that set her off, even if it had nothing to do with the stalking incident. "I think once my fight-or-flight mindset gets set off, it doesn't wanna turn off."

"I want you to try some grounding techniques next time you feel that way," Dr. Thornton said. "I think it'll help you. Try to find all the items in a room that share the same shape or color, for starters. This will remind you that you're not reliving the trauma, which will help you calm down and relax."

"Thanks," she said. "I think I'll need it."

What she didn't tell Dr. Thornton was how she was hoping to get directly involved with Hematite. She sensed that the news may be met with words of warning or caution, but Rory didn't want to hear it. No matter what anyone told her, she was going to find him—no matter what it took.

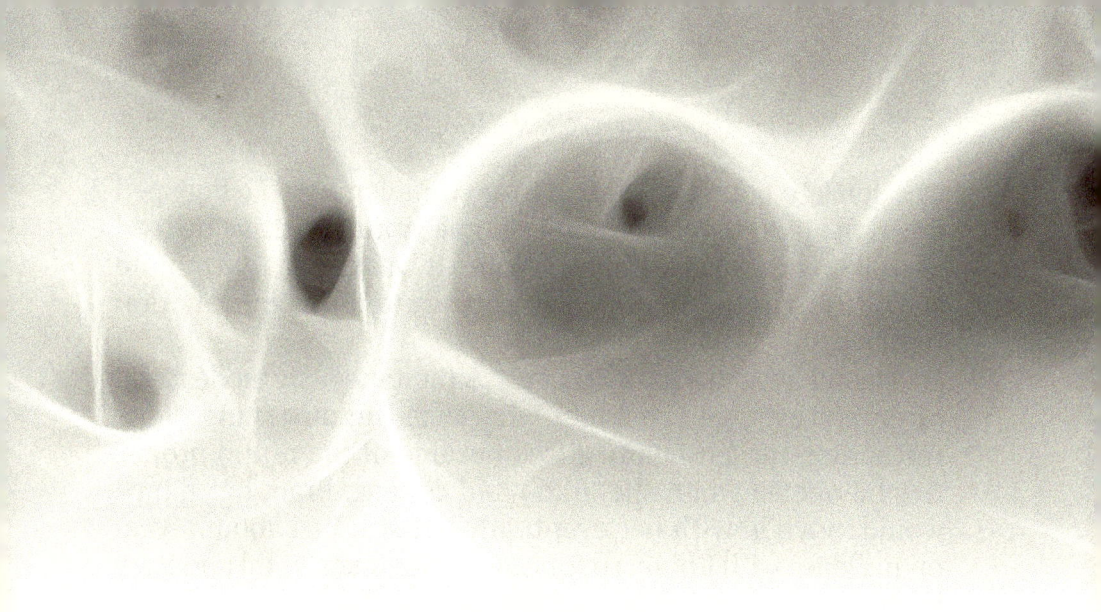

CHAPTER FIVE

Rory hadn't even finished making her coffee when Naomi called her on Saturday morning. She was half-awake, having brushed her teeth and showered but still waiting on her coffee to brew. The smell was helping her perk up, but she was looking forward to that first sip of sweetened caffeine.

"Hey girl," Naomi said. She was so fast to answer that Rory didn't even have a chance to greet her. There was a strong sense of urgency in her voice that was hard to miss. "FaceTime on purpose this time. Do you have a moment?"

Rory's interest was instantly piqued; Naomi normally cut right to the chase, and she appreciated that about her friend. "Yeah, I just got up, like, twenty minutes ago. Why, what's up?"

"You'll want to come over here and see this. I think I'm onto something big."

"How big? Like Hematite big?"

"Almost." Naomi grinned at the collection of newspaper clippings before her as she switched the camera's view to show Rory. "I think I know who Stone Breaker is."

Rory nearly dropped her phone. "I'll be there in ten minutes, tops."

Rory had never gotten her belongings together more quickly than she had at that moment. She nearly forgot her coffee but was quick to pour some into a to-go tumbler. Rory all but sped down the road to reach Naomi's home, opting to drive instead of walk to not waste a single second. It was only a ten-minute walk through the suburbs, but Rory wanted this information right away.

Naomi lived in a house that was simultaneously modest and nicer than average. Her father, who owned his own stand-alone restaurant-turned-chain, gifted her one of the rental properties he owned when she graduated college. Brad, her fiancé, would move in with her eventually but still had about a year on his lease with Elijah, so for now, it was just Naomi and Rory in the house.

"I'm so excited for you to see this," Naomi said when Rory arrived. She'd thrown her hair up in a messy bun and wasn't wearing any of her usual makeup. "There's a little self-doubt in the back of my mind, so maybe you can let me know if you think I'm onto something here, but it all adds up."

A myriad of paperwork littered Naomi's dining room table. There were so many that Rory couldn't even see the wood beneath it, but all the important ones with lines highlighted in pink were on the top.

"How long have you been at this?" Rory asked before she took a sip of her coffee. "Don't you work the night shift? Are you not exhausted?"

"I will sleep like a baby come lunchtime, don't worry," Naomi said with a wave of her hand. "Anyway, at first, I didn't believe it. I thought there was no way. But the more I found, the more I realized all signs pointed to him." Naomi pointed at a printed-out photo of a reporter for the local newspaper. His thin, blonde hair was gelled back, and he seemed awkwardly stiff in his headshot.

"Do we know him? He doesn't exactly look familiar."

"I think I do more than you. He was in a few of my journalism classes at school. I think he went to school in Riverpeak too. It's Mark Stevens."

"Okay, that name sounds familiar, at least. Wasn't he that geeky kid in your classes? His dad was the politician?"

CHAPTER FIVE

"The one who got caught sleeping with Chief Daniels, yes! Listen, I can't confirm it, but I'm sure there's a way we could if we keep going in this direction. And if you look in this video that Stone Breaker posted," Naomi grabbed a printed-out screenshot, "in the background is the city council logo. It's the same one right outside of City Hall. People have also reported seeing him drive a Harley, and the only person in town I know with a Harley is Mark."

"His dad shacking up with the police chief is enough to convince me, to be honest." Rory began shuffling through some of the documentation. Articles Mark had written for his newspaper were included in the mix. Rory began scanning them and then furrowed her brows when she saw how a few of the words stacked.

> Stone Breaker
> rising
> 19
> January

"Hey Naomi," Rory said, "do you have a highlighter?"

"Yeah, let me grab it." Naomi jogged over to her bedroom and shortly returned with one. "Did you see something?"

"Maybe it's just my history teacher brain over-analyzing something, but I think there's a message in this," she said. "It could be a coincidence, but I wanna see if this checks out. My juniors are learning about World War II, and we talked a lot about spies and how they sent codes, so I had them write a report with a hidden message inside. They had to get creative with how they hid everything. If I wasn't in the middle of grading those, I don't know that I would have necessarily picked up on this."

Rory went over the words that stood out to her. She hoped it would, in fact, result in a secret message. She blindly highlighted the stacked words in Mark's article until she reached the last line and then read over it to see what it resulted in.

> Stone Breaker
> rising
> 19
> January
> Riverpeak
> attack
> plans

"What day did Hematite get killed?" Rory asked. "Was it January 19th, by chance?"

Naomi shuffled through a few more papers and grabbed one dated January 20th. "Yup. This one from the next day is covering it since it happened the night before."

Rory set the article aside and grabbed another newspaper, doing the same thing. She followed the same pattern as the last piece, using the second word in each row to see if it lined up to form a sentence.

> Stone Breaker
> fight
> Valentine's Day
> downtown
> night

"He's hiding messages in his work," Rory said. "If he's not Stone Breaker, they're certainly working together."

"Holy crap," Naomi said. "Good catch."

"We gotta get this to Hematite. We still have about a week before Valentine's Day. He could seriously use this, and we could stop something big."

"If I get caught getting involved, my journalistic integrity will come into question, unfortunately," Naomi said. "Our news director has insisted that we stay as non-biased as possible. I think this situation falls into that category."

"That's fine; I can bring it to him. You know, speaking of journalistic integrity, this Stevens guy is pretty anti-Hematite," Rory said. "For hard-hitting vigilante stories, these

CHAPTER FIVE

all seem really soft on Stone Breaker and the city government. They've gotta be linked, which would make sense if that's his dad."

"How are you going to get this to Hematite?" Naomi asked. "It's not like anybody knows where he is."

"No, but we can find out his beat. How often does he come up on the scanners?"

"All the time. Every night the cops say the caller mentions him, but by the time they get there, he's gone."

"When you tune in next time you're at work, keep me posted. I'll be up late so just text me whenever. You know I barely sleep anymore." Rory checked her watch. "Shit, Kane will be at my house soon. I gotta go. We grade homework together every Saturday."

"Aw, cute! Here, if you're going after him, take this." Naomi slid all the papers together. "I have copies of everything. Don't sweat it."

"You sure?"

"Positive. Just stay safe, okay?"

Rory grinned and felt a renowned sense of determination she hadn't ever felt be. "I promise."

Kane smiled every time he entered Rory's house. It was a clear upgrade from his and felt more like home to him than his own place, considering how often he was there. Her single-story home was small but still made his studio apartment look like a shoebox. White curtains draped across the window in the living room and were held together at the ends with a gold rope. There was a large sill for someone to sit and look out the window at the town, which was often Rory's go-to spot. Even Kane had to admit that the view of the mountaintops from her window was beautiful and enough to almost make him forget about the problems that lie beneath them.

The open floor plan allowed for the kitchen counter bar stools to face the living room, making for an ideal space to share with company. The coffee table in the living room had a vase filled with fresh-cut flowers from the grocery store that made the whole apartment smell like summer, even in the dead of winter. Assorted photos and artifacts littered the walls, some from travels and others of her with Naomi, Brad, and Kane in college.

Kane took his usual spot on the floor of her living room, with his students' homework on the coffee table and his back against the couch as Rory made her way to the windowsill. But unbeknownst to Rory, he couldn't take his eyes off her. The sunbeams coming through the window fell on her skin and her hair, making her highlights pop in their trajectory. Her expression showed she loved how it warmed her skin, and Kane could see it in the way her lips rested in a soft smile while she worked. Every now and then, she would toss some hair over her shoulder or tuck some behind her ear. The sight of her in her element, focused on her work and basking in the sun, made Kane feel a pang of longing in his chest.

Rory, breaking the silence, interrupted him from his admiration. "What would you do if you were a superhero?"

"Me?" Kane took a sip of water to hide his nerves. "I'd probably be like Robin Hood or something. Steal from the rich but give it to the poor."

"Ooh, very noble. I like that. Anything else?"

"Eh, maybe I'd get laid for once."

Rory poorly stifled a laugh. "You'd go through all that just to get laid?"

"Hell yeah! Come on, Rory, think about it. The school pays us peanuts, and you know my family is broke as shit. That's not exactly great for a love life. I'm chronically single."

"Not all of us care about a guy's wallet, you know."

"Alright then. Can I ask you a serious question and have it not fuck up our friendship? No judgment allowed."

"Sure. I'll even pinky-promise if you want," Rory said, matching his mischief in her tone.

Kane held his finger out, and Rory interlocked hers with his. His finger was calloused, but his skin was otherwise fairly smooth. She noticed that Kane's hands were quite larger than

CHAPTER FIVE

hers, something so obvious yet somehow new to her. *Maybe,* she thought, *therapy had her seeing things in a new light.*

"Let's pretend we weren't friends and haven't known each other for years. I try to pick you up. Let's say we're out at a bar or whatever. Would you sleep with me?" Kane subconsciously licked his lips and then said, "You can say no; I won't be offended."

"Kay, you know I don't do hookups."

"Pretend you did. Don't try to skirt around the question."

"You want my honest answer?" Kane nodded and then, to his surprise, she said, "Yeah, I'd let you take me home."

"No fuckin' way, dude," Kane said as the corner of his mouth curved up into a smile. He leaned his head back against the couch. "You would?"

"Yes, Kane, I would! You're a fucking pervert sometimes, but you're funny and ridiculously good-looking, so you can get away with it."

"You think I'm ridiculously good-looking?"

Rory huffed. "You've got this, like, mid-90s-Ethan Hawke-thing going on. It works."

Kane laughed. He wanted to kiss Rory right then and there, but he settled for holding on to her pinky with his own. "I don't think I'd hook up with you."

"Ooh, ouch." Part of her felt disappointed, but she wasn't totally sure why. "Why not?"

"You're *way* too good for me. Especially morally, but in every way possible. You're the type of girl I'd intend to hit once and then end up falling in love with, only to never hear from her again."

"That is oddly specific. Thank you, I think."

"I'm glad we got that out of our systems," Kane said. He pulled Rory's pinky to his lips and gave it a playful kiss before letting go. While he hadn't been serious, it still felt good for him to let some of his feelings out, even if it was in a roundabout way.

The softness of Kane's lips on her finger surprised her. In truth, it always surprised her when Kane shared a rare moment of tenderness with her, even if it was something he tried to hide in a sea of jokes.

"What would you do if *you* were a superhero?" Kane asked. "Your turn."

"Hmm. I'd probably help other women. Beat up their shitty boyfriends and dunk the ones who catcall in the sewer."

"That is rather on brand for you. Maybe I could be your cool sidekick."

Rory smiled at him, and Kane thought he was going to melt. "Say, are you ever gonna help me and Naomi with this Hematite thing? I think we're onto something here."

Kane raised an eyebrow. "Oh yeah? What have you found?" He was genuinely curious about what Rory had to say, his own personal biases set aside.

"We're starting with Stone Breaker. I think I know who he is, but I want to get everything over to Hematite either way. I think he's this reporter that Naomi went to school with; his dad's a politician."

Kane felt a sense of relief when he heard that their focus was on Stone Breaker rather than himself.

"What would a journalist and a politician have to do with Hematite?" Rory asked. "I mean, I get they're super pro-police, but it seems excessive. What the hell are they hiding?"

Kane soaked her in as she spoke. He loved seeing the gears turn in Rory's head like this. "All I know is that he's got a really dumb name," Kane said. "Stone Breaker. What is he, twelve?"

Rory laughed. "I don't like it either. Naomi is going to be narrowing down when Hematite patrols downtown Riverpeak so I can get all these goodies to him. Maybe I can finally meet him."

Kane did his best to not tense up. "And what will you do when you meet him?" In truth, Kane was wondering what *he'd* do when he saw Rory. "What if he isn't everything he's cracked up to be?"

Rory furrowed her brows. "What do you mean? He saved my life, Kane; you know that. Your sister's too!"

"I know, I know! But what if he turns out to be just some ordinary dude? Or what if he doesn't want any help?"

CHAPTER FIVE

"Then too bad for him," Rory said. Kane could see how strong her conviction was now. While she always wanted to meet Hematite, she had never actively done much of anything about it. Now, though, she held confidence she lacked before.

"Just be careful, okay?" His teasing nature from a few moments ago faded. He kissed her pinky again but with more pressure this time. "You're my best friend, Miller. I worry about you."

"Then help us. Come on, Kane. I know you like to play dumb, but you're so much smarter than you like to lead on."

Kane couldn't help but smile. No one ever told him that before.

"I'll help in my own way," Kane said, with the hint of a promise in his voice. "I'm not about to be running into gunfire with Stone Breaker. And you shouldn't either." He was painfully self-aware of the irony in his words, but he bit it back.

Something is off with Kane, Rory thought. That left her something else to get to the bottom of, but it was clear from his half-baked responses it wouldn't be today.

That night, as he changed, Kane couldn't stop hearing Rory's voice on repeat in his mind. He pulled his hood over his head as he walked out the door, ran down the stairs of his apartment complex, and then lurked off into the shadows. He was surprised no one spotted him coming in or out of his apartment over the years, but he supposed that came with the territory. Riverpeak was a small, quiet town and much didn't happen after nine o'clock, unless you looked closely enough.

Kane entered the east side of the city with trepidation. He stopped fearing death a long time ago but still hated the unpredictability that came with the streets. City Hall was at the far end of the road, marking the division between the east side and downtown. Most of the times he had been attacked or even killed were right between the two. He even saw some spots where his old blood still stained the sidewalks.

It was eerily quiet tonight and with no real reason why, Kane was more on edge than usual. He glanced twice at each alley before turning down any intersections, trying to find any sign of life beyond the occasional prairie dog that scurried by when spooked. Based on his own chill he felt shooting down his spine, he figured most people would be bundled up indoors somewhere. But even on the coldest Colorado nights, there were still a handful of people looking for a way to get their next hit on the streets.

Kane decided after walking a few blocks that he needed a higher vantage point. There was no luck on the ground, something that usually wasn't the case. So, he found a fire escape for an apartment complex and used it to climb up a few stories before hopping over to the Chinese takeout restaurant next door, where he'd have more room to patrol. He could smell the residual sesame oil from earlier in the night, even through the multiple layers of fabric that covered his nose.

The last few times he came to the east side, there had been at least a handful of Stone Breaker's hired help waiting for him. He walked the perimeter of the restaurant's flat roof, avoiding the vents and trying to not be blinded by the neon lights of their sign, and saw no one. After doing a full lap around the roof, he sat on the spot where he started, letting his legs swing over the side of the roof as he waited for something to happen. He grabbed his cell phone and called Shawn, one of the few people in on his secret.

"Hey, dude. Where are you stationed up tonight?"

"Just a few miles outside of downtown Denver. Why?"

"It's fucking weird, man. I'm on the east side of Riverpeak, and there is literally no one here. Barely even a light on. I've never seen it this quiet."

"I think they're all here," Shawn said. "I'm keeping an eye on some pick-up trucks and beaters moving in and out of the South Main Burgers up here. Something tells me it's not just college kids with the munchies."

Kane checked the time. "They should have closed an hour ago. I'll let you go, then. Don't lose them, Jameson."

"Yeah, yeah. Whatever, dude. Don't die or whatever."

CHAPTER FIVE

Kane hung up and sighed. Knowing Shawn, that would, unfortunately, be the last he heard of it. Shawn wasn't shy about his super strength, which was the only reason Kane had approached him in the first place. When he first told Shawn that he was Hematite, Shawn laughed in his face, but believed it once Kane showed the scars to prove it. Their partnership began in college, but Shawn seemed to always seek more. As much as Shawn denied it, Kane knew it was jealousy over local fame that Kane never wanted for Hematite in the first place.

Kane squinted as he spotted someone in the distance coming from what seemed like out of nowhere. Once they were closer, he cursed to himself.

Kane knew who it was right away when he saw voluminous, tight curls he could spot in any crowd. *At least*, he thought, *she had the sense to dress plainly*. He turned his voice modifier on as he made the leap back over to the fire escape, slid down the interior of the tube, and then ran as silently as he could toward her.

Walking along the sidewalk in plain sight with a backpack over her shoulders was Rory Miller. He wasn't sure what she thought she was doing, but he had to get her the hell out of here.

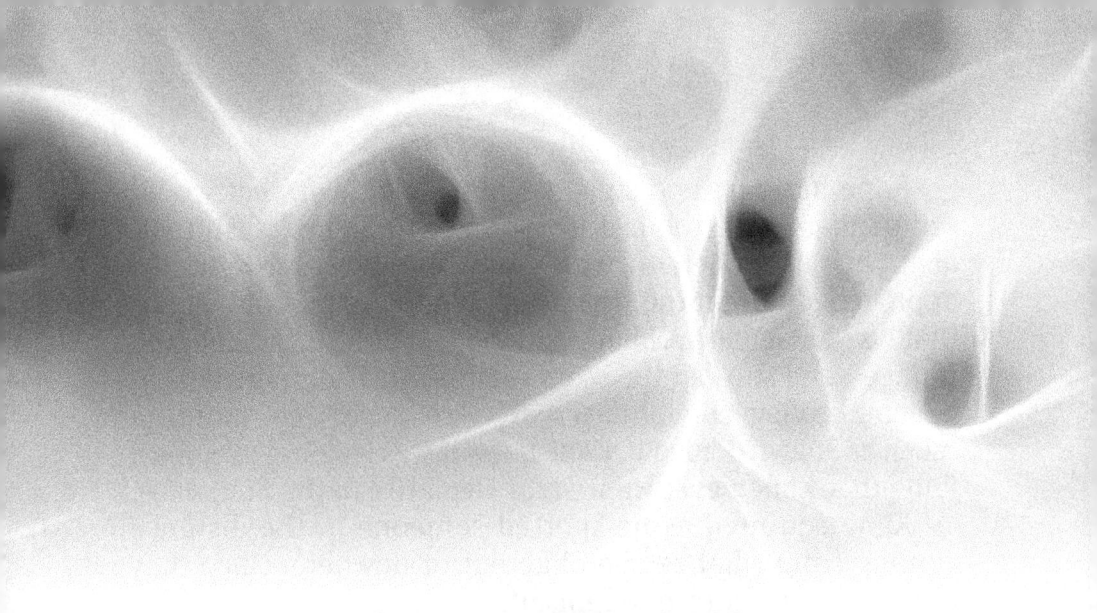

CHAPTER SIX

Rory sighed as she walked through the relatively abandoned part of town on the east side. She always got the creeps heading through this dusty corner of Riverpeak. A few people still lived here, but the city government, who viewed it as just a money pit, had largely ignored the area. Their blind eye made itself clear with the various potholes in the street, the cracked sidewalks, and patches of dead grass trying to peek out through the snow, desperate for some sunlight. There was a cop car sitting at a corner she passed, but no one was inside. Someone had tagged it with a symbol Rory didn't recognize in red spray paint.

The spookiest part of the town, she thought, was the abandoned burger takeout restaurant with its windows boarded up and covered in graffiti. She wasn't sure why, but she felt like she was being watched when she walked past it. It was Naomi's dad's old place, but she never was totally sure why he abandoned it.

She adjusted her backpack straps as they fell down her shoulders a bit, eager to share the evidence she and Naomi collected with Hematite. Rory monitored her surroundings to stay alert, not because she was afraid of the community but because she knew Stone Breaker could be anywhere. As

CHAPTER SIX

she wandered, she hoped she would find Hematite camping out. She had no luck with a police scanner, but Naomi dug up some police reports that mentioned him being here this day of the week and at the late hour. Rory was going off nothing but hope and a prayer, as she tried to ignore the chill that wouldn't seem to leave her spine.

The last time she had been to this part of town, it was much busier, with people just trying to make ends meet no matter what it took. But it seemed like the victims of the corrupt government had gone into hiding. It was actually more fear-inducing, Rory believed as she glanced around, with no one walking the streets. She hated the unpredictability of the quiet roads and run-down buildings. *What a shame*, she thought, *because it could be a charming district*. The local government just didn't care, no matter how much the people spoke up or voted for change.

Suddenly, in an instant, someone wrapped an arm around her torso. Before she could scream, a hand covered in boxing wraps and a wool glove was over her mouth and nose. The unseen figure jerked Rory into an alleyway and just as she thought she was making the biggest mistake of her life in coming down there, the person gently placed her against the wall of a building.

Her lower back felt the cool brick through her clothes; it was cold and late enough to be felt through her multiple layers, but her backpack provided some relief. Rory's eyes widened in panic, but she immediately felt relaxed when she saw it was just Hematite standing before her. He removed his arm from her body to hold his finger up to where his lips were beneath his scarves and balaclava, showing she should be quiet. Rory nodded, trusting him, and he dropped his hand.

As Rory caught her breath and let her heart rate slow down, she took in the sight of him. Hematite looked exactly as Rory remembered him, but was broader now, especially in his shoulders. His frame was still lean, though, and his outfit was more or less the same as it had always been. The only difference was the hoodie he was wearing over his usual black or navy shirt; the hoodie had a fish-mouth-shaped high neck that helped him cover his face beneath his usual balaclava and cowl. She couldn't fully make out his eyes, which were the only part of him she could see. Between the dark of the night, the shadows of the alley, and the hood over his face, it was hard to tell what color his eyes were.

"Sorry about that," Hematite said in a whisper. "We can't be seen. Follow me."

Hematite took a hold of her hand and led her down the alley. He took care to check around every corner and periodically looked up too to make sure no one was hiding on any rooftops. Before Rory knew it, they were at the storage unit facility at the edge of Main Street. Hematite led her into a unit in the back, and he was quick to close the door behind them.

The unit was mostly empty. An old laptop rested on a desk and a few newspapers hung up on the wall, all featuring stories of Stone Breaker or the town's drug ring.

"What the hell were you doing out there?" Hematite asked. "That's Stone Breaker's territory. You know that, right? You could have gotten seriously hurt."

"I was looking for you!"

"Don't look for me," Hematite retorted. "It's dangerous."

"Like I give a shit! Listen, I can help you. I have info. Like, a good deal of it."

"And what do you want in return?" Hematite asked. He already knew the answer, but he had to keep the front up.

"Nothing," Rory said. "I want nothing in return."

"Nothing comes free. Why are you really here?"

"You saved my life a few years ago and wanted nothing in return. Is it so hard to believe that maybe someone wants to help you for once?"

He didn't respond. This was not how Rory expected this to go. She could feel the adrenaline moving through her body and in their silence, she became hyper-aware of her increased heart rate as Hematite looked her up and down.

After a long moment, he finally broke the pause. "I remember you."

CHAPTER SIX

The tension she was subconsciously holding in her face released. She didn't realize how tight her jaw had become. "You do?"

Hematite nodded. "Rory, right?"

She smiled. "You remember my name?" Rory didn't think he'd remember her at all. It had been years, and he had helped more people than she imagined he could count. Rory never considered herself special enough to be worth him remembering.

"What can I say? You left an impression." He sat in the cheap, metal folding chair that was in front of the computer and leaned forward, his elbows resting on his thighs. "Alright, fuck it. You're already here. What do you got for me, Rory?"

As much as she wanted to ask him what he meant by her leaving an impression, she knew she needed to stay on target. Rory swallowed the lump in her throat and looked at the newspaper clippings of Stone Breaker. One of them caught her eye—the one written by Mark Stevens. She took it off the wall and handed it to him, pointing at the byline.

"That's Stone Breaker." As she rattled off the information, Hematite blinked at her as he comprehended what she said. She was so confident and said it so quickly that it took him a moment to digest the information. "I have proof," Rory said, as she reached for the paperwork resting in a folder in her bag. "My friend Naomi is fantastic at digging up dirt on people. She may have fallen down a rabbit hole here. Any and every kind of supporting documentation that you could possibly have is all right here. I am 100 percent positive when I say that Stone Breaker is Mark Stevens."

"I ... wow," Hematite said. "Thank you. This will help me track him and try to figure out what he's up to." He shuffled through the papers in the manilla folder. He was looking forward to telling Elijah about this information. "How did you two do all this?"

"Naomi is a reporter for Channel 10. She has access to a lot and knows who to call," Rory said. "I'm just a nosy bitch."

Hematite chuckled. "I think the word you're looking for is inquisitive."

Rory's smile grew. "Well, that certainly sounds a lot nicer. By the way, the highlighted stuff in yellow, the reports spell out a message. I found out that he stacks the second word on every line. It's been consistent, but worth noting for future articles in case he does this again. He might attack on Valentine's Day in Downtown Riverpeak. Hope you don't have a date."

He scoffed. "Guess I do now." Kane thought about how this must have been what Rory referenced when they graded papers together the afternoon prior. He was impressed—he knew Rory was sharp and that Naomi was resourceful, but he hadn't expected them to crack the Stone Breaker case so quickly. He hoped they couldn't crack his own.

"Is there any way I can help?" Rory asked.

"No, no," he said. "You've already put yourself in harm's way enough. Stone Breaker is dangerous, and I don't want you getting hurt. This is a tremendous help. If I can get ahead of Stone Breaker and Shatterstone, I might stop them for good."

Rory furrowed her brows. "Wait, who the hell is Shatterstone? There's two of them?"

Hematite nodded. "Shatterstone has been keeping a lower profile. He's the one filming all of Stone Breaker's videos."

"And I thought Stone Breaker was a stupid name. Shatterstone is even dumber."

Hematite chuckled. "Shatterstone was the one that tried to kill me. He ran before I could even talk to him and strikes me as a complete coward."

"I'd say both of them are for wearing a mask, but you know," Rory said with a nervous chuckle, "it's different when you do it."

He shook his head and grinned beneath his facial coverings. "I get what you mean. No offense taken, don't worry."

"Why is he going after you? You can't be the only one trying to clean up Riverpeak."

"Actually, I think I might be. But to be honest, I'm not entirely sure," Hematite said. "I have a theory that he's somehow profiting off the drug problem in this city. If he isn't, his father definitely is. That and the fact that he failed to kill

CHAPTER SIX

me is probably driving him fucking crazy." He looked at Rory and set the papers down. "Let me take you home."

"Oh, no, I couldn't ask—."

"I'm not asking."

"Oh." Rory released another nervous laugh; he didn't make her uncomfortable, but she still couldn't believe this was happening. "Are you sure? I'm sure you have better things to do."

Hematite smiled at her, even though she couldn't see it. "I'll feel better if I know you got home safely. But we're going my way. Do you trust me?"

Rory nodded. "With my life."

"Follow me and do as I say. Got it?"

Rory nodded again.

Hematite led Rory outside. As he closed the storage unit behind them and locked it, she made a mental note of the number to look it up later. Hematite led Rory out of the facility through the back, and once they reached the fence, he crouched down a bit.

"Hop on my back," he said. "I'll carry you over."

Rory didn't question him and just did as he said. She felt incredibly close to him as he carried her over the fence, with her arms around his shoulders and her legs around his waist. His effortlessness was a testament to the strength and stamina he'd built from years of street fighting. The muscles that Rory could feel beneath her were solid and defined, even through the layers of clothing.

Once they were back on the ground, Hematite set Rory gently on her feet. They ran behind buildings, with Hematite keeping a close eye for bystanders or anyone who might be watching. She held his gloved and wrapped hand as she trailed close behind him, so as to not get lost. The entire time they ran through the alleyways of Riverpeak, she could hear her heart pounding in her ears. Despite the risk of danger and the way the cold air stung her face, Rory couldn't stop smiling.

Once they reached her neighborhood, Kane stopped and realized he had to be careful: if he took Rory to her home, then he'd practically be giving his identity away to Rory.

"Where do you live?" he asked with feigned uncertainty.

"Come on, it's not far. Everyone's probably in bed by now."

He nodded, letting Rory walk him the rest of the way there. Now that they were out of the east side of the city, and away from Stone Breaker's reach, he felt a bit more relaxed. Rory's corner of the suburbs was quaint and sleepy. The homes lined the street in perfect rows, more or less the same style but all in different colors and sizes. Kane glanced at Rory and saw that her shoulders were rolled back, and the corners of her lips were curled upward, likely subconsciously. She let him walk on the outside of the sidewalk, farther from the streetlights that illuminated the path.

"Thanks for walking me home," Rory said. "And for everything else."

Kane nodded. "Yeah, of course." He cleared his throat as quietly as he could. "Safety first."

She fiddled with her thumbs. "Sure, sure. But for real. I've been wondering what I was going to say to you if I ever came face to face with you again. You saved my life, you know?"

"Don't mention it," Kane said with a small shake of his head. "Like you said, I'm just trying to clean this place up. Cops don't seem to want to do it, so someone has to get their hands dirty."

"Well, I'm glad it's you." Rory rubbed the back of her neck. "You're a good man."

Kane smiled beneath his mask and scarves. "Thanks." He wasn't used to this; normally he was gone before anyone could even acknowledge him, but he couldn't find the desire to walk away from Rory.

She stopped in front of her house and pointed at it with her thumb. "If, uh, you ever need anything, this is me," she said. "You're welcome here anytime. You don't even need to ask; just show up."

"I'll keep that in mind," he said. "Be careful out there. Good night, Rory."

CHAPTER SIX

Rory's closed-lipped smile was so wide that she felt it in her cheeks. "Good night, Hematite."

He didn't leave until Rory went inside. When she peeked through the blinds, she saw him linger by the front door before making his way back down the street from the way they came. She walked over to her couch, picked up a pillow, and screamed into it to release the adrenaline still pent up inside her. She thought maybe when she removed the pillow from her face, she'd find out it was all a dream, but nothing changed when she did.

She thanked him as she had always wanted, but now, Rory realized she wanted more.

"Good morning!" Rory greeted cheerily as Kane got in the passenger seat of her car.

"Morning, sunshine. You're certainly chipper today," Kane said. He noticed the pep in her tone right away.

"Aren't I always?" Rory asked with a bit of a pout. She waited for him to buckle his seatbelt and then took off for the school.

"I mean, you're definitely more of a morning person than I am, but you seem extra awake, I guess." Kane already knew why but wanted to hear what she had to say.

"You wouldn't believe what happened last night," Rory said with a goofy smile. "I found Hematite."

Time to play dumb again, Kane thought. "No shit? That's great. How'd that go?"

"I can't believe it, Kay. He actually entertained the idea of me helping him. I was hoping for a slightly less ... broody response, so to speak, but he took all the info that Naomi and I have been gathering."

"I'm glad to hear you found him. Just be careful out there, alright?"

"You're sounding like him," Rory teased. Kane didn't miss the irony. "He says Stone Breaker is dangerous, and I'm sure he is. But we found him, Kay! We can fight back if we know what to expect, you know?"

"I suppose that's one way of looking at it," Kane said. He had been up all night debating on how much he should tell Rory today, if anything at all. He took a swig of his coffee as he pondered it again and then decided ultimately against it.

Very few people actually knew who Hematite was behind the mask. He had told Elijah, plus his doctors were aware since they were the ones to discover his power with him after a near-death experience in his parent's drug shed as a teenager. The only other person who knew was Shawn Jameson, who had some powers of his own. Shawn's physical prowess was out of the ordinary and likely from the same source as Kane's inability to die. Neither of them told Brad, their childhood friend, and Elijah only knew about Kane's identity at this point.

Kane wagered that if Rory knew it was him, she'd only want to get more involved. While she was on a fast track to danger, revealing his identity to her would only put her in even more trouble. He knew Rory would do anything for him, so his love for her prevented him from saying more.

"Hey, do you want to do a joint class project this semester?" Kane offered. "I've got a section on biographies coming up for one of my English classes, and I was thinking of making them do a social studies tie-in to help them retain what they're learning. How's Hamilton sound?"

"Yes! Ooh, we could do a session on it with my U.S. History classes!" Kane was relieved that she responded so positively so quickly; the more he could monitor her, the better, even if it meant going slightly off curriculum. "I like to watch the Broadway show with them now that you can stream it online and then make them compare and contrast the show with actual history. If you want, we can work on a more robust plan later?"

"Yeah, I'd like that," Kane said. "Are you doing anything tonight?"

Rory shook her head.

CHAPTER SIX

"Come on over. I'll order some takeout and we can figure it out. Maybe even light a candle or two."

Rory rolled her eyes as she pulled into her parking spot. "I'm going to hold you to that."

Kane smirked at her, then they made their way inside the school. "Come on, you gotta at least give me credit for trying."

"I'll give you credit for trying if you ever seriously ask me out on a date. How's that sound?"

Kane rose his eyebrows. Even though she often did, it always surprised him when Rory matched his energy. "Is that permission to do so?"

"Maybe it is. I guess you won't know until you try."

"Well, I can't now; it would be expected. I like to keep you on your toes." Kane winked.

"Mission accomplished on that one."

"That's what I like to hear. See you at lunch?"

"You already know it," Rory said. They parted ways at their classrooms, which were only a few doors down from one another.

As she waited for her students to filter into her class, Rory allowed herself to get lost in thought while she prepared for the day.

She often told Kane that she never knew when he was flirting with her for real or not anymore, and she still meant it. It was hard for her to discern what was Kane's typical teasing versus him actually testing the waters. As per usual, the way he spoke to her left a feeling of butterflies in her abdomen and ruddiness on her cheeks that she tried to push down. After all, Kane was Kane, and she never wanted to get her hopes up that he would decide to settle down one day.

Rory forced herself to snap out of her thoughts when Jordan entered the classroom extra early. She noticed Jordan looked lost in a daydream, but not necessarily a happy one; her eyes lacked their usual luster and her movements seemed slower.

"Good morning, Miss Miller." Jordan's tone of voice matched her glum expression.

"Good morning, Jordan. Everything okay?"

"That obvious?" Jordan sighed. "I'm, uh, having some boy trouble. That's all. It's nothing."

"Well, there's a few more minutes before anyone else will probably come in. If I can help, I'm here, okay?"

Jordan nodded and was silent for a moment. A minute or so passed as the two of them just listened to the ticking of the clock before Jordan asked, "What do you do when you can't tell if the guy that you like likes you back?"

Rory smiled, amused by their mirrored predicament.

"You know, I've been in your shoes. I've tried waiting it out and seeing if anything would happen; it just made it even harder. So, if I had to give you any advice, I would say take the first step and see what happens. Isn't winter formal coming up soon? Ask him to go with you. If he's weirded out by the idea of a date, just brush it off as a friend-date kind of thing. Crisis averted."

Rory wished she could take her own advice but was glad to at least help someone else out.

"Thanks, Miss Miller. I think I'll try that. Are you chaperoning again this year?"

Rory nodded. "I will be. If all else fails, I'll dance with you. I keep up with the trends on TikTok."

Jordan laughed. "You do?"

"Oh yeah, or at least I try to," Rory said. A few other students came into class at this point, so Rory jotted their names down for roll call. "I can't promise that I won't embarrass myself in the process, but if you can get clout out of it, then I'll take the hit."

"Thanks, Miss Miller."

Rory internally panicked; she had almost forgotten about the winter formal coming up that she and Kane agreed to chaperone in a few short weeks. She mentally cursed herself and penciled in a note for herself to make sure she still had a dress.

CHAPTER SIX

After their assembly last month, Rory also couldn't help but wonder if Stone Breaker would make some sort of appearance at the dance.

"Oh, and Jordan?"

"Yes?"

"That *is* how you guys are using the word 'clout,' right?"

Jordan laughed. "Yeah, Ms. Miller. It is."

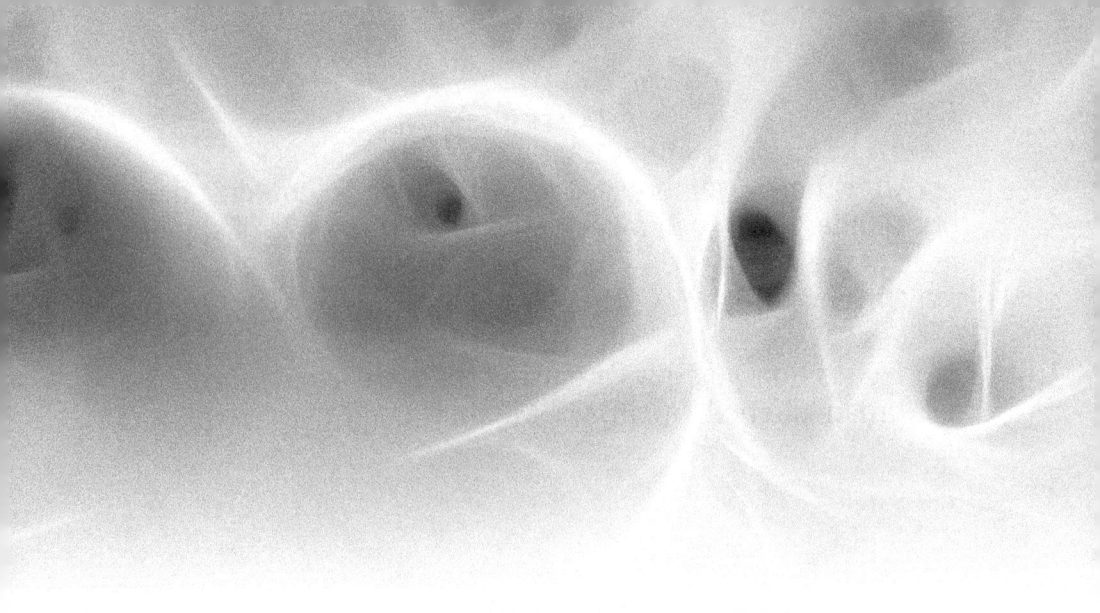

CHAPTER SEVEN

Kane, as Hematite, frowned from his perch atop one of the university's buildings. He didn't come here often anymore but still liked to make a surprise visit whenever he had the chance on a weekend. During the day, the view of the mountains was spectacular from up on the rooftops, but tonight he only saw his sister in trouble. This was the exact same spot where he had stopped Rory's stalker from hurting her all those years ago, and now Kayla and a friend were being harassed by two drunk punks wearing fraternity letters. The memories left a bad taste in his mouth.

Kayla left her blonde hair in a ponytail tonight, so Kane prepared for the men to try to use that to their advantage and grab for it. Even though she was seven years younger than Kane, people often thought they were twins with how alike in the face they looked. Kayla was tall even without heels and looked older than her years, which didn't help the twin assumptions, though Kane knew it was from the stress of growing up with drug dealers for parents.

Clearly, he thought, *the police that covered the university hadn't improved or learned their lesson.* When Rory was stalked, they didn't take any real action until the night he intervened. He wondered how many times people complained

CHAPTER SEVEN

about these two students, shifting closer so he could attack without hurting Kayla or her friend. He didn't know her name.

"Come on, pretty girl," one of the men harassing his sister cooed. "What's wrong?" He went to reach for Kayla's long, blonde hair, but he didn't have a chance.

Kayla and her friend screamed, as Hematite jumped down and slammed their attacker's head against the closest brick wall. The brick was cold beneath the man's head, the air around it even cooler. Winter was always more painful in Kane's opinion, with the air making his skin more prone to crack from dryness alongside the beatdowns. The sky was so dark that the perpetrator hadn't even seen Hematite coming.

"Run!" he shouted at the girls.

Kayla tried to follow the command, but the other guy after her—a tall yet stocky brute with sandy blonde hair and pale skin—reached out and grabbed her by the arm. Kayla started crying. In her dress and heels, she was at a disadvantage, especially with the thin layer of snow beneath their feet. Her friend wasn't in much better of a position, also dressed inadequately for a fight and fumbling for her phone in her purse.

This was precisely why Kane hated coming to the college part of town but knew he needed to. Like Rory, Kayla didn't know who Hematite actually was; she just knew that Hematite had been there for her ever since she was a little girl. He slammed the man's head into the brick wall again and then dropped him upon seeing he was unconscious.

One less asshole to worry about, Kane thought as he shifted into a boxer's stance.

Kane punched the second man in the jaw, hooking him on the side opposite his sister. The blonde man dropped Kayla's arm as he recoiled and then swung at Kane, but Kane bobbed and weaved in time to miss the hit. Kane followed up with another punch. As the man's head fell in the punch's direction, Kane used the opportunity to arch kick him the opposite way. Kane grabbed a billy club off his belt—a weapon he relied heavily on, but for good reason—and whacked him to continue the natural momentum. The attacker spat out some blood and a few teeth from where the billy club smacked him in the face.

Once the man regained his footing, he made a lunge at Kane, but Kane grabbed the guy's sloppy punch and used the opportunity to get him into an arm bar. The man tried to struggle out of it, but Kane shoved him to the ground and hit him in the head with his billy club again. He hit his temple, and the man passed out. Kane sighed as he stood up, just glad that the fight was over with.

Kayla's friend gawked. "Oh my God, is he dead?"

"Probably not. He's just gonna take a very long nap." Kane patted the man's pockets until he found the one with his cell phone and dialed a number.

"Nine-one-one, what's your location?"

Kane wasted no time. "Two pricks tried to attack some women on campus. They're both passed out behind the dining hall by Lynx Crossing. They're alive."

"Sir, may I get your name?" the voice on the other end asked. But Kane hung up and tossed the phone on the ground next to the blonde. He looked at the two girls, who were frozen in shock.

"You again," Kayla said with a smile. She exhaled and her body slumped in relief.

"You know this guy?" her friend asked.

Kayla nodded. "He's been protecting me since I was a little kid."

"How many times do I have to tell you to stay out of trouble?"

Kayla smiled at him, picking up his teasing. She sounded out of breath but relieved. "Thank you, again. I think I owe you my life twice over at this point."

He nodded. "It's no problem. Don't think anything of it."

Kane knew his mother hadn't been using drugs when she was pregnant with Kayla, so the likelihood that Kayla had any of the abilities Kane did was slim to none. It was a large part of why Kane felt it was his duty to protect her beyond just being her older brother.

"You know, I still have that ring you gave me. The hematite one." Kayla held her hand up to show it on her pinky.

CHAPTER SEVEN

Kane grinned beneath the mask. "I'm surprised. I hear they break pretty easily."

"I guess it knows I still need it." She shifted her weight as she fidgeted with the ring, something she did out of nervous habit. "But seriously, thank you."

"Is it true that you can't die?" Kayla's friend piped up. "There's been rumors ever since you were on the news a little while ago. That's so cool."

"It's not cool," he said. He kept his rage within, not wanting to snap at a stranger. "It's a fucking curse." He looked back to Kayla and just nodded. "Take care."

Kane left at that, returning to the shadows and making a break for it before the girls could follow him. He internally groaned, as Kane understood he benefited from his powers but wished he never had them. Kane was becoming numb to the pain of it all, which in itself was something that disgusted him. But he wasn't sure if his power applied to aging or just when he was attacked. He physically felt himself getting older, and he dreaded the idea of being a decrepit immortal whose body never seemed to stop deteriorating. Worse, he wasn't sure what he would do if he had to outlive those he loved. Kane knew he couldn't fight forever, and once they were gone, he wouldn't want to anymore. The idea of outliving his sister and not getting to grow old alongside Rory was one thought he liked to try to keep out of his head.

About a year into Kane's foray as Hematite, he was still nameless. Everyone had just been calling him the masked vigilante, unsure of what his motives were and just speculating who he was. It amused him whenever he'd turn on the news that no one suspected he was just a teenager wearing whatever clothing he could throw together from the thrift store and the depths of his closet.

Most of what he did when he started wasn't newsworthy, beyond people noticing he was beating the cops to their jobs. Everything had changed, though, when his sister's elementary school made the headlines.

Kayla had been sick for a few days and had to stay after school to make up some tests she missed out on. Kane used the opportunity to patrol the school, resting on the rooftop in his Hematite outfit.

Thirty minutes had passed before Kane heard a helicopter flying overhead. It had approached the school quickly, and the police weren't far behind it. The sound of the helicopter blades in the air and the police sirens dominated his ears, but once they passed by—seemingly taking a lap—he tried to listen in to what was happening.

He then heard the faint pitter-patter of gunfire and a few screams on the other side of the building. He tried not to panic but, knowing his sister was in there, ran into the building. He wasn't worried. He was mostly positive that any bullets wouldn't kill him; he had died twice before that and lived to tell the tale after all.

Kane ran until he saw someone standing in the hallway, kicking at the doors. They were obviously too old to be a student, but too young to be a faculty member.

"Drop your gun!" Kane shouted. He didn't have his voice modifier yet, but the multiple scarves he had wrapped around his face and neck muffled his voice enough to be unrecognizable when he dropped his tone.

Kane was only sixteen and had no clue what he was doing, but it didn't stop him from charging at the other teenager. His punches were getting better than they had a few years ago, even from before he donned this mantle, but it had still been considerably sloppy. Luckily for him, his opponent wasn't much better. Their knowledge of gun-handling had been essentially nonexistent, making it easy for Kane to disarm them.

Once the shooter was disarmed, he grabbed a knife and went for Kane's arm. Kane winced but kept moving, letting the blood slowly drip onto the linoleum of the school floors.

When Kane met his eyes, he saw that they were dazed; it was like there was nothing behind them. His eyes had been bloodshot and dilated from liquid courage, a look Kane knew all too well from his father.

CHAPTER SEVEN

Kane's jaw clenched as he grabbed the discarded gun, hit him in the head with the butt of it, and let him fall to the floor. He dropped the gun again and kicked it down the hall just in case the shooter would wake up, but from the looks of it, he would be out until the police arrived.

Kane looked up to the classroom with a fresh boot print on the door from the dirt on his shoe. He recognized it as Kayla's classroom and thought he'd faint. He grounded himself, knocked on the door, and then said, "It's safe now."

Kane heard his sister's voice through the door. "My hero!"

He smiled beneath his mask. Kayla didn't know, and since he didn't have a name, that's what she called him.

He heard her teacher call her name, but Kayla came running to the door and pushed the black paper covering the window back. Kane could see her peering through the bottom of the glass to look in.

"See!" Kayla exclaimed. "It's really him!"

The teacher glanced up at her spot from behind her desk and saw that it had been, in fact, the masked vigilante from the news.

The teacher approached the door and opened it, seeing that Kane was right: the student who brought the gun was passed out behind him.

"Thank you," the teacher said. "I already called 9-1-1. They should be here soon."

"They were checking the perimeter when I got here. I'm sure they will be too." He turned to Kayla. "You need to stop getting into trouble, alright?"

She laughed. "Trouble seems to find me, but I'm okay. You're always there."

He was planning on giving her the hematite ring in his pocket for her birthday later that week but happened to have had it with him. Despite her insisting that she was fine because he was there, Kane saw her small body trembling and her pupils blown wide, so he reached into his pocket and handed her the box.

"It's hematite," he said. "For protection. I think you need it more than I do, kid."

The attempted shooting made the news that evening. Thankfully, no one had been seriously hurt or killed. What really *struck Kane, though, was the interview the stations did with Kayla. A nine-year-old's witness statement was like media gold.*

"That hero came and rescued my class! And he even gave me this ring! It's made from hematite, see? Isn't it pretty?"

As the news anchors explained that hematite was a stone symbolizing protection, they all began to call him the Hematite Hero, eventually shortening it to Hematite with time. Kane still wasn't sure what he thought of the name, but it certainly stuck.

The next day at work, Kane felt like he could barely function. While he patrolled often, his nights out were becoming more and more frequent. Whenever Rory saw him, he'd have a cup of coffee or an energy drink handy in an attempt to stay awake. What he really needed was a full night's sleep, but Kane didn't think he could afford that anytime soon.

Juggling his usual search for answers, looking after his sister, and dealing with Stone Breaker was starting to burn him out. If Kane had to be completely honest, he didn't want to fight anymore, but he knew it wouldn't be an option for a long time. He thought maybe one day in a few years, he could finally settle down and hope Rory was still single so he could make good on his promise to marry her, if she wasn't dating anyone by the time they turned thirty. He wanted to just enjoy the way the sun felt on his skin as he held her hand instead of spending all of his time out in the night. It would all be worth it, he thought, if that was what was waiting for him at the end of the superhero tunnel.

"You okay, Kay?" Rory asked when he got in the car the next morning.

"Mhm, I'm fine," Kane grumbled as he buckled his seatbelt. Her voice had snapped him out of his daydreaming. "Late night, that's all. The usual."

"Are you sure?"

Kane nodded. He hated lying to Rory as it was but lying to her when she knew he was bullshitting her made it even worse.

CHAPTER SEVEN

Rory had never felt more worried about Kane. Something was going on that he wasn't telling her about, and she wasn't sure if she was more concerned or hurt that he wasn't fessing up. Rory thought Kane would tell her anything, but maybe she had been wrong. She missed her usual Kane, the one who always knew what to say to make her laugh with a crude joke in private or a wink across the room. The more she thought about it, the more she realized that Kane didn't smile as much as he used to anymore.

On their lunch break, Kane didn't seem much better than he had that morning. His eyes still looked sunken in from lack of sleep. His hair was falling out of the half-bun he kept it in so it would stay out of his face. He said little as he ate lunch, seeming to just enjoy his food and any energy it might provide.

"Come with me," Rory said once they finished eating.

"Huh?"

"Come on. We still have twenty minutes until our next classes start. Don't question it."

Kane just shrugged. "Okay." He didn't have the energy to fight, so he just followed Rory from the teacher's lounge to her history classroom. It was clear simply by looking around the room that Rory knew what kept her students' attention. One wall had a signed poster from a production of *Hamilton* that was performed in Denver. She had stitched together side-by-side photos of the characters from the show with their real-life portraits, with short bios of each historical figure.

Rory pulled a blanket out from a trunk she kept by her desk. It was fleece and had some cartoon kittens on it. When she handed it to Kane, he looked at her blankly.

"What are you doing?" Kane asked. "What's this?"

"I keep this in case any of my students don't get enough rest at home," she said. "It's clean. I just washed it last night, and no one used it today. Take a nap. You look exhausted. I'll wake you up when we gotta get back to it, okay?"

He smiled at her. Despite his smile, Rory could see the bags forming beneath his normally bright eyes. His skin seemed more pale than usual, even for the dead of winter. "I could kiss you right now, you know that, Miller?"

Rory laughed and just ruffled his long blonde hair. "You really are exhausted."

Kane chirped his thanks and then curled up in her desk chair. He fell asleep without a problem, despite what Rory would consider him being in an uncomfortable position.

Rory sighed as she looked on, wondering what was going on with Kane. *Surely there was more to his partying than met the eye*, she thought, and she wondered if he was more involved in the Hematite and Stone Breaker situation than he led on. An intrusive thought suggested he could work with the other side, but then she remembered how he comforted her after Hematite rescued her and dismissed it. *There is no way*, she concluded. Rory simply made a mental note to tell Naomi that Kane was acting strangely so they could get to the bottom of it.

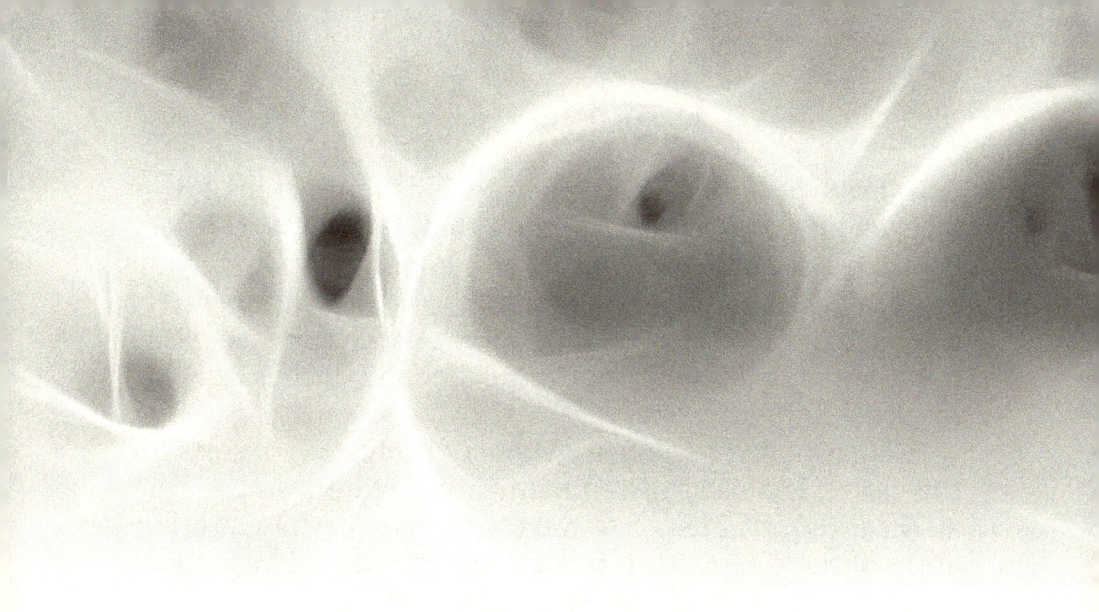

CHAPTER EIGHT

Mark Stevens sighed as he scrolled through his email inbox in his cubicle. He wasn't even sure why he continued showing up to work anymore; every time he did, he just felt more and more deflated. He crafted his latest story discussing Hematite's ever-growing presence in the community—and questioning what that meant for Riverpeak—in such a way to inspire doubt in the vigilante's helpfulness.

Unfortunately for Mark, it had the opposite effect. He clicked through dozens of emails calling him a fraud. They questioned how he still had a job at *The Riverpeak Times* after consistently showing biased journalism. A few took the time to detail instances where Hematite made a personal impact on their lives, but Mark largely ignored them.

Mark knew he was on thin ice with the paper he reported for. The only reason he could get away with it so far was that his father was providing exclusive interview access to *The Riverpeak Times* on the condition that Mark was employed there.

Mark often wondered if he'd even have a job if his father's money wasn't a factor. He'd always felt like his voice had been drowned out by his father and this time was no exception. His relationship with nepotism was a complicated one: he had no issue using his father's name, status, and money to his advantage, and he was the first to admit that. But on the contrary, he wished he could make a name for himself without relying too heavily upon the Stevens family status. He desperately wanted to be accepted for who he was and what he had to say, but that reality seemed to grow further and further from his reach as the years went on.

Hematite had become a symbol of protection of sorts for the city of Riverpeak. Even many other writers and editors at *The Riverpeak Times* became wrapped up in the sensationalism of their hometown hero. Whenever they'd hear about Hematite activity on the police scanners, they'd all gather around to listen closely and rushed to send a reporter that way.

But for Mark, Hematite represented everything that made him feel bitter. Mark often still felt like the dorky boy in his grade school classes who struggled with coming into his own. He saw his inner child whenever he'd look into the mirror or saw his reflection in another late-night cup of coffee. The only difference was that the sadness in his eyes had become hollower.

He picked up his phone as it buzzed. Dougie had texted him again. Dougie was the only one in school who didn't pick on him, likely because he was also another target of the kids who were too cool for them. When Mark told him about his idea to take on the identity of Stone Breaker and try to knock out Hematite so his father's top lobbyists could stay afloat, Dougie had immediately offered to help.

Mark knew he could rely on Dougie when he told him he needed a name to go along with Stone Breaker's own identity. After all, it would be over for both his and his father's careers if the world knew what they were up to in trying to take down Hematite. Dougie's first choice was Shatterstone, something to show unity between the two of them by their similarities. Mark had never been more touched in his life.

[Dougie: Nothing new on Hematite. There's legit nothing on him online. I'm not sure we're going to find him.]

Mark groaned internally. He was getting more frustrated with the lack of information available on Hematite.

CHAPTER EIGHT

[Mark: Nothing at all? Not even on anyone he might be close to?]

Dougie took no time to reply.

[Dougie: There is that girl we saw him take into the alley. It looked like Rory Miller. Remember her from school?]

[Mark: Not well. I don't think I had any classes with her. Maybe one back in elementary school? But if you think she's the one we spotted with Hematite that night before we found them, then go for it. I'm down for anything to make him suffer TBH.]

[Dougie: She was really quiet in school. Let's see what she's up to these days. Don't worry, I'm on it.]

Mark looked at the clock on his computer and realized it was time to head home. Whenever the clock read six, he tried to brace himself for his return to his family's house. He took his time packing his bags, trying to prolong every second until he returned home. Mark still lived with his parents, and while his father promised him a bountiful reward for going against Hematite, he had yet to see much of it beyond his usual cruelness subsiding. *Perhaps, Mark thought, he shouldn't ask for much more than that.*

When Mark came home, he announced his arrival with a quiet hello. Mark wished to not be perceived, but it never worked out that way. While their house was one of the nicest in all of Riverpeak on the outside, he certainly felt like there was a lot to be desired once you stepped inside.

The best way Mark could describe the interior was subtle opulence. Their decor showcased his father's wealth without being tacky or too flashy. Tom Stevens was convinced that this style would give them the illusion of belonging to an old-money family. While they certainly had more privileges than others in Riverpeak, most of their money came from Tom's shady business dealings as a councilman. Elections didn't pay for themselves, Tom would always tell Mark, and the campaigns never stopped just because the season was over. If he had his way, he'd be running for mayor next.

Mark's mother's sing-song voice called from the kitchen, and he could see the back of her blonde bob from where he was standing. Overall, he had inherited her constitution. As per usual, she was the picture of the perfect housewife. "Hello, Mark sweetie! Are you joining us for dinner?"

Mark swallowed. His mother Lydia couldn't cook to save her life, but he knew what would happen if he denied her. "Of course, Mom."

His father came down the stairs at that moment, almost as if on cue. Mark could tell by the lightness of Tom's footsteps that he was in a good mood today. Mark felt his shoulders shrug back and relax at this discovery, but his voice still felt stuck in his throat.

"Hi, Dad."

"We're celebrating tonight, my boy!" Tom laughed, a boisterous sound that came straight from his gut. "You won't believe what we found out today."

"Is this that project you were telling me about?" Lydia asked Tom. Mark moved to the kitchen to help his mother set the table, as his father took his seat at the head of it.

"It is. We've been running some tests over the last few weeks. Ray did some extra testing on his boy this week and last, and to say it's been going swimmingly would be an understatement. We fed him more of the drug in his daily doses, and he's getting more control over his powers now that we found just the right amount. He can finally use a lighter now, not just a matchstick."

"That's great!" Lydia exclaimed. Mark could tell just by looking at her that she didn't understand a word of what Tom said. The only thing that rested behind her eyes was emptiness. Mark used to hate her just as much as he hated his father, but now he wondered how much she had suffered at Tom's hands alongside him.

"Hey, Dad? What is the drug, anyway? We always talk about it, but I don't even know what it is if we're being completely honest."

His father shrugged. "Oh, I don't know. It's some new thing on the market." Mark realized the irony in this, given how long they'd been in business with the drug ring, but didn't dare correct his dad. "I think they blended a bunch of things

CHAPTER EIGHT

together, meth included, but I'm not sure what else. I don't keep up with it so long as it's still moving. We have supply coming in from Denver and directly here in Riverpeak, so we don't have all our eggs in one basket."

"I suppose that makes sense. Is it ready for others to use yet?"

"It will be soon, at this rate. That's great news for you and me, Mark, isn't it? If we can sell the drug as the very thing that's giving people superpowers, you know what will happen? Instant profits in Ray's hands, which means more money in our pockets."

"That's wonderful!" Lydia said with a little clap. Mark's empathy for her was waning thin.

"It is." Despite his agreement, Mark found his words to be hollow. He hoped his father didn't notice. "Dougie and I are still working on the Hematite problem."

"Good," Tom said. "Did you find him yet?"

"No, but we found someone close to him. Dougie's looking into it tonight."

"We'll take what we can get when it comes to that little punk," Tom said. "Talk about a thorn in our sides." Mark knew that "our" referred to Chief Eliza Daniels. "I can only pay her off so much before it becomes a waste. You boys are doing good work."

Mark yearned for the day when his father would acknowledge him as a man, not a boy, but he knew that today was not that day. He wasn't sure when he would earn it, but he was determined to. He picked at his lamb, trying his best to pretend it was an excellent meal but struggled to swallow it due to lack of flavor.

Once their meal was over, Mark was free for the evening. His father would succumb to his shows, and his mother would fall into a trance on her tablet, which meant that Mark didn't have to worry about their watchful eyes for once.

Mark settled into his room with the door shut as he called Dougie, who answered right away.

"Hey, man," Dougie said. "Ready?"

"I'm ready." Mark opened his web browser. "What do you have on Rory Miller?"

"She's a teacher at Riverpeak High School. I think she lives alone. I found her voter registration with her address. According to her Facebook profile, where she goes by her first and middle name instead of last, she's single. It's fairly private, but there aren't any photos of her with any guys, except for Kane Kelly."

Mark scoffed. "Kane Kelly? Fuck that guy."

"Whoa, I didn't realize you hated him."

"Shawn Jameson never left me the hell alone in school. Kane, Elijah, and Brad would just watch as I got the shit kicked out of me by Shawn. If Elijah and Kane told Shawn to stop, he just took it as a suggestion to ignore. They never actually did anything."

"Jeez, what pricks. No way she's dating him."

"No, he's not that type to be in a serious relationship, especially with someone like her. I remember in school she was too much of a goody-two-shoes. It looks like they're just coworkers who hang out sometimes. Who else does she hang out with?"

"I did find a photo of her with Kane, Elijah, Brad, and Naomi. Looks like it was at Elijah's birthday party."

"Wait, Naomi Sato? The reporter?"

"Yeah, her."

"I'm friends with her on Facebook! Let me go to her page. Maybe I can see more," Mark said and quickly opened Naomi's profile. Her cover photo gave away no details—it was just a childhood photo of her with her parents and brother standing in front of a lake by Mount Fuji—and her profile picture was an engagement picture of her and Brad.

Mark opened Naomi's photo albums and began poking around. He found one with the University of Colorado as the title, so he opted to start there. "Yup, Naomi and Rory are definitely best friends," Mark said.

"I remember them hanging out in school too," Dougie said. "Do you think Naomi's in on this?"

"I'm not sure, but she's too high-profile. She's the darling of Channel 10, and her dad is super famous locally. I doubt she'd risk her career."

CHAPTER EIGHT

"So, Naomi Sato is off the table," Dougie said. "What about Rory's family?"

"Let me see..." Mark clicked back to view all of Naomi's albums. "Oh, I found more photos from the birthday party. Let me see who else was there. Maybe the families went too."

Sure enough, there was a photo of Elijah's mom and dad standing alongside Rory's, Brad's, and Naomi's parents.

"Her parents are both tagged," Mark said. He opened both of their profiles up in new tabs. He started with Naomi's mother. "Susan Miller's page is private. I can only see her profile photo, which is a selfie she took with Rory. Doesn't help us at all." He closed out of that tab and then went to Rory's dad's page. "Ah-ha! Bingo! Dad's is public."

"Send me the link," Dougie said. "I'll work my magic and get all the info we need out of this guy."

"Already sent it to you. Looks like Dave Miller isn't super active on social media, but it should hopefully do the trick."

"I think it'll be fine," Dougie said. "Thanks, Mark. How's everything with the drug doing?"

"Not ready for us yet," Mark said. "I'm wondering when my dad will finally let me try it. I think he wants it to be safe before we try to get powers from it. But they said it worked on Ray's son; his powers are getting stronger. It took some torturing to get him there, though. I don't think the process has been pleasant."

"What do you mean?"

"You didn't know? Ray's kid wasn't born with the powers they've been testing. I thought I told you that. They just pumped him full of the drug to see what dosage may or may not work and to see if they could replicate how it happened naturally."

"Holy shit."

"My dad said they think Hematite might have been born with it. They're trying to determine who some of the other kids might be, but if they have powers, they think Hematite's the only one that's actually done anything about it. There are so many people he could be that it's pretty impossible for them to narrow it down. Lots of clients and all. But Ray's family hasn't had an easy go of it."

"Poor guy," Dougie said. "But it'll be our time soon enough."

"I hope," Mark whispered. "I'm thinking that my dad's just saying he'll let us try it but never actually will. Especially if he gets in a bad mood. He was good today because the tests on Ray's son have been going well, but that's not the norm, you know?"

"Let's just put our trust in the process," Dougie said. "And even if he doesn't give it to us, we can always take matters into our own hands together. Right?"

Mark nodded. He wasn't sure that he'd ever have the courage to face off against his father in a situation like that, but he said, "Yeah, you're right, Dougie. I guess all we need now is to figure out what we're going to do with Rory Miller."

"I could try to kidnap her or something. She doesn't look that tough. I could probably handle it."

Mark expanded on that. "We could bring her to my dad's office in City Hall and then make a video for Hematite."

"Oh, I like your thinking! Sort of like a ransom note, but in digital form."

"And even if they aren't connected, it's a great way to lure Hematite in," Mark rationalized. "She's a high school teacher. Hematite says he wants to help the community, right? Then let's see what he does if he leaves one of its educators behind."

"I didn't even think of that! That's brilliant!"

"Do you need me with you when you make your move?"

"I don't think so," Dougie replied. "So far, what I've found beyond her address is that she's just a teacher who lives alone. She made the news in college when Hematite rescued her, so that explains her connection. But I don't think she's doing anything other than pencil-pushing for him."

"If you need backup, call me," Mark said. "I don't want to underestimate anyone involved with Hematite."

"Roger that. But it'll be fine. Just you wait. I'll get to work and see you tomorrow for Valentine's."

CHAPTER EIGHT

Mark waited for both of his parents to leave for their Valentine's Day dinner plans before he left the house. His mask was in his messenger bag, which he slung across his shoulder before he hopped onto his motorcycle.

Dougie was waiting for him at the church in front of the pond. Mark put his 3D-printed mask on, the band lightly pinching at the hairs on the back of his head, as he approached Dougie. Mark made a mental note to touch up the lightning bolt paint job on his mask since the edges were chipping again.

"Did you bring it?" Mark asked.

Dougie nodded. "I've got the ice in my trunk."

"Good," Mark said. "My parents are on their way to Denver, so we don't have to worry about them. What are yours up to tonight?"

"Same. I recommended a place out in Colorado Springs for them to try. We're clear."

"Perfect," Mark said with a grin. "Alright, let's go."

They each grabbed a bag of ice and made their way across the street. The local French restaurant, Le Petit Chateau, was the most popular in Riverpeak. Dougie's car was only about a block away, but with the weather, they weren't worried about the ice melting.

"Man, this is fucking freezing," Dougie muttered.

"It'll be better once we're not holding these bags," Mark said. "Come on, almost there."

Mark set his bag down once they were at the back door of the restaurant. He reached into his messenger bag and grabbed the hammer in the bag. He swung it down, and the door handle ripped off with a thwacking noise.

"That was too easy," Mark said as he put the hammer back in his bag and picked the ice back up. "Come on. Let's start a riot."

"I can't believe we saw this on a meme," Dougie said with a chuckle.

"Right?" Mark laughed. "It's perfect."

The first employee to spot them once they opened the door screamed. Her shout made the other employees all freeze, despite being the busiest they'd ever be all year.

"Is that Stone Breaker?"

"What are they doing here?"

They didn't speak but beelined it for the deep fryer.

"Sorry about your beignets," Stone Breaker said through his voice modifier before he and Dougie as Shatterstone chucked the ice toward the fryer from a safe distance.

Everyone ran back as quickly as they could to avoid getting burned by the splattering oil. A few people who couldn't get out of the way in time were hit with some of the backsplashes. As soon as the ice hit the boiling oil, the fryer bubbled over. Oil leaked directly into the burners, causing the fryers to go up in flames. A trail of flaming oil quickly traveled across the floor toward a rack of towels. One employee scrambled in the chaos to salvage them and prevent the spread, but they were too late.

"Let's go!"

The two of them ran out the way they came and made their way to the front of the restaurant to witness the ensuing chaos. A few patrons seated near the kitchen began running out, which caused a chain reaction of sheer panic.

"That should draw him out," Shatterstone said. "At least the fire feels nice."

"It does, doesn't it?"

The two of them watched from across the street, knowing that they were untouchable at this point. Stone Breaker tried to not laugh beneath his mask as he watched people call for help, knowing that the help wouldn't arrive, all thanks to his father.

"Hey, jerk-offs."

The two of them turned at the sound of the deep, mechanical voice. Hematite was standing behind them, still in the shadows, hands by his sides.

"Aw, look who decided to show up," Stone Breaker said. "Nice of you to join us, Hematite."

"I knew you'd be up to something tonight, but this is low, even for you. What the fuck do you think you're doing?"

"Thought we'd grab your attention with a bang," Shatterstone said.

CHAPTER EIGHT

"How'd you know we'd be here tonight?"

"Your code in the newspaper was pretty easy to crack." Hematite shrugged, to Stone Breaker's surprise; he hadn't accounted for his hidden messages to be uncovered. "Tell your buddy Mark I said thanks for the heads-up."

Stone Breaker swallowed. "You've got a choice to make, Hematite. Help those people or take us on."

Hematite laughed. "How do you think they all got out?"

Stone Breaker's smile dropped beneath his mask. "What?"

"You really don't notice much, do you?"

Instead of responding verbally, Stone Breaker reached for the hammer in his bag and swung. Hematite grabbed Stone Breaker's wrist before he could attack and made quick work of disarming him. Shatterstone dove for the hammer as Stone Breaker recoiled to prepare for his next move.

They both swung to attack Hematite at the same time, so he ducked. While he was lower, he elbowed Shatterstone in the stomach, to which Shatterstone doubled over and dropped the hammer.

The sudden oncoming of fire trucks nearly blinded Hematite, but he grabbed the hammer as it dropped. He aimed for Stone Breaker's knee, but Stone Breaker moved just in time. He lunged at Hematite and brought an elbow down onto his back, putting all his weight into it to make up for his overall lack of physical strength. Hematite winced, but he had been hit worse many times before. Shatterstone used the opportunity to gang up on him, as the two of them stomping at Hematite while he was down, but their kicks caused Hematite to slip out of Stone Breaker's grasp.

"That the best you got?" Hematite taunted as he got up. "What are you gonna do, kill me?"

As Hematite laughed at his own joke, Stone Breaker and Shatterstone both stopped to look at one another.

"Oh my God, we didn't think of how we'd grab him," Shatterstone mentioned out loud to Stone Breaker. "Fuck, what do we do?!"

"Just kill him! Even if he comes back, we can at least get him to your car!"

It was just enough time for Hematite to take a step back and grab both of their heads from behind. He got a good grip on their hair as he swung them both, banging their heads together. He grabbed his billy club, not wanting to use something as potentially lethal as the hammer and whacked both of them on the way down for good measure. Before he could reach down to grab Stone Breaker's mask, police sirens interrupted his train of thought. The blue lights illuminated the night, along with the pre-existing red ones from the fire trucks that were working on Le Petit Chateau.

"Shit!" Hematite muttered to himself. If his usual detective wasn't there, he knew he'd be screwed. Instead of sticking around and unmasking Stone Breaker, he had no choice but to run off, cutting through the woods before the police could find him.

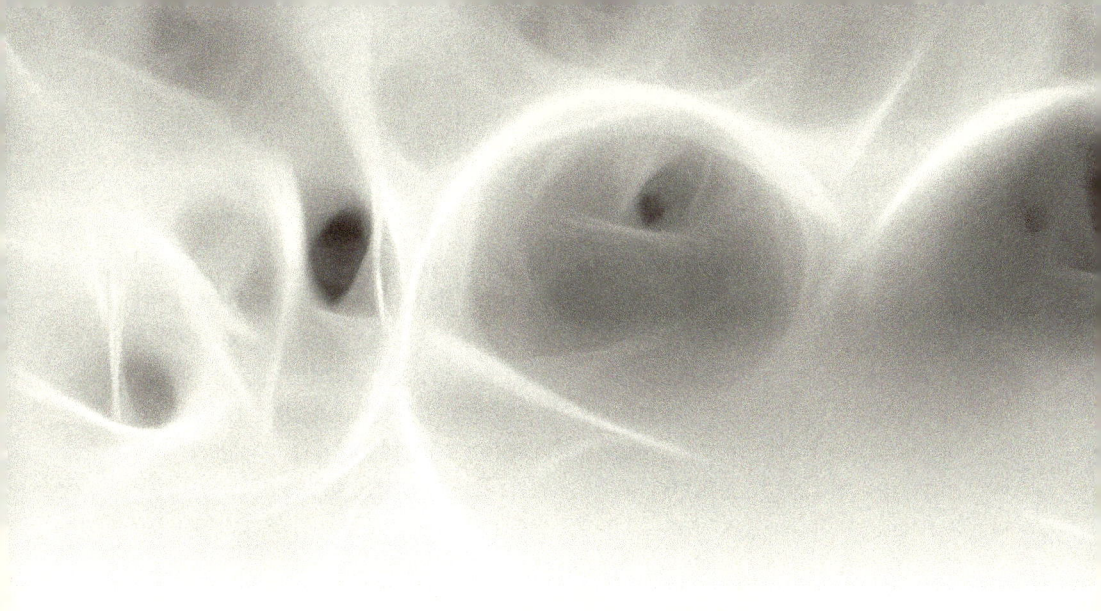

CHAPTER NINE

Kane as Hematite rushed up the steps of his apartment complex, not stopping until he was inside with the door locked behind him. He rested his back against the door for a moment as he collected his breath. He was certain he lost the cops before they even caught sight of him, but close calls with law enforcement always made him anxious.

Kane tossed off his gloves and unraveled his boxing wraps as he walked over to his bedroom. He plopped the long strings of fabric in his laundry basket before he removed his cowl, balaclava, and voice modifier. He made his way over to his bathroom to wash his hands and face, taking his time with the job. Luckily, there were no fresh scars on his already bloodied knuckles, but he knew he'd be worse for the wear when he continued to undress.

Once he tossed off his fish-mouthed hoodie and shirt, he looked at himself in the mirror to check the damage. He didn't feel like any bones were broken, and there was only some mild redness on his stomach. Kane suspected at least a few of those spots would be bruised by the morning, but Stone Breaker and Shatterstone had both been fairly weak, so he knew it wouldn't be anything major. When Kane spit into his sink, he was relieved to see just saliva and no blood on the white ceramic.

Kane picked his hoodie up and quickly sniffed it. The smell of smoke still lingered from Le Petite Chateau, and he frowned at it. He was glad that he had been waiting right outside the restaurant when it caught fire so he could usher people out right away, taking some of the slack off the staff, but still wished he had caught Stone Breaker sooner. As he tossed his clothes in the laundry basket with his boxing wraps, he made a mental note to wash them right after he showered so he could get the smoke stench out.

Kane stood in the shower aimlessly for a few minutes, enjoying the feeling of the hot water against his skin. He didn't rush washing his hair, feeling meditative as he gently scrubbed the dirt, grime, melted snow, and ash off himself. There was something euphoric about a post-fight shower, like he was rinsing away the events of the evening. He looked at his hands as he bathed and wished he could wash everything away. He often wondered if it was all worth it or if it would amount to anything when he allowed himself to get lost in his thoughts. When that happened, his mind wandered to Kayla and Rory.

When he finished his shower and tossed his laundry in, he plopped onto his bed. He made another mental note that he'd need a new mattress soon; as much as he hated to splurge, his back needed the support more than ever.

He held his phone up in front of his face, not straying from the lock screen right away. It was a photo of him and Rory that Naomi took on Elijah's birthday. He smiled at the sight of her face, her joy at the moment clear in her expression.

He opened the contact and called her. He usually didn't call this late, but his selfishness won over as he figured it would be worth a shot.

"Hey, Kane!" Rory was a bit taken aback by his call, but she was happy to hear from him nonetheless. "What's up? I figured you'd be out by now."

"Happy Valentine's Day, pretty lady," Kane said. "Are you doing anything? Anyone?"

CHAPTER NINE

Rory laughed from her spot on the couch. "You too. But no, none of the above. I'm surprised you're not."

"Nah. I'm not that wild. Besides, the best place in town kinda caught on fire."

"I saw that! Thank God Hematite was there. I'm glad I stayed in tonight."

"Do you wanna maybe stay in together? I can cook if you haven't eaten yet. I promise you, you're not some last resort booty call. If I *did* have any booty calls, you'd be top of the list." If he was being honest, he hoped a relaxing evening with her would take his mind off his fight with Stone Breaker and Shatterstone. Seeing her in a normal sense would help him feel at ease.

"You know, I was just debating dinner. Is this you asking me on a proper date?" Rory felt some heat rising to her cheeks that she'd never admit to him or herself.

"It's whatever you want it to be," Kane said. He smiled, afraid of defining it despite knowing how much he needed her company. "It can be nothing serious and nothing casual all at once. Deal?"

Rory's blush instantly faded at his words. "Sure, whatever that means. Why the hell not?"

"You said I've been worrying you lately. Consider this me making it up to you."

"My place or yours?" Rory asked.

"Here's fine. I've got food to whip up. Come over whenever," Kane said, trying to hide the longing in his voice. "I'll get decent."

"Get decent?"

"Yeah. I just showered. You want a picture?"

Rory could practically hear his smirk. "Maybe another night."

"You know what? I'll take that. That's not a total dejection. See you soon?"

"I'll be right over."

Rory rushed to her closet, unsure of what to wear, but settled on jeans and a decent blouse to go along with Kane's theme of nothing serious and nothing casual. She kept her makeup simple, not wanting to make a fuss in case Kane didn't want to either, and was relieved to see him answer the door dressed similarly. He wore an old pair of jeans with a hole forming in one knee and a button-up shirt left undone over a graphic tee. His hair was still wet from his shower and slicked back, highlighting the details of his face. Rory noticed a few freckles that dotted the top of his forehead by his hairline.

"Beautiful as always," he said as he let her in. "I don't have any roses or chocolates or anything, but I make a bitchin' tofu Pad Thai."

"That's already more than I anticipated for the evening," Rory said. "It's all commercialized crap, anyway. It smells great in here."

Kane was relieved to hear her say that. He was hoping the smell of dinner would cover any lingering scents of smoke from when he returned earlier.

"I'll plate everything up. You just sit there, look pretty, and pick your favorite cheesy romance movie for us to watch over dinner in the spirit of love."

"Even if it's from Hallmark?"

"Their Christmas ones are my guilty pleasure, so go for it." It wasn't a lie, but not for the reason Rory might think. Their idyllic outline and predictable happily-ever-after formula always gave Kane some comfort and escapism from his life.

"Okay, now this is a side of you I have never seen," Rory said with a laugh as she grabbed the remote. "Even after all these years, I'd never have pegged you for the type."

"There are a lot of things you could peg me for." Kane winked.

Rory rolled her eyes, understanding what he was implying.

"But in all seriousness, you can thank Kayla. You can actually thank her for any good traits of mine."

Kane joined her at the small dining area table; since his apartment was a studio, it was easy to see the television from anywhere. Kane paid little attention to the movie, looking mostly at Rory—especially once they had moved over to his

CHAPTER NINE

couch after eating—out of the corner of his eye. He didn't dare get caught staring at her, but he placed his arm around her shoulders as they watched. Rory relaxed into Kane's embrace and scooted to be closer to him on his couch. Kane was glancing down and smiling at her when she looked up to meet his eyes.

"What's your dream guy like?" Kane asked. He added as he pointed to the TV. "This guy doesn't seem your type. I can tell that much."

"Nah, he's not," Rory said. The question caught her off guard. "Hmm." She took a moment to contemplate her answer; the more she thought about it, the more she realized she would just be describing him. Between how he presented the evening and what he just asked her, she wasn't sure if she should be completely honest. "Someone kind who makes me laugh. That's my only criteria these days."

Kane smiled. "I like that answer. I think that's reasonable."

They enjoyed a comfortable silence together for the rest of the movie, only occasionally chiming in with commentary about the ridiculous plot. By the time the movie ended, Rory realized she didn't want to go home, even though she knew she should.

"We have to get up early for work tomorrow," she said. "It's criminal to have a holiday on a Thursday. But thanks for having me over. We should do this more often."

Kane beamed. "I'd like that. I'd like that a lot, actually. Come on, I'll walk you to your car."

They were silent on the walk down. The winter night was practically silent, save for a thin layer of snow crunching beneath their feet. When she reached her car, she asked Kane, "What was tonight?"

"Like I said, it's whatever you want it to be." He winked at Rory and leaned down to kiss her cheek. "Happy Valentine's Day, Miller."

She smiled at him, despite how puzzled she was at his cryptic-ness. "Happy Valentine's Day, Kane."

On the ride home, she mulled over what Kane could have meant. His mixed signals from insisting the dinner was whatever to kissing her cheek had her feeling dizzy. She knew she should have been more direct with him too but also wondered what that may mean for their friendship if he really meant nothing by it and she was just overthinking it, like she had a tendency to do.

As Rory settled into Naomi's apartment the next evening, she said, "I'm glad you could do this with me tonight. I'm surprised you're not spending time with Brad."

"His older brothers are in town for the week, so he's on family duty. But I'm glad too. It gives us a chance to work uninterrupted. How was your night? I hope you didn't just sit at home alone watching bad romance movies like you usually do."

"You know, I did exactly that, just not alone," Rory said. "Kane invited me over."

"Wait, he did?!" Naomi jumped on the chair and crossed her legs to settle herself down. "You spent the night with Kane? Kane Kelly?"

"Yeah, what other Kane do we know?" Rory asked with a shrug. "I don't think it was anything serious. Kane doesn't take anything seriously."

"Why else would he invite you over on Valentine's Day?"

"It was just two friends hanging out, Naomi, I swear. You're making a bigger deal of this than it was. He cooked, we watched a movie, and I went home. No frills."

"He cooked for you, and you wanna call it no frills? Oh my God, you're helpless!"

"Kane's not like Brad. He's a lot more laissez-faire," Rory said. "And we've been friends for so long. If he wanted to pursue me like that, you figure he would have already."

"Maybe he's got the same fears as you. I know you've mentioned not wanting to ruin the friendship you guys have. He might feel like that too. I dunno. Come on, let's grab what we've got and get to work."

CHAPTER NINE

They pulled out the stacks of relevant paperwork from the files that Naomi had been keeping in her closet. They left the ones focusing only on Stone Breaker behind, pulling only what little they had on Hematite. Compared to the Stone Breaker pile, the stack was unimpressive.

"Alright," Naomi said. "I'll see if I can find any public records that give us a hint. Maybe arrest reports related to drugs if he's going after the drug rings."

"I'll check out some police reports from incidents he was involved in. Maybe someone who he helped saw something."

"Ooh, good thinking!" Naomi began typing away at her laptop.

After a few minutes, Naomi groaned from her spot on the lounge chair in her living room. Her black hair was falling out of the braid she had loosely tied it in before Rory had arrived.

"I'm not finding anything!"

"I'm not having any luck, either." Rory frowned. "I hoped that me having actually met him in person would help, but so far, it's a bust."

Rory suddenly had a revelation. She shifted the position she was sitting in from slumped to upright. Rory's sudden rapid typing on her laptop alerted Naomi to this.

"What's happening?" Naomi asked. "I'm sensing a light-bulb moment."

"He has a storage unit," Rory said. "There's gotta be some record of who bought it, right? I remember the number from when he took me there."

"Yeah, but we're not the FBI," Naomi said. "That's not gonna be public record. We'd need a warrant and a badge to pull that one off."

Rory sighed and slumped back into her previous position. "Damn it." *So much for that good idea*, she thought. "How the hell are we not finding anything? Like, anything at all?"

"He's either great with computers or has a guy that's helping him stay completely blacked out on the internet," Naomi said. "We run across that at the station sometimes. Some people just have no digital footprint. We should call Elijah for help."

"Does Brad know you're doing this?" Rory asked. Looping in Elijah would likely result in clueing Brad in, given they lived together.

"Yes ... and no. He knows I'm looking into who Stone Breaker and Hematite are, but he thinks it's for work. I wasn't sure how much I should say," she said. "Brad gets it. I just don't want him to freak out, you know?"

"I'm in that boat with Kane," Rory said. "And he's been off lately. I dunno. It's hard to explain. I'm thinking he might be wrapped up in this and we don't even know it."

"You think? What do you mean by off?"

"He was so exhausted the other day that I let him take a nap in my classroom during our lunch break. And he's just made a few comments that make it sound like he knows more than he leads on. I don't know. Maybe he's just super hungover half the time. Either way, I'm worried about him."

"I'll ask Brad if he's heard anything. He tells me everything. We'll get to the bottom of it." She winked as she set her laptop down so she could redo her braid. "But I think it may be better if we don't ask for Elijah's help after all. I think Brad's chalked a lot of my stress up to wedding planning lately. And with his anxiety, I don't wanna do that to him if I don't have to."

"You don't need to justify it, Naomi," Rory said. "That's totally valid. I know how Brad can be. Good heart, would be understanding, just a nervous wreck."

"I'm glad we're doing this, though. So many people in the news industry get off to the idea of helping people. They think they're making some enormous difference, and they sell us that too. But a lot of them really aren't. A lot of them actually just make things worse." She huffed. "They don't make 'em like Cronkite anymore."

Rory smiled at her friend and reached out for her hand. She gripped it. "I'm glad we're doing this too. I don't think I could have made it this far without you. Who needs Cronkite when we've got Naomi Sato, huh? I'm proud of you."

Naomi laughed. "Thanks. The imposter syndrome is real." She took a sip of wine and then said, "I'm proud of you too. You've overcome a lot."

CHAPTER NINE

"Thank our therapist," Rory said with a laugh. "She acts all buddy-buddy with me and then, bam! A hard-hitting question that feels like a punch to the gut."

"I'm serious!" Naomi said. "I'm so glad you like Marissa, though. She was awesome with me and my mom when we went for therapy after my dad's restaurant fire. But you did that yourself! Healing isn't pretty, and you've really put yourself out there. Now look at us," Naomi said. "We're swimming in a sea of papers."

Rory grabbed her glass of wine from the coffee table and raised it for a toast. "To actually making a difference."

Naomi held her glass up alongside Rory's in an act of cheers. "To actually making a difference."

"Your brother would be proud of you," Rory added.

Naomi smiled at the memory of her brother. "I bet Noah would have loved to have been a part of this. I miss him so much. You know, I always thought there was more to his death than what my dad said."

"Yeah? You've never told me that."

"Mm." Naomi nodded and took a sip of her wine. "The fire he was in, the one my dad made it out of. Obviously. You know that already. But it just never sat right with me that Noah just died in a random freak fire one day. And I know that denial is part of the grieving process, but it's been years now and I've never shaken that."

"If I've learned anything lately, it's trusting my gut. Maybe you're right."

"Once we're done with this and the wedding is over, that's my next goal. Maybe this whole Hematite and Stone Breaker thing will open up a whole can of worms, and I can get to the bottom of things. Maybe we'll get some justice for Noah."

"Something tells me that this," Rory said, as she gestured at their iPads and scattered newspaper clippings, "is only the beginning of something much bigger."

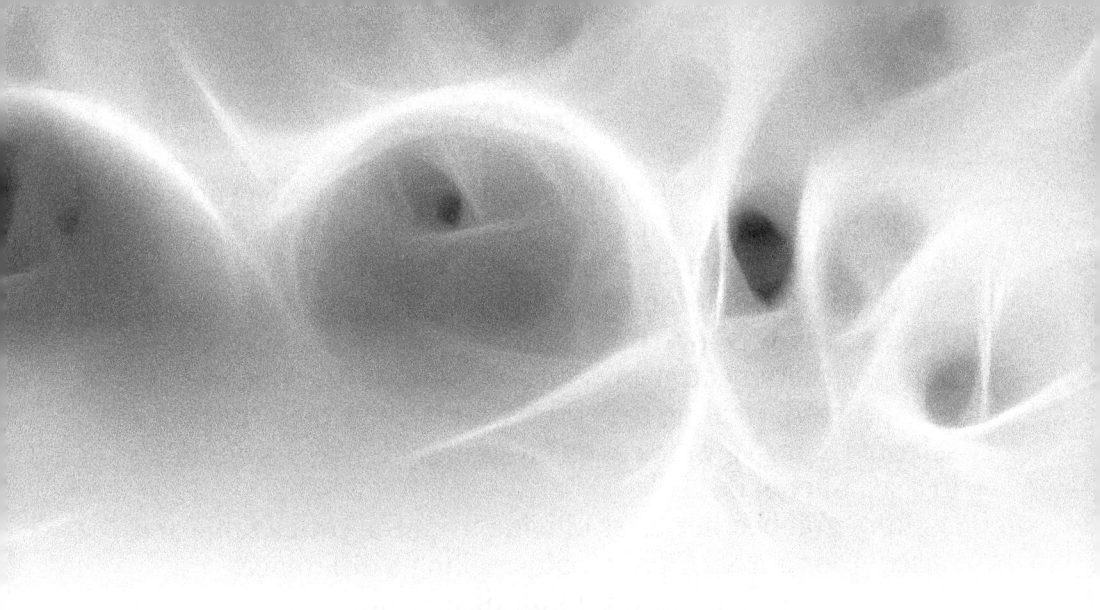

CHAPTER TEN

Naomi's house wasn't far from Rory's, so Rory usually just walked whenever she'd visit, if the weather was nice. The air still had a bit of a bite to it, but it finally stopped snowing, so Rory enjoyed the outdoors for the first time in months. While the cold weather wasn't her favorite, she never minded the way the chilly air hit her skin after being cooped up in the heat. It was hard to see the tops of the mountains in the distance at night, but their snowy caps were just bright enough to make out their shapes.

Halfway back to her home, she couldn't explain why but she felt her fight-or-flight response kick in. Thanks to Dr. Thornton, she was getting pretty good at identifying the racing of her heart and increased paranoia. Her instincts were telling her to run, but when she looked around, no one was around to clue her into what might have triggered her response. She tried to shrug it off as her post-traumatic stress overacting in a moment of loneliness, but she just couldn't shake off the way the hairs on the back of her neck stood up.

"Rory Miller," a voice called. It was a man's voice that Rory didn't recognize. She didn't turn around, just picked up her pace, but he caught up to her. A gloved hand touched her shoulder.

CHAPTER TEN

Rory turned and saw a lanky, awkward man with short hair and wearing a cheap mask. Rory deduced that this must be Shatterstone, Stone Breaker's assistant. The mask looked 3D-printed, similarly to Stone Breaker's, but with less time or effort put into it, as there wasn't anything painted on the front. He wore black clothing with a red-and-yellow puffer jacket that looked brand new but scuffed up, as if he had gotten into a fight while wearing it. Rory thought his color scheme was an odd choice, given their whole point was anonymity and to stay undercover.

Rory shook his hand off her shoulder and said, "How do you know who I am?"

"We've got eyes everywhere," Shatterstone said. "You'd be surprised."

Rory tried to ignore the chill that went down her spine and her increasing nausea. "This isn't your usual spot." Rory tried to keep her voice strong, so as to not show her fear. "You really wanna do this in front of the whole suburb?"

"You really think anyone would notice? It's getting late, after all."

Shatterstone opened his mouth again to continue speaking, but Rory didn't give him a chance to start. Rory rolled her shoulders back, remembered everything she learned in her boxing classes, and threw a punch. It landed right in Shatterstone's face. She could feel the thin, 3D-printed mask crack beneath her knuckles and could hear his jaw pop along with it.

Shatterstone stumbled, so Rory hit him again. The second hit knocked him down and slid his cracked mask off his face. He was a different man now unmasked, but something about his constitution reminded Rory of her stalker all those years ago.

She didn't know what came over her, but she didn't stop punching him. All she knew was that it was her or him, and it was more important to her that he stayed down. She found herself on top of Shatterstone as she continued to land more blows, repeatedly hitting his face.

"What the hell did you think was going to happen?" Rory asked him between punches. He couldn't answer. "You think you can just fucking attack people in the middle of the goddamn road? Who gave you the right, you little punk?"

Rory was only stopped by the sudden force of someone dragging her off Shatterstone's body. Their arms moved beneath her armpits to snake around her body and yank her back.

"Hey, hey, hey!" It was Hematite. Rory huffed as he helped her stand up. "Rory, relax. What happened?"

Rory didn't answer him right away. She took a few moments to collect her breath. A few people peeked outside their windows. Hematite let go of Rory and turned her around to face him.

"Give me your hands." The words came out so fast that Rory could barely make them out. "Now."

Rory simply held her hands up in front of her, not questioning him. She couldn't tell if he sounded angry or not, thanks to the way his voice was distorted. Hematite ripped off an edge of his cowl and used it to wipe the blood that came from Shatterstone's face off her knuckles.

"Are you okay?" He spoke more gently now, keeping his gaze on her knuckles; Rory had never seen someone so focused.

Rory shrugged. "I thought it was him. He tried to attack me, and I thought it was him. I…" Rory released a shaky breath. "I don't know what came over me. It's like I blacked out or something."

Hematite knew Rory didn't like to say her stalker's name, but he knew she meant Daniel.

"Wash your hands with some antibacterial soap when you get home. But this should do the trick for now." There was a tenderness in Hematite's tone and his movements as he wiped the blood off Rory's knuckles with his cowl. Their closeness wasn't doing her any favors as she tried to calm down after the adrenaline rush.

"Will do." Her heart still felt like it was beating a million miles an hour, but she regained control of her breathing as she spoke to him. There was something about the gentle way he tended to her that helped her relax in an instant and made her feel safe. "Thanks."

CHAPTER TEN

"Are you hurt?" Even with his voice modifier and no way to see his facial expression, it was clear to Rory that he was genuinely concerned. If she didn't know any better, she'd say he almost sounded desperate.

When he looked up from her knuckles, their eyes met. It was the first time Rory was close enough to Hematite with proper lighting that she could make out his eye color; they were a beautiful shade of blue. She couldn't see his eyebrows, though, as they were covered by his hood and balaclava.

Rory shook her head. "No, I'm fine. He didn't even have time to hurt me."

Hematite just nodded. "Good." He stopped wiping Rory's knuckles clean but was still holding her hands in both of his. They could both hear the sirens and see the lights of the police cars pulling up to the street, but at that moment, it felt like time was still between the two of them. "I'm glad you're okay. You did the right thing. I'll handle the police, okay? Just keep your hands in your pockets. It's freezing out, isn't it?"

She nodded, understanding what he was getting at. Hematite dropped her hands when the police arrived, and she shoved them in her coat before they could arrive.

"Who do you got for us, Hematite?" The cop was a short man with red, slicked-back hair and a thin mustache. He hadn't shaved in a few days and seemed more friendly than any of the other cops that Rory had encountered.

Hematite acknowledged him with a nod. "Detective McMahon. I caught Shatterstone, Stone Breaker's sidekick, attacking this woman."

"Looks like he took quite the beating," Jon McMahon said, as one of his men dragged Shatterstone's unconscious form, now handcuffed, to the car. "So much so that his mask broke."

"It's just pretty thin plastic. It was him or her, and I wasn't about to let an innocent woman get hurt. Quick decisions had to be made."

Rory chose to not say anything. Perhaps Hematite feared what may happen if she was outed as the one who attacked Shatterstone. The way they bantered told Rory that Hematite had a silent agreement with Detective McMahon, so it granted him a certain privilege they both knew that Rory could not afford. It could put her career at risk if the truth got out.

"You're on thin fuckin' ice, Hematite." McMahon's narrowed gaze conveyed seriousness, but there was a hint of playfulness in his tone as he smirked and held up a piece of the broken mask.

Hematite laughed. "Maybe, but you need me too much. Are we good here?"

"Yeah, I'd say so. Everything he said true, miss?" When Rory nodded, McMahon said, "Good enough for me."

Hematite looked at Rory and said, "I'll take you home, okay?"

Before Rory could respond, McMahon asked, "Are you alright, miss?" He made eye contact with Rory, searching her eyes to sense her comfort level with Hematite's offer. "We can bring you home if you'd prefer."

Rory nodded and forced herself to smile at McMahon; it was hard for her to feign any sort of happiness at the moment but didn't want him to fret. She could feel some tears pooling by her bottom lids, but she swallowed hard as she tried to hold them back. "I'm fine, thanks to Hematite, yeah," she said. "I'd rather go with him, but thank you, detective."

McMahon nodded. "Understood. Take care." He grabbed a business card from his wallet and handed it to her. "In case you need anything, alright?"

Rory took it and shoved it in her coat pocket. "Thank you. I'll hang on to this just in case."

After the police left, Rory and Hematite were silent on their way back to her house. They walked side by side, shoulders close enough to feel each other's warmth but not enough to touch. Hematite wanted to say something, but whenever he'd glance at Rory, he'd see that her eyes were on her shoes and deep in thought, so he opted to say nothing at all to let her process everything on her own terms.

Even though Rory had mostly calmed down thanks to Hematite's presence, the only thing she could hear was her heart thumping a mile a minute in her ears. She couldn't even hear the shuffling of their feet as they walked side by side. She

CHAPTER TEN

was surprised that Hematite kept quiet, but his being there was enough to help her feel not so alone.

Once they reached her front step, he finally spoke. "Be sure to ice your hand too. Your knuckles might be sore tomorrow." There was a stiffness to his words, like he was holding something back, but Rory didn't think to press it.

"Thanks for the pointer. I... I'm sorry. It all happened so fast. I don't know what I was thinking. I feel like I wasn't thinking."

"Don't apologize." Hematite placed a hand on her shoulder, making her look up and into his eyes. "It's not your fault. You did what you had to do."

Rory nodded, feeling mesmerized by the way the shades of blue seemed to swirl around his pupils. "I guess so." She swallowed. "Thanks for taking the heat for me too."

"Any time. It's better that I do than you." Rory noticed he spoke to her differently than he did to McMahon or to others, using a tone with a sweet softness that shone through his voice modifications. "I've worked with McMahon before. He lets me do my job. I won't be far in case you need me, okay? Just say the word."

Rory nodded. "Okay. I appreciate that." She smiled at him, more genuine than she had at McMahon, but Hematite noticed her smile didn't quite reach her eyes. "Good night, Hematite."

"Good night, Rory."

Once Rory closed the door, Hematite snuck up to the roof of her home. Shatterstone's arrest would certainly strike a nerve, so he didn't want to leave her alone so quickly. As he sat over the corner where her bedroom was, he could faintly hear her sobbing into her pillow.

Rory held her pillow against her chest, her knees sandwiching it between her. She wrapped a fleece blanket around herself as she wept, fully processing everything that happened to her. As she sobbed, Rory felt a sharpness in her lungs, letting the pillow muffle the sound and provide softness against her skin. She tried to blink away the images of Dougie and

Daniel's faces, but as she did, they just merged into one, like a weird amalgamate from a bad sci-fi movie.

She got herself into this mess, she thought, and there was no turning back now. She tried to remember the words that Dr. Thornton told her in that first therapy session—"It's not your fault"—but Rory couldn't help but feel like this would have never happened had she never stuck her nose where it didn't belong.

Hematite wanted nothing more than to burst into her window and hold her. He felt a huge twinge of guilt, knowing there was nothing he could do about it as he heard her cry; it was his job to watch over the community, and he wasn't sure how Shatterstone got away with this without him knowing. Kane wanted to assure her that she was safe, even though it was a lie to do so. But he knew he couldn't.

The next morning, Rory called Dr. Thornton right away. The drive to Denver was feeling shorter with each visit, and Rory was just glad that Dr. Thornton could squeeze her in so quickly and on such short notice.

"Let me start off by saying that I am so glad that you're physically okay," Dr. Thornton said, after learning what happened the night before. "What exactly is going on?"

"Thanks, Marissa." Rory used the frigid February air to her advantage and wore gloves to hide a few scrapes on one of her knuckles. "It... it was a rough night. I'm not sure if I handled it better or worse than I would have a month ago."

Dr. Thornton sadly smiled at Rory as Rory recalled the night prior. "Something like this is anyone's worst nightmare, even without a history like your own. I hope you're treating yourself with kindness."

"I'm trying," Rory affirmed. "And, well, I guess I should mention why this came about." Rory paused before she confessed, "I found him."

Dr. Thornton raised her eyebrows. "You found Hematite?"

CHAPTER TEN

Rory nodded as she adjusted her glasses; she hated the feeling of contacts on irritated, puffy eyes. "I did. The letters for Kane and Naomi are on my phone, but I haven't had the chance to share them. It's been so busy, and the timing has felt all wrong. I never wrote one for Hematite. But I found him!"

"How did it go?" Dr. Thornton asked. "Did it meet your expectations?"

"It went great. I'd say it met most of my expectations, if not exceeded them. We've been tracking down Stone Breaker together. I just... I thought finding him would help me feel some closure," Rory said, "and so far, I still feel like something is missing."

It was the first time Rory had spoken that truth out loud. She was glad to be alongside Hematite, but there was still a hollow feeling that lingered in her chest and that kept her up at night.

"While trust should be earned and not freely given," Dr. Thornton said, "I think you need to give in to your trust more fully. Do you trust anyone? You don't have to answer right away."

Rory took a moment to think about it. She trusted Naomi and knew that without a second thought. "Definitely Naomi. She's been helping me too, with the Hematite thing."

"And what about your friend... Kane, was it? His name has come up a few times."

Rory allowed herself a moment to consider it. Normally, she would have said yes without a shadow of a doubt. She trusted Kane with her life. But lately, things had been different with him. Rory could sense that they were both hiding things from one another, despite likely fighting on the same side of the battle.

"I do," Rory said. "I do trust him. Kane's always been there for me."

"I sense you're hesitant," Dr. Thornton said. "Your next homework assignment is to evaluate your trust. Start with Kane. I think it'll help you with your feeling of something being missing. Have you told him everything?"

Rory shook her head. "Most of it, but not all of it."

"Start there. It's clear that he cherishes you based on what you've told me so far. What's the worst that could happen?"

Mark Stevens felt like he was going to throw up, as he watched the morning newscast with his father. He took a long sip of his coffee in hopes of not having to discuss anything with his dad, but the coffee just churned in his stomach, along with his nerves.

"Breaking news. Shatterstone, a masked figure assisting Hematite's nemesis, Stone Breaker, was arrested last night," the male anchor said.

"Riverpeak Police tell us that Hematite stopped Shatterstone from attacking a woman only steps from her home," his female counterpart reported.

"Police tell us that Douglas Doerr was the man behind the mask."

"That's your friend, right?" Tom asked. His voice was still calm, and his body was completely still on the couch next to him; Mark wasn't sure if that was a good or a bad thing.

"Yes, sir," he replied. He wasn't able to meet his father's eyes and didn't dare see what lurked beneath his calm facade.

"Let me make a call," Tom said. "Should be no problem." He stood and walked over to the other side of the living room as he waited for the phone to ring. It wasn't on speaker, which only made Mark feel like he was going to bring his coffee back up even more. "Chief Daniels! Hi. How are you doing? Good? That makes one of us," Tom said on the phone. "Listen, it's come to my attention that my son's friend was arrested last night. What's his bail? How can we work something out?"

Mark's palms felt clammy as he waited for his father to continue speaking. He kept his eyes forward, focusing on the news; they had long since moved away from the news about Dougie and were now talking about some new restaurant that had opened.

CHAPTER TEN

"What do you mean there's nothing we can do?" It was a question, but Tom asked it more like a statement. "You've got to be fu—are you joking?"

Tom hung up and tossed his phone on the couch. It bounced next to Mark, who grabbed it before it could fall off the edge.

"After everything I've done to build a relationship with her, and this is the fucking thanks I get." Tom looked at his son, which forced Mark to finally meet his father's gaze. Tom's brows were furrowed so much that there were extra wrinkles on his forehead. His mouth was usually in a permanent scowl when he was behind closed doors, but the frown was even deeper than usual. He pointed at Mark and said, "You better have some good ideas about how we're going to move forward. You promised me we'd take down Hematite, not the other way around. What the hell are you two doing?"

"I... I know, sir, I'm sorry." Mark winced. "Dougie told me he had it covered. He did his research. Rory just wasn't what we expected."

"She's working with a goddamn vigilante! Why the hell wouldn't you expect this?" Tom sighed as he placed his hands on his hips and huffed. "I want both of their heads on a silver platter. You got that?"

Mark nodded. "Understood, sir. I'll make it up to you. This won't be a setback."

"Good," Tom said. "It better not be. Ray tells me they're struggling to get shipments in from Denver of materials they need because no one wants to deal with this Hematite bullshit. When his pockets hurt, our pockets hurt."

"It'll be handled." Mark had little confidence and wasn't sure what he would do next. But he said, "I promise."

Tom's phone started ringing again. "Oh, fuck me. It's Ray." He answered it as he walked to the back door and eventually outside. Mark wished he could hear their conversation but didn't dare risk following his father when he was in this type of mood. He closed his eyes, hoping something would appear to him, but the only thing that came to his mind was Rory Miller.

Mark was certain of only two things anymore. The first was that Rory Miller was a force to be reckoned with. The second was that she had some sort of personal connection to Hematite well beyond just being a big fan. If Hematite had been there to rescue her before anything could have happened, then Mark had a feeling she was the key to hitting him where it really hurt.

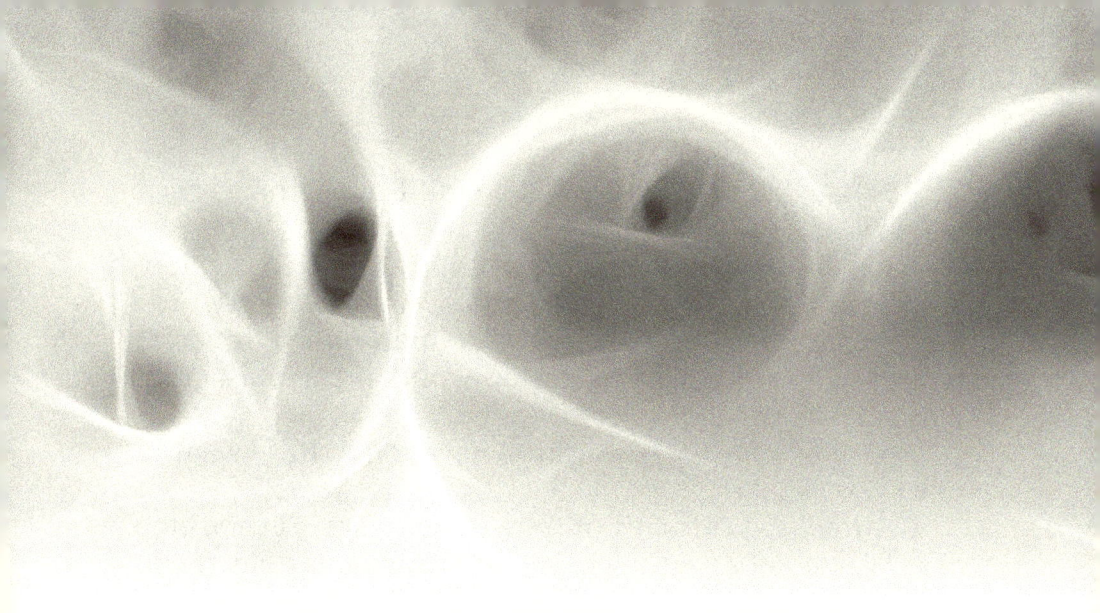

CHAPTER ELEVEN

Rory was relieved to see Kane looking more like himself when he arrived at her home on Saturday afternoon. He held a paper to-go bag in his hands from Jefferson's Coffee and the dark circles under his eyes finally faded. He was dressed casually in a graphic T-shirt and sweats, allowing himself to be comfortable before having to change for the school's winter formal that night.

Kane noticed right away that she was wearing her glasses but wasn't surprised.

"You look refreshed," Rory said.

"I took your advice and got a good night's sleep." Kane did actually let himself sleep in for once. While Shawn wasn't his favorite person, he had asked him to cover for him, given the increased activity in town last night while he watched over Rory. They had been working together more frequently as of late during their patrols, which Kane wasn't thrilled about, but it helped to have the extra set of eyes and someone with super-strength to scare off the members of the drug ring. "In thanks, I come bearing lunch."

"Thanks. I was getting worried about you, man."

"I could tell," Kane said. "You're the only one I listen to these days, so do with that information what you will."

Rory laughed at his teasing. "Careful! The last thing I need is a power trip."

Kane dropped his backpack in his usual spot on the floor in front of her couch. "I'd trust you with it, don't worry."

Rory swallowed the feeling of a lump in her throat. It reminded her of her conversation with her therapist from only a few hours ago.

"Speaking of trust," she said, "I have some stuff I want to talk to you about."

Kane sensed the shift of tone in her voice. "Everything okay? Come on. Over lunch. We both think more clearly on full stomachs."

Rory nodded in agreement. Over the last few weeks, she had sensed their dynamic shift as she got more and more involved with Hematite and Stone Breaker. Rory wasn't sure why, but it bothered her that she and Kane didn't see eye to eye on this beyond him just being one of her best friends.

"What's going on? Is it the Hematite stuff?"

"Yeah," she said. "Don't get me wrong; I've been honest with you. Lying to you is something I wouldn't ever dream of. I just haven't shared every detail." Rory grimaced. "Naomi and I are actively trying to find who he is now. We trust he can handle the Stone Breaker stuff, but … it's getting serious." Rory took a deep breath. "I don't know how, but I think Stone Breaker is on to me."

"He knows you're working with Hematite?" When Rory nodded, Kane asked, "Do you think he saw you when you went to go find him? That's gotta be the only way."

"Probably. Hematite told me I walked right into his territory," she said. She ran her hand over her face in exasperation. "And Shatterstone told me the other day that they have eyes everywhere. He, uh… he came after me on Friday night."

Kane's lips formed a thin line. "What?" He already knew this, of course, but he had to play dumb. His anger from the night prior never subsided, but he had done a decent job at hiding it.

When Rory looked past some of the loose wisps of blonde hair that fell in his face, she could see a storm silently raging

CHAPTER ELEVEN

in his eyes. She told him what happened, then held her hand up as she paused for a bite of her sandwich. She wore Band-Aids beneath winter gloves earlier that morning when she saw her therapist, but they were on full display now for Kane to see some light bruising and scrapes by her middle knuckles.

"Oh my God," Kane said. "I'm so sorry."

"I beat the shit out of him, though. I didn't get hurt beyond, well, this." She gestured to her fists. "I iced them this morning, but they're still stiff as shit."

"Rory, what would the school think?" Kane tried to keep his voice soft, so as to not appear angry with her. "You could get fired if they found out!"

"Hematite took the heat for me, so it worked out. I guess he's buddy-buddy with some detective or something."

Kane sighed. "While I am proud of you for kicking his ass, this isn't safe. I don't think relying on Hematite is a viable, long-term strategy." He hoped that if he could sow some seeds of doubt, Rory would walk away before it was too late.

"Why not? He's proven himself to be reliable. And I think he's been looking over me personally ever since I gave him the info on Stone Breaker. He always seems to show up when I need him lately."

Kane frowned. "He can't be everywhere at once, Rory." Despite how calm he was, Rory saw his brows furrow as he picked at his nail beds, something he did when he was frustrated. "He's just one guy. I know he saved your life and I understand why you really look up to him, but he's just a man. Any single one of us could start wearing all black and kicking the shit out of the junkies on the east side of town. Don't you think now is a good time to walk away?"

"How could I walk away, Kay?"

"I am literally begging you for your own safety. It is so amazing that you and Naomi found out who Stone Breaker is and that you've been feeding Hematite what you found. I cannot understate how in awe I am at you," Kane said, "but I can't see this ending well. It's reckless."

"And who are you to lecture me on recklessness, huh? Kane, you passed out in my class the other day because you're out every night doing God knows what with Jameson like you're still twenty-one-years-old. I think you're hardly one to talk."

"You're right," Kane said with a single-shouldered shrug. "I do a lot of reckless shit. But at least I'm not risking my life."

That much is true, at least, he thought, *in a roundabout way.*

"I just want you to be safe. For everyone's sake. For yours, for mine, and for your students."

"I can't walk away, Kay," Rory reaffirmed. "My therapist recommended I open up to you about all this so I can work on building trust."

Her words hit Kane like a gut punch. He frowned and then asked, "Do you trust me?"

Rory nodded. "With my life. That's why I'm telling you everything, even if I don't like what you have to say about it." She sighed, scared of what might follow, so she added, "I want you to be honest, but please be gentle. I'm trying here."

"I trust you too." Kane grabbed a hold of her hand and gave it a light shake. "And I trust you know what you're doing. But these guys... they're unpredictable, Rory. Shit's scary out there. At least promise me you'll remember that."

"Alright. Fair."

"I just don't want to see you get hurt. Like, seriously hurt. You don't have to save everyone, you know?"

After their talk, they graded papers in silence. Instead of her usual spot by the window, Rory sat beside Kane on the floor. Some of the tension still lingered between them, but the quiet was still ultimately comfortable. When Kane glanced over at her, he wanted nothing more than to press his lips to her temple and swear that it would all be okay. He opened his mouth to speak but decided on something else.

"Hey, Rory?"

"Hmm?"

"You... You mean a lot to me. You know that, right?"

They made eye contact. Rory wasn't sure what she was seeing behind Kane's dynamic blue eyes, but there was a softness in them today that was usually masked by mischievousness. Today, he was gentler. The tempest in them from earlier had faded now, showing a beautiful sea.

CHAPTER ELEVEN

"I know," Rory said. "You mean a lot to me too, Kane. I'm sorry if I've been kinda rash lately."

"I understand why you have been," Kane said. His heart felt like it was going to burst out of his chest. He desperately wanted to tell her right then and there how much she really meant to him, how he'd loved her for as long as he could remember now, but he refrained.

For Rory, she wished she could see this side of Kane more often. She smiled at him and ruffled his hair. "I've got it under control, Kane. Don't worry too much about me."

"Easier said than done," Kane said with a laugh. "I'll try to be better about being there for you through this, alright? I know it's important to you."

"Thanks."

"Besides," Kane said, as he cupped her chin with his thumb and index finger. "We can't have you upset at the winter formal tonight. Those kids are going to be looking for a smiling face after they get yelled at by their math teacher for not leaving room for Jesus."

Rory laughed. "You're right. They'll be looking to us as the cool teachers that actually let them dance."

"Just no making out behind the bleachers," Kane said with a wink. "You know, I never went to any of the school dances."

"You didn't?"

"Nah. Too poor. And by the time I was old enough to get a part-time job, if I had the money, I'd just give it to Kayla so she could go to hers. Her friends were nice enough to let her borrow their old dresses."

"I didn't go, either. Naomi tried to drag me along once, but they were just never my thing. I dunno."

"What? You? Avoiding a big party? Color me shocked," Kane said with playful sarcasm. Rory nudged his shoulder as Kane said, "We should have gone together. Though I'm glad we didn't know each other back then. You'd have hated me in high school."

"Oh, I doubt that," Rory said with a laugh. "I'm shocked we never had a class together, though, after all those years."

"No, you would have seriously hated me. I was a fucking asshole who spent way too much time with Jameson."

"You still do. But I doubt you were ever an asshole."

"Suit yourself," Kane said as he shook his head. "But I'm glad I met you when I did."

"Likewise. I was too shy for my own good growing up. You've brought me out of my shell a lot, you know?"

"You're gonna make me blush. Save it for later when you wanna make out behind the bleachers, okay?"

Rory couldn't help her grin. "I'll keep that in mind."

"Wait. Does that mean you might want to make out behind the bleachers?"

The longer she looked at him, the more she thought did. "Don't test your luck."

―――――

Rory and Kane were the first chaperones to arrive at the school for the winter formal. It was "Winter in Paris"-themed, so the gymnasium was decorated in white-and-blue-colored streamers and fabrics, with a faux-crystal chandelier hanging from the center, in a sad attempt to look somewhat sophisticated. Rory thought the only Parisian thing about it was the hors d'oeuvres if frozen foods from Costco counted.

Kane wore a simple suit and Rory wore a basic black cocktail dress and brown trench coat, not wanting to outshine the students but still fit in. They did this together every year; while they had their work cut out for them, Kane enjoyed the free food and Rory enjoyed Kane's company. They started the evening making sure their students came in sober and strait-laced, with only a handful of students having to be turned away—something Kane took note to check on the next time he went on patrol as Hematite.

"Do you think anything is going to happen tonight?" Rory asked Kane, once the crowd was mostly inside. "With all the vigilante stuff going on?"

"I hope not," Kane said. "It would blow if Stone Breaker got a bunch of kids wrapped up in it."

CHAPTER ELEVEN

She did a great job of putting on a cheerful show for her students to act like nothing was wrong, taking photos with students when asked. But Kane could see the tightness in her shoulders and the way she was fidgeting with her thumbs when they'd watch the students along the gymnasium wall. To anyone not paying attention, everything was fine. But if you looked at Rory long enough, you could see the increasingly rapid rise and fall of her chest through her cocktail dress and how quickly she'd glance around the room. She was on high alert, and Kane was positive he was the only one who noticed.

"Hey," Kane whispered in her ear. "I know I'm no Hematite, but if anything happens, I've got your back, okay?"

Rory looked up at Kane and smiled. She saw no hint of joking in his expression, but that he was being dead serious for once. She nodded and said, "I know. Thanks, Kane."

The DJ interrupted them. "We've got a request from your senior class president. It's Lil Nas X!"

But Lil' Nas X didn't play. A lightning bolt sound effect rippled through the speakers. Kane saw Rory's brows furrow and lips slightly part.

"*Bon soir,* Riverpeak High School. How's your winter formal going?" The distorted voice was undoubtedly Stone Breaker's. "I believe someone here is helping Hematite. Now's your chance to give yourself up. I—."

"Sorry about that, folks," the DJ said as he cut the message off. "I don't know how that got in my playlist. I'm making sure it's gone now. That must have been a mistake."

But Rory knew it wasn't a mistake at all. She looked up at Kane and saw that he was already looking at her. She felt a lump in her throat as she said, "We gotta get out of here."

Kane just nodded. "Come on. I'll go with you."

As Kane rushed through the crowd alongside Rory, he glanced down when he felt her take a hold of his hand. He gave hers a squeeze, letting her interlock their fingers together. Kane made eye contact with the principal from across the room and she met them halfway, blonde curls in an updo for the evening so it was easy to spot her.

"I'm taking her home," Kane said when they came together. "Stone Breaker isn't after the students. He's after her because Hematite helped her with something back when we were in college. It's a long story."

Rory was glad that Kane had taken charge of the situation. She was too busy trying to collect her thoughts and get her breathing under control without hyperventilating. All the color and warmth had long since drained from her face.

"Rory, are you okay?" the principal asked.

"I'll be fine. But if he's keeping tabs on me, I don't want any of the students to get hurt."

"Call me in the morning, okay? Not as your boss. As your friend."

"I will. Thanks, ma'am."

Kane continued to hold Rory's hand as they bolted to her car. She grabbed her keys with the other hand and only released from Kane's grip when she got to the driver's side door.

"I'm calling Elijah," Kane said as he entered the car's passenger side.

"Okay." Her hands trembled as she tossed her keys in the cupholder and hit the start button in her vehicle. She didn't realize how clammy they were until she gripped the steering wheel. Kane normally would have harped on her about letting the engine warm up before she immediately took off, but he knew now wasn't the time to pick on her about those sorts of things. As they drove by the snow-covered grasslands, she swerved to avoid a mule deer that was too close to the side of the road, but her four-wheel drive did its work and kept her in control.

She drove while Kane called Elijah.

"Hey, Elijah. Listen, dude, can I ask you to do me a favor?"

On the other line, Elijah frowned. "Are you on speaker right now?"

"No."

"A Hematite favor or a Kane favor?"

"Yes." Kane hoped Elijah would understand that he meant both.

CHAPTER ELEVEN

"Got it," Elijah said. "Rory's with you, I take it? Isn't winter formal tonight?"

"Yeah, that was tonight. Here, I'll put you on so she can hear you too." Kane switched to speakerphone. "She's driving. But something weird just happened at the dance. The DJ went to go play a song request but a message from Stone Breaker played instead. The hell is that about?"

"I'm willing to bet that the DJ was set up on Bluetooth. Let me grab my keys; I'll drive over to the school and see if anyone's connected. If it is set up via Bluetooth, I'll start bluejacking and try to scare him off. I'll let you know if I find anything."

"You're the best. Thanks."

"Anytime. You okay, Rory?"

"I've been better, but I've been worse," Rory said, trying to convince herself that she was fine. She hated how a stupid message on a speaker was all it took to get her heart racing. "And I have no idea what bluejacking is, but thanks for trying in advance."

Elijah chuckled. "It's like when you AirDrop people things unsuspectedly but with an added layer of anonymity. I've got my ways. Don't worry; we'll figure something out and I've got Rick Astley bookmarked."

When Rory pulled up next to Kane's car in her driveway, he took a hold of her hand before she could turn the car off. Rory snapped her head at him in response, unsure of what Kane might say or do next. She normally loved Kane's spontaneity, but she was too on edge for unpredictability.

"Do you want me to stay here with you for the night? Like good ol' times?"

Rory smiled at the memory and nodded, still struggling to form words as she processed everything that had happened.

"No funny business, I promise," Kane teased.

Rory wasted no time in removing her trench coat and heels when they got inside. Kane kicked his dress shoes off as Rory plopped on her couch. Kane could see the stress seeping out of her in the way she sat, with hunched shoulders and lines on her forehead. Part of him thought he should urge her to go to sleep so he could go back to the school and look for Stone Breaker, but he decided to put his trust in Elijah for the evening so he could be the friend Rory needed.

"Hey."

Rory looked up and saw Kane standing before her with both of his hands in his slack pockets. He removed his suit jacket a few moments ago, leaving him in his button-up shirt. Kane had rolled the sleeves up, showcasing his muscular forearms and a few mostly faded scars. As he removed one of his hands from his pocket and extended it out to her, Kane smirked.

"Can I have this dance?"

Rory blinked in response. "Huh?"

Kane smiled at her. "I never went to any of our school dances; neither did you. I'm all dressed up. You look beautiful, and it'd be a shame to waste that. Come on. Dance with me." She continued to stare at him, so he added, "It'll cheer you up."

Rory responded only by smiling at him and giving him her hand. Kane whisked her up and gave her a quick twirl before taking her in his arms. He held one of her hands up with his own as his other rested on the small of her back. Kane felt a warmth flutter in his abdomen as Rory's free arm wrapped around his shoulders.

Kane turned his head toward her television stand and said, "Hey Alexa, play mellow romantic songs."

Rory didn't even know the song that played, but it had a pleasant rhythm that was easy for her and Kane to sway to.

"You clean up nice, you know," Rory said.

Kane chuckled, and she felt the vibration of his laugh against her own chest. "You think so?"

"Mm. Nineties Ethan Hawke-kind of thing, remember?" She was silent again for a moment and then said, "Thank you. For everything tonight."

"Don't thank me. I'd be a pretty shitty friend if I hadn't. This was, like, the bare minimum as far as I'm concerned."

CHAPTER ELEVEN

Rory appreciated his trying to brush it off. She had so much she wanted to say to Kane, but the word "friend" stuck in her mind, so she decided to just enjoy the moment as it was. "I mean it."

Kane softly kissed her hair, so gently that she almost didn't notice. Before Rory could call him on it, Kane said, "I made a promise to myself a few years ago when Naomi filled me in on what had happened to you in college. She let me into your dorm to keep an eye out so she could get some sleep. You were so distressed, and you wear your heart on your damn sleeve, so it was hard to not notice. Internally, I said I was going to make sure a girl as pretty as you would laugh at least once a day every day, so long as you knew me."

Rory felt like her heart practically melted when he said that. "You've made good on your promise, that's for sure."

"And I intend to." He thought about telling her the rest of his feelings, despite his identity, but didn't want to overwhelm her. "Between me and Hematite, you're safe, okay?"

Rory pressed her face against his chest as they continued to dance along to the song in her living room. "I know. I've always known that, Kay."

Kane said nothing else, so Rory pushed her feelings back down like she always did, not wanting to read too much into what Kane was doing and saying. She knew she should take her own advice, but so much happened that she didn't think she could take it if she was wrong.

When she woke up the next morning in her bed, Kane was still asleep beside her. While they had fallen asleep back-to-back, he must have shifted in his sleep because she woke up with his arm draped around her waist and his head against her neck. His breath was warm against her skin, tickling her shoulder with every slow exhale.

When she moved a bit, Kane woke up. He quickly shuffled to retract his arm. "Shit, I'm sorry. Good morning."

"It's fine," Rory said with a wave of her hand. "Thanks for staying with me. I don't think I would have gotten much sleep if I were alone."

"No way was I ditching you. Elijah texted me once you fell asleep. Stone Breaker was still there when he got there, and he followed him. Some guy left on a motorcycle after Elijah bluejacked him. He said he followed the sounds of 'Never Gonna Give You Up' to City Hall, but Elijah couldn't get much further without going in."

"It's gotta be Councilman Stevens' kid," Rory said. "I'll have to text him my thanks later. Are you staying for breakfast?"

"I have an appointment, but not until eleven. What time is it?"

"Only nine."

"I'll stay, sure."

As they sat across from each other at Rory's dining room table—Kane in his sweatpants and T-shirt from yesterday and Rory still in her pajamas, glasses, and hair tied back—they both just savored the moment. Unbeknownst to the other, they both pretended that every morning could be like this. But both knew without saying anything that this was just the calm before the storm, leaving everything in their minds left unsaid.

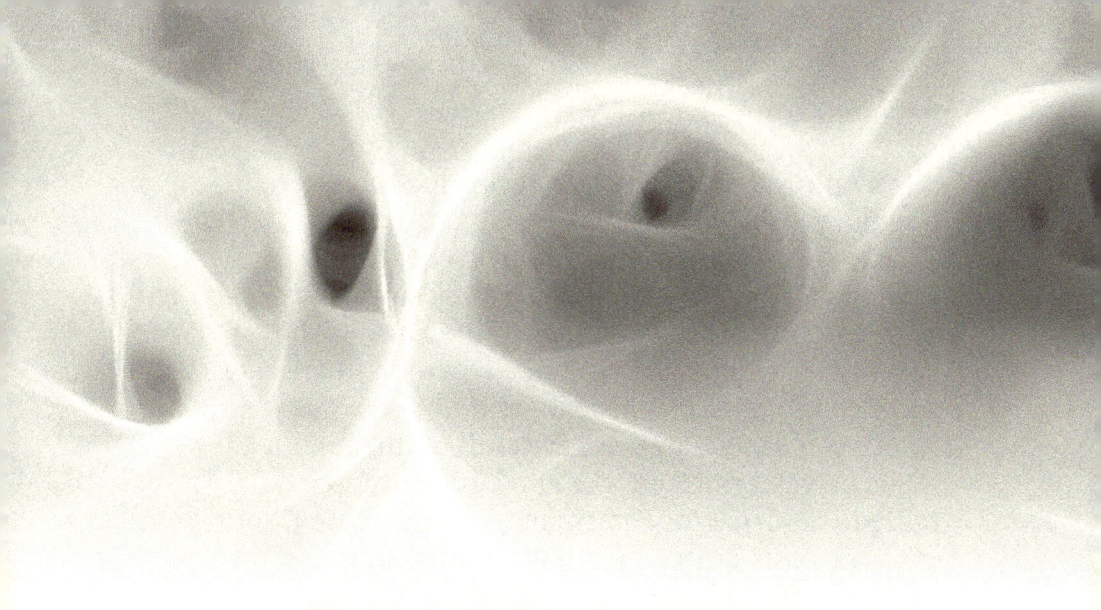

CHAPTER TWELVE

Kane always had a weird feeling when he arrived at Potter Laboratories, and late Sunday morning was no exception. It rested on the outskirts of the town on a large, isolated plot of land. The sign showing where the property started was about a mile out from the actual building, with only the occasional moose showing face between the sign and Constance's Pond a few blocks away. Hardly anyone ever came out here, leaving Kane alone with the physician, Dr. Potter himself. The building was all slate on the outside; its interior lacked any color too, varying from shades of white to grey. The only part of it that felt real was the view of the familiar Pikes Peak in the distance.

Dr. Potter was waiting for Kane in the lobby upon his arrival. He was a lanky man whose lab coats were all a bit ill-fitting for his stature; they were either awkwardly short or strangely loose, but never both. His skin was nearly as white as his coats. Kane wasn't sure if Dr. Potter was a real medical professional, but his lab on the far reaches of town had certainly provided Kane with more answers than his own doctor.

"Mr. Kelly," Dr. Potter said, "welcome back. How has your investigation been going?"

"It's going, I suppose. I've recently received some help along the way."

"That's excellent to hear. Come, come."

Dr. Potter pushed his glasses back up his nose and led him to the usual, private room in the back of the lab. Kane could hear the light whirring of a machine in another room. Gooseflesh formed on his skin, and he wasn't sure if it was from his uneasiness or from the chill of the building.

"So, we've confirmed you can't be murdered," Dr. Potter recalled, "at least not permanently. Watching your cells regenerate was quite the show. You are aging at an appropriate rate, though, so you may not be explicitly out of the woods as far as mortality goes. Has your investigation provided any answers yet?"

"A few." Dr. Potter seemed actually relieved to hear that news. "The city government's involved. I think they're profiting off that drug that's been pumping through the west side of town. And I think that drug is why I can't be killed."

"A blood test and a quick swab should be all I need for now," Dr. Potter said. He excelled at two things: fast work and showing no emotion, which always left Kane on his toes. Dr. Potter went through the motions, swabbing Kane's cheek and pricking his finger, and then announced he'd return shortly.

Kane picked at his nail beds as he waited for Dr. Potter and the results. Dr. Potter used a lot of experimental methods that Kane couldn't explain. He tried to swallow any questionable morality that Dr. Potter may have, aware that judging Dr. Potter would make him a bit of a hypocrite himself. He was just grateful to be getting answers and to be getting them quickly; Dr. Potter's tests typically took only a few minutes. With how small Riverpeak was, everyone knew about Dr. Potter's lab, but it seemed like no one had actually ever been inside or knew anything about him. Kane had initially gone out of an act of desperation, but so far, he was pleased. Primary care physicians didn't have the right tests, but Dr. Potter did. Kane hadn't bothered to ask how, mainly since Dr. Potter had yet to give him reason to.

CHAPTER TWELVE

Dr. Potter said as he returned to his room, "Well, Mr. Kelly, you continue to amaze me. Once again, brilliant."

Kane forced himself to not roll his eyes. "I'm glad you find this entertaining. What is it?"

"Your theory was right about your mother," Potter said. "What you're experiencing can best be described as a semi-distant cousin of Neonatal Abstinence Syndrome. The main difference, though, is you're not experiencing withdrawals. It didn't show up in the blood test, but I did get it from the cell swab. That's in line with our past tests that explained the how. Now you have the why."

Kane swallowed and took a deep breath. He didn't want to get too emotional, especially in the lab. "And what about other kids who were born like me?"

The words felt strange. He always suspected it had something to do with his mother's drug addiction—the substance she used was largely a mystery to him, despite his work to eradicate it over the years, but it was still cycling around Riverpeak. However, his longtime suspicions didn't make the confirmation any less jarring. He wouldn't wish this recurring pain of immortality on anybody.

"Do you know anyone else with abilities like your own?" Dr. Potter asked.

"Not that can't be killed, no. But I do know a guy with super strength like the world's never seen. He helps me sometimes when I'm on patrol. His mom's ... like mine."

"Do you think he'd be willing to undergo the same blood tests as you've undergone?" Dr. Potter asked. "I could compare your samples, see if there's any overlap and if the drugs are causing it."

"I'm warning you now, he's kind of a dick. But Shawn Jameson will come if I ask him to."

Dr. Potter grinned. "Excellent. A pleasure, as always, Mr. Kelly."

"Yeah," Kane said half-heartedly, "likewise."

Kane didn't even turn the radio on as he drove home from the lab on the west side of Riverpeak. The winding road back was lonely, especially in the dead of winter, but it allowed him to collect his thoughts as he made the trek back. The moose he sometimes saw didn't even make an appearance today, although it would have been a welcome distraction.

He felt like he was at war with himself. He and Kayla stopped speaking to their parents the moment they moved out; given their childhood memories of drunken fights and dodging needles, their fractured relationships weren't a surprise. Part of him wanted to go back to the family's home on the east side of the city, where Stone Breaker was running amuck among the run-down homes and abandoned businesses. He yearned to sit down with his mother and father and ask them why: why he was born; why they couldn't stop using when they were expecting; and why this was the life they ended up living.

But he couldn't. He knew it would be a waste of time and energy, and that he would only leave more frustrated than he started. Kane wasn't even sure if his parents were still using or not.

He thought about driving by the house at least, hoping that looking at it would spark a revelation; he'd be there the following weekend to see his sister when she visited from college, but he was growing more and more impatient in finding answers. But instead of going out of his way to that side of the city, he just pulled into his apartment complex and sat in the parking lot, feeling numb. Kane thought he might cry, based on the lump in his throat, but he felt a void inside of him instead. The tears he desperately needed to release never came. Instead, the pressure just continued to build in the back of his throat and beneath his eyes before it eventually reached the bridge of his nose.

He rested his head against the steering wheel as he sat in silence, wondering how much longer it would take to get the answers he needed. Stone Breaker was his key, he knew that, but he felt like he was at an impasse. If Stone Breaker was, in

CHAPTER TWELVE

fact, Mark Stevens, then he had a shield. If Hematite broke into a councilman's office, that would be the end of it.

But he knew for certain now that Councilman Stevens had to be at the heart of his problem. He just wasn't sure yet exactly how he would find out why Councilman Stevens was involved.

As excited as Kane was to see his sister the weekend after, he still dreaded every moment. Kane stared at his parents' house for a few moments from his car. He knew in the worn-down jeans, cheap shirt, and old winter coat that he'd still be cold, but it was critical to fit in on the east side of town. He felt naked without his Hematite gear, but he was here strictly for family.

Sometimes, he dreamed of what his life might look like had he been born into another family. When he did, he didn't envision a fancy home or anything extravagant. He simply envisioned something with windows that were actually properly sealed, a tablecloth on the dining room table, and an absence of mice in the winter.

In Kane's dream, his mother and father didn't scream at each other. It would be a place where he could take Rory to meet his parents. There was no clashing of beer bottles or used needles in the trash bins that he'd have to be cautious of when taking the garbage out. He wouldn't have to worry about Kayla.

The thought of his sister made him snap out of it. She was the reason he was here, after all. She had only been back in school for about a month but was home for a long weekend.

When he got out of his car, he grimaced, but he was better prepared for the way the air bit at his face than he expected. All the late nights out with only some long sleeves and some thermal undergarments made winters easier for Kane than for most people, even fellow Colorado natives.

When Kane opened the door and walked into his family home—they never locked the door—he was greeted by just

Kayla. Her blonde hair, the same shade as his own, sat in a messy bun on top of her head.

"Oh, thank God you're here," Kayla said, as she all but ran to her brother. Kane could tell by the way she gripped at his shoulders in their hug that she desperately needed it.

"How many times do I have to tell you that you can stay with me instead of this dump?" Kane said with a laugh.

"It's like I always forget how bad it is when Mom says she misses me," Kayla said. "I'm crashing your couch for spring break, though."

"I'm holding you to that. How is everything? Any better?"

Kayla shook her head as she pulled away from their hug. "No. I wish. Come on, Mom and Dad are out back. I'll catch you up."

Kane knew that meant they were in the shed in the backyard. "They're working again, huh?"

"Gotta make money somehow, I guess." Kayla's voice trailed off as she said it and her eyes found the tops of her shoes.

Kane shook his head. "Grab your shit. Let's get outta here."

"Won't Mom–?"

"She can yell at me later," Kane said with a shrug. "Come on. I don't feel like fighting today, and you know how Dad and I can get when he's out of sorts."

"Fair enough," Kayla agreed. "I didn't pack much. I'll be quick."

"I'll wait in my car to get the heat on."

"Thanks!"

Kayla was true to her word; she was only gone about three minutes before she was tossing her duffel bag in the backseat of Kane's car and then hopping in the passenger side.

"You're a lifesaver! When's the last time you talked to them?"

Kane sighed as he backed out of the driveway. "Is it awful that I couldn't tell you?"

"No, not at all," Kayla said. "I gotta be more like you about it. Maybe it's a mother-and-daughter thing, but I swear to God she always knows how to get in my head."

"It's not your fault. She's good at that."

"Seriously, how do you do it?"

CHAPTER TWELVE

"I realized you can't save everyone. So, I just gave up. But enough about them. What's going on?"

"I... Do you ever just feel like you can't catch a break?"

Kane nodded. "Do I ever. What happened?"

"Maybe we're both cursed. Maybe it's genetic." Kayla laughed. "I'm doing well in my classes, and I'm on track to graduate in a few months; it's not that. But it's like, at what cost, you know? I thought I was having an existential crisis, so I figured that heading home would clear my head. That was a fucking mistake. Seriously, thanks for getting me out of that hellhole. It's like all the awful shit that happened during our childhood comes back." Kayla sighed. "Looking back ... you really protected me from a lot of that."

"Somebody had to look out for us, right?" Kane said with a smile.

"I guess so. I started seeing a therapist too. Just the counseling services at school. They're nice, but I dunno, I feel like I have a lot to unpack. I haven't told any of my friends, though. I don't know what they'd think."

"You are the second person I know to start therapy this year. Maybe it's the universe saying I should too," Kane said.

"Wait, really?"

"Yeah. You know Rory. She started going last month. Said she loves it."

"Oh, I love Rory," Kayla cooed. "Speaking of her, did you ask her out yet?"

Kane grinned. "Nah. She's way out of my league." They pulled up to his apartment complex as he said that. "I'll grab your bag. I should have some extra blankets and pillows."

"I don't think I've been to your apartment."

"It's nothing special, but it's home for now."

As Kane helped Kayla get settled, she looked at her brother. "I'm really proud of you, you know? Given everything we've been through, you've really done a good job for yourself. I look up to you a lot."

"I'm proud of you too, kid," Kane said. He gently elbowed her shoulder. "Don't get too sappy on me now."

"You know, some of my friends say that you're this big-shot party guy," Kayla said. She had a cocky grin on her face, like she knew she was about to uncover some massive secret. "But that doesn't sound like you. You've never been a big-shot party guy."

"Should I be insulted?"

Kayla laughed. "No! I mean, you know. Look at where we came from. That's not really either of us, no matter how much we might try to pretend. What's really going on?"

"That is classified information," Kane said, as he grabbed a can of Diet Coke® with lime—his sister's favorite—from the fridge. "It's complicated."

"Come on!" Kayla said. "I just told you my deep, dark secret that I'm going to therapy. Your turn. Why do you party?"

"I don't party."

He said it with such bluntness that Kayla froze. "Wait, what?"

"Yeah," Kane said as he sat on the couch next to her and handed her the can of soda. "I should have told you this a long time ago."

"Told me what?"

"Look around. You're smart. You'll figure it out. If you can, I'll tell you my deep, dark secret. But it stays between us. Got it?"

"Of course," Kayla said. Kane could tell that she understood the severity of it all. Her voice trailed off again as she stood from the couch and immediately wandered the apartment.

Kane propped his feet up on the coffee table as he ran his hands through his hair, pushing it out of his face. Part of him wasn't sure if this was the right move to make, but he knew he would eventually have to tell Rory. He figured practicing by letting Kayla in on it would be a good start, especially since he knew his sister well enough to know that Kayla would take that information with her to the grave.

"I'm not gonna find anything weird in your drawers or closet, will I?" Kayla asked from his bedroom.

"Depends on what you define as weird."

"Fuck's sake," Kayla mumbled. Kayla started with his bedside table, hoping she wouldn't stumble upon anything she

CHAPTER TWELVE

wouldn't want to imagine her brother using. To her surprise, there wasn't much in there: just some writing utensils, a notepad, and a sheathed pocketknife. She closed it and moved on to his closet. She didn't want to invade her brother's privacy, but he made it a sort of game, so she figured all cards were on the table when she slid the door open.

There were mostly button-up shirts he wore to work and some jackets. She thumbed through a few of them until she reached the far-right side of the closet. Her fingers came across what felt like a scarf, but when she pulled it out, she noticed it was more like a hooded cape. The ends were frayed and tattered as if pieces had been ripped off, both with and without purpose. She held it in one hand as she continued on until she saw the black-and-navy uniform pieces that she recognized as Hematite's: the navy-and-black long-sleeved shirts he alternated between and the black joggers with pockets that cinched at the ankles.

"Holy shit." Kayla put the cowl back and took a step back, staring at the clothes in the open closet. She lifted her hand up so she could glance at the hematite ring that she now wore on her pinky—she once wore it on her thumb and then ring finger, but as she got older, she nearly outgrew it.

Kayla glanced to her left as she heard the shuffling sound of her brother's footsteps. He leaned against the doorframe and with half of a smile, Kane said, "I see you found it."

"It was you all along?" Kayla asked. Kane nodded. Kayla wasn't sure what else to say as she glanced back and forth between her brother and the clothes she found. She said, "Are you fucking joking with me right now?"

Kane shook his head. "I'm not. I'm serious. That's mine. It's always been me."

Kayla closed the closet door, deciding it was too much to process. "Everything makes sense, how Hematite was always there at just the right time." She glanced at her ring. "Oh my God, I fucking named you when I was nine."

Kane chuckled. "Yeah, you did. I didn't want anyone to call me anything originally, but your nickname had a nice ring to it. Pun not intended."

Kayla didn't know what else to say. She simply charged at her brother, wrapping her arms tightly around him, and burying her face in his chest. She didn't intend on crying, but she couldn't help herself.

"Didn't you die a few weeks ago?"

"Nah, you don't have to worry about that," Kane reassured her.

"I won't tell a soul, Kane. I promise."

"I know you won't. I knew I couldn't help Mom and Dad. But I knew I could help you." He patted her shoulders as he pulled away. "But I have to do something late tonight. Whatever you do, you stay here. Got it?"

Kayla wiped her tears with the back of her hand. "What are you going to do?"

"I'm going back to our parents' house," Kane said, "and I'm breaking into that fucking shed once and for all."

Kane tried to stick to the darker alleys as he weaved through the east side of town. His Hematite getup helped him stay disguised in the night, blending in with darker surroundings. Every time he came through the east side of the city, he felt an immense level of sadness.

Growing up, he blamed his parents for their shortcomings; he still did, to a degree. But now, as an adult, looking at the condition of his hometown, he knew there was more to it than people simply making poor life choices. Riverpeak City Council and the police department often worked but brought no real help beyond fattening their own wallets, even if it was at the cost of their constituents. Kane saw his family and the people in this part of town as the victims that they were, hoping that he could find a solution alongside the answers to his own abilities.

He slunk through the shadows to stay hidden on the way to his family's home. He was just glad that Kayla was out of there and sleeping soundly in his apartment. When he lingered by the pine tree across the street, he noticed that the

CHAPTER TWELVE

lights to the house were completely out. He could see, however, that the lights to the shed in the backyard were still on. The memories from the last time he entered the shed came flooding back, but he pushed them back. He had grown a lot since then.

Kane made his way over, hoping he wouldn't have to fight his own family but bracing himself for that possibility. He opened the front door, still unlocked from earlier, and tiptoed his way through his childhood home. He paused at a picture frame that held a photo of him and his sister when Kayla was first born. The frame was cracked. Kane took the photo from it and pocketed it for himself before moving forward.

He opened the backdoor. It squeaked a bit, and he hoped it wouldn't alert anyone to his presence. There was nowhere for him to hide, so he darted for the shed and put his back against a wall by the door. He waited a moment, surprised that no one came out, and then moved to a window to peer in.

He saw both of his parents passed out on the floor. Some smoke was billowing from a burner, so Kane tried for the doorknob. It was the only one they cared enough to lock, so Kane grabbed his billy club and broke a window with it. Even with the sound of shattering glass, his parents didn't stir.

Kane propelled himself up through the window, trying to avoid the broken glass as best as he could. He first approached his parents, using his foot to roll his dad over from his stomach onto his back. His father was wearing a ventilation mask, but it clearly hadn't been enough to do the job right. When Kane found a pulse, he sighed in relief.

Kane did the same for his mother, seeing she was wearing the same type of mask as his father. Once he realized they were both alive but just unconscious, Kane moved on to the drug on the shed's counters. There were blenders, beakers, and a variety of jugs. He wasn't sure what they contained. He turned the portable burner off before grabbing a small vial from a stack of them and pouring some of the liquid inside. To make sure the temperature wouldn't break the glass, he started with a small amount before he filled and capped it.

Kane unlocked the shed door and made his way outside, using the snow to cool the vial enough to pocket comfortably. He went back into the house to cut through to the front. He moved his way back to the pine tree before he took his burner phone out to call for emergency services.

"Nine-one-one, what is your emergency?"

"My neighbors have been in their shed in the backyard for a long time, and I'm afraid they might be hurt in there. Can you send an ambulance to check on them? I'm seeing some smoke come out from there too."

"What's the address? We'll send a crew right away."

"Well, I'm at 98 Greenfield Avenue. They're the yellow house next to me."

Kane lingered by the pine tree across the street as he waited for someone to arrive. From his position, no one could see him, even with the few streetlights a few feet ahead. Only a few minutes passed before an ambulance and fire truck wailed on by, stopping right in front of his parents' home. Once he knew they'd be taken care of, he left for his apartment, not wanting to stick around any longer than he needed to.

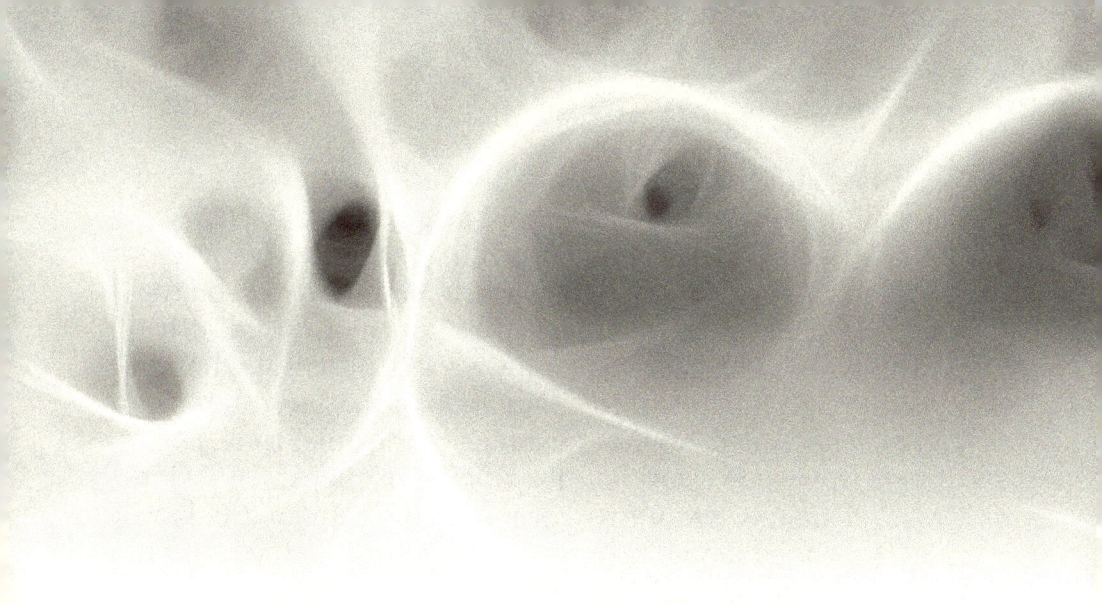

CHAPTER THIRTEEN

About two weeks had passed since Rory's encounter with Shatterstone. If it were up to her, she would still stay between home and school. She was still shaken to her core about what had happened and felt like someone was watching her every move. Rory didn't want to think of anything as a setback, but she knew in her gut that some of her progress in healing had definitely taken a few steps back. If it weren't for her picking Kane up on their way to work every morning, she would have been completely alone.

So, when Rory received an invitation to her friend Carla's birthday dinner, it provided an opportunity to be around friends rather than to carry on in isolation, something that Rory knew would ultimately make matters worse. The less she could be in her own head, the better, and Carla's party was the perfect distraction.

"Drive safely!" Carla called to Rory as Naomi walked her to her car.

"Thanks, Carla! I'll see you later, Naomi."

"Text me when you're home," Naomi said, as she got into the driver's side of her own vehicle. At that, Rory closed her car door and took off from Carla's birthday night-out.

It was later than she was usually out, but it was a Friday night, and her students didn't have any homework assigned that she needed to worry about grading. Her drive home was relatively uneventful since there wasn't really anyone on the road from Denver to Riverpeak. The hour-and-a-half drive on the populated back roads always felt peaceful when it was quiet. Rory listened to an audiobook that her therapist had recommended, taking advantage of the quiet time. Even though the words often felt like ripping off tight Band-Aids, it was ultimately meditative for Rory, especially on the long ride. Her elated mood from seeing old friends helped soften the blow from the audiobook too.

When Rory hit a red light closer to town, she felt like something in her peripheral vision was out of place. She glanced over to the alley between the empty warehouses where the dumpster was normally left wide open. But tonight, she noticed the lid was down. It was odd enough that she paused her audiobook to pay closer attention.

She glanced back at the light to make sure it was still red, and when she looked over again, the light flashed. The sudden shift in light was enough to cause a flicker over the shadows along the spot where the dumpster met the wall.

Rory looked in her rearview and confirmed she was the only one on the road. She rolled the window down, grabbed her cell phone, and turned on the flashlight so she could look down the alley more clearly. No one was in the warehouses at this time of night.

"Holy shit," she whispered to herself.

It was Hematite.

Rory tossed her phone on the passenger seat and backed her car up a bit. She then pulled forward and to the left, parking her car so it was blocking the alleyway before she climbed into the backseat. When she got out of her car, she pocketed her keys and left the back door open.

"Hematite?"

He didn't answer Rory's call, and the figure before her didn't move. When Rory got closer, she held her phone with its flashlight still on over his body. She covered her mouth

CHAPTER THIRTEEN

with her hand so she wouldn't be too loud when she saw that there was an abundance of blood pouring from his abdomen and staining the concrete beneath them.

"Fuck."

She put her phone in her other pocket and moved his limp body so she could grab him from beneath his armpits. His body felt cold and stiff. She remembered the CPR training she had when she first started teaching and checked for a pulse, breathing, or any sign of life, but had no luck.

Despite his body being stiff from the cool air, Rory dragged him down the alley. She cursed herself for wearing heels and a skirt to Carla's birthday dinner instead of something slightly more casual and practical. His body left a trail of his blood behind in thin streaks. It took her a few moments and all of her strength, but she managed to reach her car where the back door behind the driver's side was open.

She hoisted herself into the backseat and brought him with her, figuring it would be easier to rely on her own body weight for the momentum. Once Hematite was slumped in the backseat, Rory leaned over his body to close the car door, trying not to feel dirty about the whole thing. She grabbed her keys, awkwardly climbed back into the driver's seat, and then took off.

"Fuck," she muttered again. She grabbed her phone when she hit the next red light—they were all on timers, even at one in the morning—so she could plug in directions to the hospital.

Suddenly, Rory heard a familiar, gruff voice from the backseat. "Whatever you do, do not take me to the emergency room."

Rory yelped in shock. "Holy shit! Oh my God. You're alive. I thought you were dead. Are you sure?"

"I'm absolutely positive." Hematite grimaced through the pain. "They'll unmask me. I can't let that happen. Got it?"

Rory nodded as she turned the GPS off on her phone. "Right, right. I, uh, I think I have a first-aid kit at home. My friend Kane is pretty good with that stuff. I could call him—"

"No!" Hematite quickly caught himself after he interrupted her. "Don't call anyone. The less attention this draws, the better. I don't need the media going into another frenzy. If you have a first-aid kit, that's all I need."

Rory nodded. He could tell by her uneven breathing and the uncontrolled pitch in her voice that she was still panicking. "Okay, okay. Right. Okay, I'll take you to my house."

Kane thought about telling Rory the truth, but then remembered the fact that he was bleeding out in the back of her car and thought it might just worry her more. Besides, Rory already seemed determined to put herself in more danger than she needed to be, and Kane didn't want to amplify that risk. Her safety mattered more than her curiosity.

"What happened? Who did this to you?"

"I got jumped. There were five different guys, all amped up and out of their heads. I think they were sent by Stone Breaker. Whatever it is they're selling, it's getting worse. A bunch of them held me down, and then one of them introduced me to his knife."

"Can you at least explain to me how you came back to life on your own after that?" Rory asked. "I checked for a pulse, breathing, everything. You were legit dead."

"My parents did a lot of drugs, including when my mom was pregnant with me. My doctor thinks that has something to do with the fact that whenever I die, I come back within a few minutes. It's usually only ten or fifteen. It's a real pain in the ass."

"How so?" Rory asked. "Does it not heal you?"

"No... Imagine you're playing a video game," Hematite said. He found that talking to her was distracting him from the lingering pain in his abdomen where he had been stabbed. "You have two save points before a boss battle, but you forget to save at the second one. So, when you get your ass kicked, you remember everything but the character doesn't, and you have to gain some of your experience points back and whatnot. My body remembers everything; my memory is often hazy, depending on how long I'm out for."

CHAPTER THIRTEEN

They hit a pothole that made Hematite groan and cough. His cough caused him to spit up a little blood, but he wiped it away with his scarf.

"That and it really fucking hurts, even after I wake up."

"I'm sorry. We'll be at my place soon, okay?" She tried to hide the higher pitch of her voice but failed to mask the fact that she was freaking out. "I don't know that it totally makes sense, but I won't make you explain again. You must be exhausted. I took a shortcut, so it shouldn't be much longer."

Once they were inside, Rory rushed to help Hematite patch himself up. Kane noticed that the frenzied panic Rory was feeling in the car seemed to have melted away once it came time to help him, replaced with a steady determination. Rory was always fairly quick to take action, something that he always loved about her.

Rory started with his face, which meant Kane could keep most of his disguise on. He winced at the Neosporin® but sat still for her on her couch as she touched up a cut on his face from a knife wound just below his eye; she was careful to not remove his facial coverings entirely out of respect for his desired privacy. The two of them were still in silence as they sat side by side on her couch. While it was quiet, it was still comfortable between them. Rory had a fleeting thought that it felt familiar, but she shrugged it off.

Rory was the one to break their silence first. "Why did you become a superhero?"

Hematite exhaled. "I have a sister. She's a few years younger than me. We ... didn't exactly have a good home life growing up. Like I told you, my parents did a lot of drugs. They drank and fought a lot."

He paused and saw that Rory was still listening intently as she continued to adjust the balaclava and dab at his face. While Kane over the years hadn't told her a lot of the details of his and Kayla's childhood, she knew it was rough. He figured she was in the dark enough for him to share more.

"I wanted to make sure my sister was okay. I learned how to fight from having to fend for myself against my father. Started with keeping my sister safe from bullies and our parents, and then that just snowballed into what I'm doing now. I just don't want kids to grow up like we did."

"I really respect you, you know," Rory said. "Most people don't care enough to do anything; it's refreshing, though I'm sorry to hear that happened to you."

Hematite smiled beneath his mask. "Thank you." He glanced down at his hands as Rory took a hold of them.

"Can I take these off?" Rory asked. "I want to make sure your knuckles aren't bleeding or anything."

Hematite's heart was racing. He and Rory held hands many times, but their closeness as she tended to his wounds had him feeling like his head was spinning. So, he simply nodded his response to let her take the gloves off and unwrap his boxing wraps. Rory delicately held his hands in her own as she helped clean them up and treat the wounds on his knuckles. Bruises were already forming on some of his fingers. Hematite didn't even notice how the Neosporin® stung; this was a tender side of Rory that he had never experienced.

"Where did you get stabbed?"

"Oh, here," Hematite said, as he lifted up the bottom of his shirt. He revealed toned abs littered with different stab and gunshot scars. "I should, uh, probably invest in some protective gear. But you kinda don't care to bother when you can't die, anyway."

"Good God, they had it out for you." Rory's eyes widened at the sight. The wound by his stomach was a deep gash, but the bleeding had stopped.

"Eh, I've had worse," he said with a shrug of his shoulders. He helped her patch up the spot and once she was done, she bandaged it tightly. "Thank you for all your help." They were so close that he could see the little details of her face: the curve of her brows, the way her highlighter rested on her cheekbones, and the light mascara on her lashes. "I probably would still be over by that dumpster if it weren't for you."

Rory lightly laughed. "Don't mention it."

Their eyes met, and Hematite couldn't take it anymore. He placed a hand behind her head, fingers weaving through

CHAPTER THIRTEEN

her hair, and quickly pulled his scarf down and balaclava up as he leaned in to kiss her.

Rory thought she was dreaming when Hematite's lips met hers. They were dry and cracked from his rough night, but she didn't even care. Rory could faintly taste iron, likely from some blood he coughed up earlier. His fingertips felt rough yet comforting against her scalp.

Rory parted her lips enough for Hematite's tongue to slip between them. Part of her brain was furious with herself. After all, she didn't know Hematite's name or what he looked like beneath the mask, hood, and scarf. But her heart knew that she didn't need to know those things. He meant more to her than she could say, not just for those times he saved her, but because of everything he stood for.

"I... I'm so sorry, Rory," Hematite said when he suddenly pulled away, quick to push his balaclava back down. He glanced down and dropped his hand. "I shouldn't have crossed that line with you. My being here and you helping me already put you in enough danger as is."

"I know you already warned me to not get too deep, but it's too late for that." Rory gently cupped his chin with her fingers and forced him to look back up at her. She could see the sadness in his eyes as she surveyed them. "You have nothing to apologize for."

Rory pushed his balaclava back up and brought their lips together that time. Hematite, to his own surprise, didn't stop her. Part of him felt relieved that she kissed him again. Rory couldn't explain it, but kissing Hematite felt as natural as breathing or eating. To avoid craning her neck any longer, Rory shifted by moving one of her legs across his lap, settling in a position where she was straddling him. Hematite's hands fell to her sides, running first down and then up her back.

Kane as Hematite never imagined that he would actually be like this with Rory. He had wished for it, sure, but never thought it would be a reality, so he just soaked it all in. He admired the natural, feminine curves of her body and how plush her skin felt in his hands.

Rory had never felt so close to someone before, even without knowing his name or face. She knew there was only one place for their actions to go, and she knew that what she wanted to do would certainly elevate that. She mentally thanked herself for remembering to take her birth control medication that morning and then followed through with what her heart told her to do.

Rory ground her hips against Hematite's lap, to where Kane thought he was going to choke.

"Rory, I—"

"It's okay," she said against his lips.

He was the one to pull away completely. "Are you sure?"

"I trust you. And I promise, I'm not normally like this," she said with a nervous chuckle.

Hematite just smiled at her as his hands gently gripped her ribs. "Don't worry. I know." He swallowed a lump in his throat. "Listen, It... do you mind if I keep the mask on? If that changes things, I'll understand."

Rory nodded and placed her hands on his shoulders. "It's okay. I get it."

That took Hematite by surprise. "Wait. You do?"

"Yeah, to a degree. As much as I'd love to see the rest of your face... I don't need to." She did desperately want to see who was beneath the mask, but she also trusted him, regardless of who it was. She recognized the uniqueness of their situation and wouldn't dare disrupt it.

Hematite felt his heart swell in his chest; for a moment, he thought it would creep up his throat and leap out of his mouth. Out of fear of revealing all his feelings, he opted to kiss Rory again in response. Her nonchalance about him keeping his face covered didn't shock him as much as he thought it would. He had fully expected her to ask him to remove his facial coverings, but he also knew how much Hematite meant to Rory, not just as a symbol but on a personal level.

There was a hunger in his kiss as he gripped at her body tighter, pulling her closer to him so she'd buck her hips against him once more. One of his hands fell to her thigh

CHAPTER THIRTEEN

and slowly crept up it. It was clear to Rory that he had been holding back before but wasn't anymore. As Rory moved her hands to undress herself, Hematite turned off his voice modifier and removed his shirt, careful to not remove his cowl. He moved the voice modifier down by his neck, disconnecting it from his balaclava, and knew he'd have to be careful without having it as a crutch. Usually, when he was unprepared, he could change his tone enough to not sound like his usual self. But he knew he couldn't get lost in his feelings and lose control.

When Hematite discarded his shirt, Rory noticed even more scars littering his torso. Unsurprisingly, he was built like a boxer with strong shoulders and well-defined abs. Her fingers gently feathered over his pale skin, tracing the slight dip between his pectoral muscles where a few scars were mostly faded. She wondered how many of these were simple injuries versus times he had died.

The fabric from Hematite's hood and scarf felt soft against her skin as he left rough kisses on her body. She glanced at his face, but his hood cast a shadow over his eyes and covered his face just enough for her to not be able to make it out entirely, especially when paired with his balaclava that still covered his hair, nose, and forehead. In fact, with the way it was bunched up, she couldn't really see his eyes and was surprised he could see much of anything. The nagging voice in the back of her head telling her this was wrong had been effectively silenced when their lips connected, and bodies united.

The rush that Hematite was experiencing had him feeling, for the first time in a long time, very much alive. He thought his heart was going to beat straight out of his chest from a combination of anticipation for Rory's next move, the nervousness of exposing his true identity, and the pleasure of the moment. There was so much he wanted to say, and he was half-tempted to rip his mask off, but he thought it was for the best if he just left it on at this point. The last thing he'd want to do was break her trust right after earning it so wholly.

Hematite's arms wrapped around Rory tightly to hold her close to him. His cowl nearly got in the way, but both of them felt attuned in a way that they could not compare or explain. Rory almost forgot he was wearing his mask until her hands cupped his cheeks during their embrace. As they both finished, they took a moment to soak each other in before they moved. Hematite didn't release his grip on Rory, but only slightly loosened it. She looked into his eyes again, seeing the shade of blue clearly now.

Hematite decided he'd tell her his identity eventually, but not tonight.

"If you have to go, I understand," Rory said.

Hematite cleared his throat. Rory sensed he was struggling to hide his actual voice. "I'll stay for a while. Stone Breaker is looking for you, after all. It's probably safer if I'm here for a bit."

Rory smirked; she knew he was justifying his actions, maybe more to himself than he was to her, but she didn't want to make him uncomfortable by calling that out. "Like I've said before, you're always welcome here. And you don't need an excuse to come either, you know."

He smiled at her, but only halfway. "Thank you."

That night, he held her until she fell asleep. Hematite enjoyed the moment while he could, dreaming of enjoying this every night, but he knew he couldn't. He glanced at her resting peacefully in his arms, sleeping soundly. Hematite knew Rory had been struggling with sleep lately, so to see her so comfortable touched his soul.

When Rory woke the next morning, he was gone. She wondered if the night prior had been a dream as she remembered what happened, until she saw something scribbled on a sticky note on her bedside table. She figured Hematite must have fished out from her backup stash of school supplies. It simply read:

Had to go.
Stay in touch.
-H

CHAPTER THIRTEEN

Rory smiled as she read the note over, especially when she saw the black heart scribbled in the bottom corner, but her smile faded the longer she stared at it. The realization of last night hit her like a tsunami, with no warning and all at once.

"Oh my God," she whispered to herself.

She stared at the sticky note a little while longer before grabbing her phone with her free hand and making a call.

"Hi! Dr. Thornton? Hi, sorry, I know. Marissa. Marissa. Listen, any chance in hell we can bump my next appointment up? I think I took your advice about trusting people a little too far."

"Rory, take a deep breath. You're talking really fast. What happened? Are you okay?"

Rory took a deep breath and then said, "I don't wanna give you TMI."

"Rory, I'm your therapist. As far as I'm concerned, there is no such thing as TMI, and I've probably heard worse than whatever it is you're about to tell me."

"Okay. Okay." Rory took another deep breath. "I slept with Hematite last night." Rory wasn't sure why, but she said it in a whisper. "Mask on. Didn't know his real name. Still don't. I couldn't even tell you the last time I slept with someone. Why did I do that?"

"Can I ask you something? Do you regret it?"

"Do I regret it?"

"Gut reaction. Don't think about it."

"No," Rory blurted out. "Oh, God. Is that bad?"

"Not at all. Maybe get tested just to be safe, but I'm sure you're fine. I know you know that sex is perfectly natural."

"Right, right."

"It sounds like you're self-aware and you have a history with this guy. This wasn't a stranger, and I'm not worried about this becoming a self-destructive behavior. I actually consider this good news coming from you."

"You do?"

"Hematite's been there for you. It's good that you trust him enough to be in that situation. I think it shows progress, just in a roundabout way. But we all grow differently. There's no wrong way to heal. Well, within reason. No wrong way to heal so long as you're not hurting anybody, but you get my drift."

"Thank you for talking me off the ledge."

"That's what I'm here for. Listen, if you still feel the need to come in this week, I had my Thursday lunch break slot open up. Call me on yours then, okay?"

"I will take you up on that," Rory said. "Thanks, Marissa."

As Rory hung up, she couldn't help but smile.

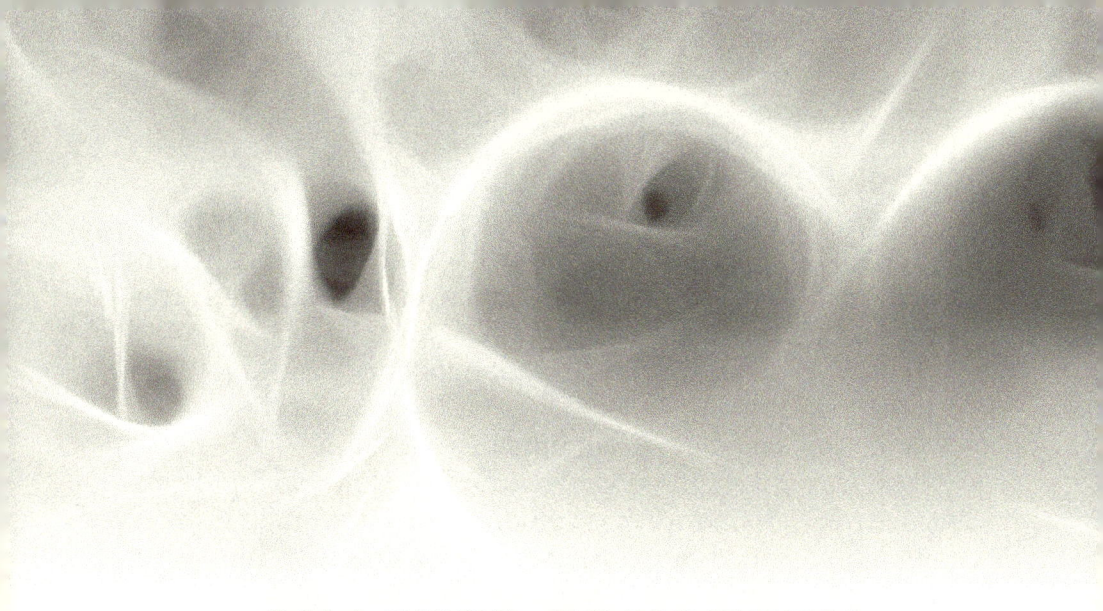

CHAPTER FOURTEEN

A few days later, when Kane opened Rory's car door, Rory expected the morning air to be much more frigid. But she was met with a pleasant surprise by the warm breeze. March's end approaching meant that spring was coming too, though the snow still wasn't letting up and wouldn't any time soon.

"How was Carla's birthday party? That was this weekend, right?" Kane already knew the answer but was curious about how much Rory would say.

Rory nodded. "Yeah. It was good! It was nice to get out of the house again."

She paused, and the excitement in her voice naturally faded when she did. She wasn't sure if she should tell Kane that she found Hematite and brought him home. Kane didn't need to know all the details, but she also wanted to be transparent with her closest friend.

Kane immediately noticed her mood drop but tried not to take it personally. "Rory? You okay?"

Rory glanced over at Kane at the red light. Their gaze met and when she looked Kane in the eyes, she could have sworn she was gazing into Hematite's eyes again. They were that same striking blue, like the sky on a clear day holding back storms.

"Rory?"

"Yeah, I'm okay," she said with a gentle shake of her head. The green light prompted her to keep driving and gave her an excuse to look away from Kane. Their eyes were definitely the same, of that much she was certain.

"I can tell something is up. What happened? You know you can tell me anything."

"I'm, uh, just a bit shaken up still, that's all."

She was still taken aback by the fact that she had been intimate with Hematite. She couldn't help but wonder if she'd completely ruined her working relationship with him after that, but she told Kane only half of the truth.

"I found Hematite dead last night. I got him in my car, and he came back to life in the backseat before I could take him to a hospital. If you look back there, you'll probably find some blood stains. I tried to do a deep clean this morning but was running later than I wanted to."

Her therapist wouldn't be happy about her omission after working on some trust exercises, but Rory felt it was a necessary step back.

"Holy shit." Kane once again feigned his surprise; he wasn't sure where his acting abilities came from, but he was especially grateful for them lately. "I mean, I guess it's a good thing you found him and not someone else."

"It was still kinda freaky. At the moment, I was so pumped with adrenaline from just trying to get him out of there. But looking back ... it was pretty intense."

Kane reached for one of Rory's hands and held it. It was large enough to engulf her own, both in size and warmth. "That must have been. I'm surprised you didn't call out today."

"He's okay; that's ultimately all that matters," Rory said with a shrug. She glanced at his knuckles and mentally compared them to Hematite's; there was some discoloration in the same spots that Hematite's were bloodied or bruised the other night. "I might have nightmares for the rest of the week about it, but I guess I find some comfort in knowing that he can't die so easily."

CHAPTER FOURTEEN

"There you go." Kane gave her hand a gentle squeeze, and she turned to smile at her friend. She couldn't help but think how much Kane's eyes reminded her of Hematite's. Rory tried to shake the feeling in both her heart and her gut, but there was no other plausible explanation.

It has to be coincidental, Rory thought. Kane and Hematite were so fundamentally different as far as their personalities went that she thought it couldn't be Kane.

"Also, Stone Breaker made a video about me," Rory said. "Naomi sent it to me this morning, hence me running later than I wanted to."

"I saw it when I was getting ready this morning. I wasn't sure if I should bring it up."

"I think you're right. He must have seen me with Hematite when I went to go drop that evidence off. It's especially concerning given that Naomi and I are ninety-nine percent positive that it's Mark Stevens. He's a reporter, which means he has easy access to anything he wants to know about me."

"I think he's too much of a chump to actually do anything for now," Kane said. "But don't worry, Rory. I got your back. Why haven't you guys reported him to the police?"

"We don't have any hard proof. What we have is just theory and speculation based on what we both know, plus some cryptic messages in newspaper articles that Mark wrote. And given his father hooked up with the police chief... I'd say our chances of getting a warrant are slim." She frowned. "I could barely get the police to take me seriously when I reported the guy stalking me in college, and there wasn't even some weird connection going on there. Naomi and I both went together, but I think they saw two college girls and just laughed. We have to leave this one to Hematite."

"Yeah, that's true. You're right. Unfortunately, looks like a lot of crime in this town has to be left to him."

The corruption of their local police department never escaped Kane; the fact that he was still able to perform his vigilante duties for the last twelve years was a testament to that. But he suspected a much bigger picture than the police liked to paint. Detective McMahon always worked his cases lately, and Kane was certain that it was intentional.

Kane had a revelation. "Here's something you and Naomi can look up," he said. "Look into his father. See where he gets his money from. Who his lobbyists are should tell you a lot."

Rory smiled. "That's brilliant. Thanks, Kane."

Kane grinned. "I told you I'd come around eventually to help in my own way, right?"

Rory stood before her class with her hands clasped in front of her. "Alright, you guys, are you ready for some current events? We'll start with Jordan, as we usually do."

Jordan, who sat in the front row in the left corner of the classroom, unfolded her newspaper clipping. "I brought an article about Stone Breaker. I don't exactly have much commentary on it, but I thought you should see it anyway, Ms. Miller. Is that okay?"

"Yeah. I've seen it." Rory leaned back against her desk, barely sitting on it, as she sighed. She hoped her casual body language would put her students at ease. "Go ahead, Jordan."

"Stone Breaker released a new video Sunday night threatening a Riverpeak High School teacher," Jordan read. "Stone Breaker spoke directly to Rory Miller in the video uploaded to his YouTube channel Stone Breaker Rises." Jordan paused before she said, "Hey, Ms. Miller?"

"Yes, Jordan?"

"Are you okay?"

The question stopped Rory in her tracks. She tried to hide her surprise to not further alarm her students, but as she looked at the crowd of twenty faces before her, she could already tell they were all thinking the same thing.

"I'm okay, Jordan," Rory said with a smile. "Thank you. You guys don't need to worry about me, okay? Nor do you need to worry about yourselves."

"Ms. Miller, we're not kids. Don't lie to us," Jordan said.

They are kids, she thought; *they are only fifteen*.

CHAPTER FOURTEEN

Another girl asked, "Stone Breaker isn't gonna come to the school, is he? My parents are getting nervous."

"Stone Breaker isn't coming to this school, and he will not hurt me," Rory insisted. "That isn't a lie, nor is it just wishful thinking."

"Then why did he upload that video addressing you last night?"

"Because I have ... a friend that Stone Breaker wants to hurt," Rory said. She chose her words carefully and didn't want to get the students too riled up. "And no, I don't know who Hematite is. So don't even ask."

"Is that your friend?" one of the boys asked. "What can we do?"

"Nothing," Rory said. "You will all make me very happy by not worrying and not getting involved. You're safe as is. Let's keep it that way, okay?"

Rory swallowed back her genuine feelings, something her therapist would frown upon, but she had to stay strong in front of her students. She let their class move on without further ruckus, but when Kane joined her in her classroom for their lunch break, Rory's bottled-up emotions were on the brink of spilling over.

Kane could tell just by looking at Rory that everything had caught up to her. She was maintaining her composure well enough to the naked eye, but he could see the worry in her face in a way that only someone who had known her for a decade would recognize.

"We'll stay in here," Kane suggested. "Let's talk."

Once Kane locked the door behind him, Rory burst into tears. Kane rushed to grab a tissue from where she kept them on her desk and pulled one of the student's chairs up so he could sit beside her. His hand ran gently up and down her back.

"Hey, hey," Kane whispered. "I'm here. I got you. What's really going on, Rory?"

"They're just fucking kids," she managed between her sobs. "They shouldn't have to worry about this."

Kane knew she hosted current events as part of her curriculum every Monday. The Stone Breaker video, which was posted late Sunday night, must have been a hot topic.

"But what about you?" Kane stressed. "What's going on in that pretty head of yours, huh?"

Rory gave herself a moment to take a few deep breaths. Kane let her take them without judgment and just continued to rub her back.

"I know I ran into this on my own," Rory said, "but I feel like I can't ever catch a break, you know?"

Kane nodded. "Rory, it's not your fault. Stone Breaker being a piece of shit is not your fault." He leaned in to kiss her temple, so softly that Rory almost didn't feel it. "And you're right. It's bad enough for someone to be stalked once. I can't even imagine going through it twice." Kane paused before he added, "You're the strongest person I know, you know that?"

Rory released a nervous chuckle through her tears. "I don't feel very strong. I feel like I'm holding on by a thread."

"Yeah, but you're still holding on."

Rory looked up into Kane's eyes and was met by Hematite's once again. When she looked at Kane, she felt everything she had when she and Hematite first embraced. The coincidences would explain everything: why he was acting strange, his sudden increased exhaustion and nights out, and his resistance to getting involved.

"Kane, you trust me, right?" Rory asked.

"Of course, you know that."

They never broke eye contact. Rory gave herself another moment to catch her breath after her breakdown and then asked, "Are you Hematite?"

Kane felt like his heart sank into his stomach. "What?" he asked, trying to play dumb and cool.

"Please don't lie to me," Rory said. She held eye contact with him. Kane was too afraid to break it in fear of revealing himself.

"Rory, why would you think that?" Kane asked. He was trying desperately to skirt around the issue; lying to her

CHAPTER FOURTEEN

always ate at him, but he wouldn't be able to live with himself if he lied to her now.

Rory shook her head. "I dunno," she said. "Just a hunch."

"I wish I were as cool as he was."

"Maybe I'm just delusional right now," she said, recognizing that her emotions were running high. On top of it all, she was seeing Kane in a new light. Maybe, she thought, she was just desperate for him to be Hematite after the weekend's events. She shook her head and grabbed a new tissue. "Forget it."

Kane internally relaxed, but not entirely. The gig would be up soon, he thought, and he needed to do something about it—he just wasn't sure if that meant upping the ante or finally coming clean.

When Kane suited up in his Hematite disguise that night, he beelined it for Rory's house. Even if her safety wasn't hanging in the balance, he was deeply concerned for her to the point where it was making him nauseous.

Hematite scaled her single-story home to get a 360-degree view of her property. After Shatterstone had already stopped her on her way home, he wasn't sure what Stone Breaker would do next. Kane took out both his cell phone and a burner phone. He used his phone to pull up Rory's contact information and plugged her number into the burner.

When Rory heard her cell phone buzz against the coffee table, she set her tea down to look at it. She didn't recognize the number, but the text message was reassuring.

[Unknown: A little birdy told me you need some extra help this evening. I'm camped out for the night. Sleep well and let me know if you need anything. -H]

Rory smiled. She wondered if it was Kane's doing.

[Rory: Do you want to come in? It's like 35 degrees out there.]

Hematite smiled as he pocketed his cell phone and kept the burner in hand.

[Hematite: I can see everything from my spot. Don't worry; I'm plenty warm enough.]

[Rory: The second step by the front door has a loose brick. Spare key's in there. Come in if you change your mind.]

[Hematite: I'll take a note of that. Thank you.]

Only a few minutes later, Hematite heard Rory's front door open. He shifted to glance over and saw Rory stepping outside. She had a stainless-steel mug with a lid in her hand. She wore her winter coat over her pajamas, unprepared for the cold but still smiling.

Rory heard the sounds of shuffling on her roof and looked up toward it. She waved as she saw Hematite perched there. If she didn't know to look for him, she wouldn't have spotted him, since his outfit blended in with the night sky.

"There's this local tea shop up in Denver that my therapist got me hooked on," Rory called up. "They made this blend; it's kind of like an English breakfast, but with lavender and honey. I hope you like it."

Kane tried not to laugh. *Leave it to Rory*, he thought.

He shifted to the edge to jump off her roof, made sure his voice modifier was turned on, and met her by the doorway. "Thank you." He accepted the mug. "That's very thoughtful of you."

"I don't think I'll be able to sleep if I know you're freezing your ass off out here all night. It's the least I could do."

"I'll head in if it gets too cold. First, I want to be sure of a few things. I promise."

"I'll hold you to it." She smiled at him as she went back in. As the night went on, she tried to stay awake in case he changed his mind but sleep eventually won that battle.

When she woke up the following morning, the only sign of Hematite was the cleaned mug resting on her dining room table. Rory held the mug in her hands and brought it to her chest, using it to feel close to Hematite for a moment as her drowsiness subsided.

She pondered her situation as she drove to Kane's house on the way to the school. She still had so many unanswered

CHAPTER FOURTEEN

questions, but she knew she was sure of a few things now that helped narrow her search for Stone Breaker.

The first was that Mark Stevens was Stone Breaker; there was no other explanation. She also was sure that Hematite's theory about the Stevens family profiting off of the drugs would turn out to be correct.

The second was that Kane was involved with Hematite and not telling her the full truth. She still wasn't convinced, despite their conversation the day prior, that Hematite and Kane weren't one and the same. But even if Kane wasn't Hematite, after last night, she knew Kane had some sort of connection to the masked vigilante.

It simultaneously made sense to her and made no sense at all. Hematite always seemed so stoic and stern, despite his heroic acts of helping people in need throughout Riverpeak and other towns near Denver. Kane, however, was usually joking around and didn't take much of anything seriously.

But Kane's late nights and bright blue eyes would make so much sense. How Hematite knew to look after her last night would be explained instantaneously if it were Kane.

Just as she pulled up to Kane's apartment, she received a text from Naomi.

[Naomi: Let's meet up this weekend. I have four candidates for Hematite.]

[Rory: Add a fifth. I'm still not sure of it but add Kane Kelly to our list.]

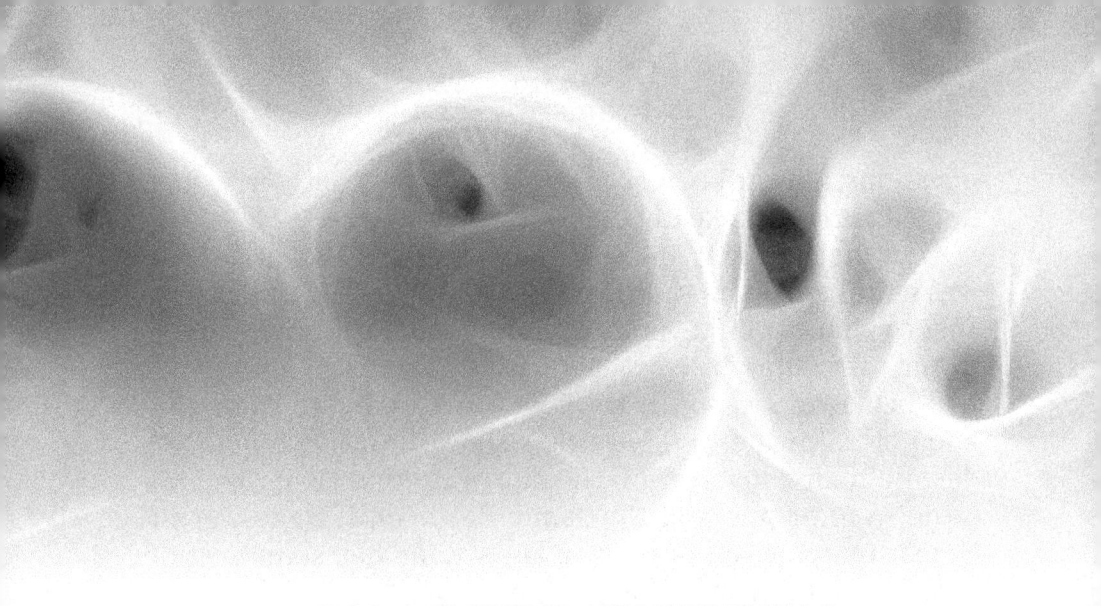

CHAPTER FIFTEEN

Rory wasn't sure how to feel when she got the text from her mom inviting her over for dinner and to catch up, but she still found herself at their front door. Rory's parents' home looked no different than how it did during her childhood. They, like everyone else in Riverpeak, set their roots there and let them grow deep enough to be permanent. As a child, she didn't understand the appeal of the small town, despite its general suburban safety. As an adult, she valued and appreciated it deeply.

She wasn't in the door for more than a few seconds when her father, Dave, embraced her. His skin, only a shade or so lighter than her own, was dry. Rory made a mental note to get him a nice moisturizer for Christmas.

"We saw the news. We've been so worried, Rory."

She offered her parents a sad smile. "Thanks, Dad. I'm okay, I promise."

"Come on, dinner's ready," her mother, Susan, said as she pulled Rory in for a hug. "You know you can talk to us about these things, right, honey?"

Rory just smiled. "I know." It was a lie. In truth, she didn't think she could. She knew thanks to a few therapy sessions that her parents meant well but didn't know how to process

CHAPTER FIFTEEN

their daughter's trauma. Rory mentally reminded herself that it wasn't her fault as she sat down at her parents' dinner table. As her parents talked about the YouTube video where Stone Breaker mentioned her by name, Rory just blankly stared at her meal. She spun her spoon in the small bowl of butternut squash soup for a minute before finally taking a small slurp. She hardly tasted it in her trance.

Her father's change of inflection as he asked a question made her snap out of it. "I mean, why does this Stone Breaker guy even want to go after you?"

Rory took another sip of soup as she composed herself. "Because I know who he is and told Hematite."

The only sound was Rory's father's fork dropping. She took another sip of soup, finally tasting it now. It was perfect: the flavors of butternut squash, salt, and cream all completely balanced, just like everything else in her family's life.

"You what?" her mother asked in nearly a whisper. There was no anger in her voice, but simply pure shock.

"Yeah, I've been working directly with Hematite. Surprise, I know."

Her father asked, "Does your boss know?"

Rory shrugged. "She doesn't need to."

Her mother gasped. "Rory!"

"What? She doesn't," Rory said. She surprised herself with her calmness; *maybe the therapy is working*, she thought. "I haven't broken any laws, and I'm not in violation of my contract. I simply found evidence to support the identity of an attempted murderer and told his victim."

"And not the police?"

"Yeah, Dad, because that's worked out well before." Rory shot her father a glance, and he nodded his head, remembering her past. "I know this is alarming. But I meant it when I said you didn't need to worry about me. I'm an adult. I'm capable of making my own decisions."

"The last thing we want is for you to get hurt or fired," her mother said. Rory could tell that her mother was attempting to be empathetic; it was mostly working. "But this ... I find this extremely concerning."

Rory met her mother's eyes. Her conviction came from her mom's side of the family, which anyone could tell simply by looking at them both in a room together.

"You taught me to fight for what I thought was right, no matter what the stakes," Rory said, without breaking her mother's eye contact. "This is me doing just that, whether you like it or not."

Her mother sighed and nodded. "Please tell me you know what you're doing."

Rory grinned. "I do. And I'm not alone."

"Let me guess, Naomi too?" her father said. "You two were always thick as thieves."

Rory just nodded. The rest of their dinner was quiet, save for the sounds of silverware. Rory couldn't tell what her father was thinking, as his posture was oddly stiff. Her mother, however, seemed to be deep in thought. Rory was both grateful for the silence and unnerved by it.

"I'll help with the dishes," she said when they finished. Her mother stood side by side with her by the dishwasher as her father took care of putting away leftovers.

"Rory," her mother suddenly said, as she passed her a rinsed dish. "I'm proud of you. You know that?"

Rory stopped to look at her mother. "Thanks."

"Seriously, I'm really proud of you. I know when you were deeply hurting a few years ago, it wasn't easy. This can't be, either. But I hope you give them hell."

Rory blinked. She saw her own face in her mother's, but a bit more hardened.

Her mother continued. "We moved to Riverpeak before you were born because we were told this town was safe. And it is. But what's been happening lately has been out of control." Susan sighed. "But I have faith in our next generation knowing that you're the one teaching them."

Rory swallowed back some tears that built up. "I think that's the nicest thing anyone's ever said to me. Thanks, Mom."

"I will always worry about you. I'm your mother. But I trust you are doing what you know is best in this … unusual situation."

CHAPTER FIFTEEN

Rory couldn't help her smile. She wasn't exactly sure what her mother was thinking, but she knew that Susan's strong sense of justice mirrored her own. "That means more to me than I can even say."

Rory left her parents' home feeling renewed. She wasn't sure what had changed over the years, but it threw her for a loop as she made the short drive back to her own home. She decided to not think about it too much and to just be grateful for the fact her parents at least partially understood.

As she drove through the suburbs, she noticed taillights behind her the whole way. Before she reached her street, she took a random left turn to see if they'd follow. She took three more, feeling increasingly uneasy as the taillights maintained their distance and knew she was being followed once she made the complete square.

She grabbed her cell phone and quickly scrolled in her contacts to the phone number that Hematite had texted her from. It rang a few times before she heard his altered voice on the other end.

"Rory?" Hematite was surprised she had called. "What's going on?"

"Yeah, hi," she said. She forced herself to slow down her breathing before it could get too out of control. "I'm driving home right now, and I'm being followed. I confirmed that after taking four left turns. Think it's Stone Breaker? It's not his usual Harley, but I'd be willing to bet he borrowed one of Daddy's nice cars."

"I'd bet on it too." He shifted his stance, so he was no longer sitting on the edge of the library's rooftop but crouched to be more alert and ready to move. "Where are you?"

Rory glanced at the street signs as she drove by. Her foot put a bit more pressure on the gas pedal. "Driving on South Street. Just passed River Road heading toward downtown."

"I'm not far. I'm on my way from Main Street. Head toward Jefferson's Coffee, and I'll meet you there."

"Got it. See you there soon."

"Stay on with me just in case," he said. He waved his hand at Shawn, who was sitting with him, to tell him to follow. Shawn got up and did as instructed. "You said it's another car?"

"Yeah, I see two headlights." She looked in the rearview mirror again. "It's too dark for me to see what kind of car, though."

"That's alright. We'll know it's you."

"We? Who is 'we'?"

"I have a strong friend," Hematite said. "Very strong."

"What does that even mean? Since when do you have friends?"

"I take offense to that. I have friends."

"No, you don't, dude," Shawn said from behind him.

Hematite rolled his eyes.

"Alright, I'm almost at Jefferson's. I can see it."

"Make a sharp turn into the parking lot. Jefferson has cameras. We've got you covered." He turned to Shawn and said, "Go ahead, dude."

Rory pulled into the parking lot. The car behind her didn't make the turn in time. Rory heard it screech, as it made a quick turn in a doughnut shape. As Stone Breaker's swung into the parking lot, a large body jumped on top of the roof. Rory jumped a bit in her seat as she heard the crushing noise from across the parking lot. The person on top of the car had a wide frame with muscular arms and a strong back. Their build reminded her of a powerlifter in a Strongman competition. They punched above the driver's seat where they were standing and it made another loud, crunching sound.

"Don't leave your car," Hematite said to her on the phone. "You're safer in the car." At that, he hung up.

Hematite followed suit, leaping on top of the car to join his companion. Even though Hematite himself was mostly muscle, he was significantly leaner than his friend, who made him look even smaller. Something about the larger one's silhouette looked familiar to Rory, but with his face covered in the dark, she couldn't say why.

The car backed out of the parking lot and swerved, likely in an attempt to shake Hematite and the second hero off. Rory

CHAPTER FIFTEEN

wasn't sure who he was, but she sensed he was like Hematite, in that he was born differently than his peers.

"Get the window!" Hematite suggested to Shawn. "I can get in!"

Shawn nodded and leaned over to punch the window on the passenger side. Rory could hear the glass shatter even from her spot in the parking lot.

Hematite used his legs to slip into the car through the broken window. He could feel the shattered glass beneath him as he tried to weasel his way in. He was greeted by Stone Breaker behind the wheel. Stone Breaker tried to reach for something in the center console, but Hematite didn't waste any time. He threw a punch at Stone Breaker's face, feeling the ABS plastic beneath his cloth-covered fist; unfortunately for Hematite, this mask was much thicker than Shatterstone's had been. It gave Stone Breaker just enough protection to not completely lose control, but his swerving got worse.

"Crash the car, dude!" Shawn shouted from above. "I'm good up here!"

Kane grabbed the wheel and gave it a hard turn. The car spun out and eventually crashed into a pole, the back end taking the brunt of the impact. Shawn jumped off just in time and broke his fall with a roll, using his momentum to his advantage.

The airbags prevented Hematite from seeing much in the car, but he reached for Stone Breaker and grabbed his shirt. "Leave Rory Miller out of this," he said. "Do you understand me?"

"You think I'll listen to you?" Stone Breaker coughed. "Tough shit, asshole."

The passenger side door opened. Hematite glanced back and saw Shawn standing there. They nodded at each other, and Hematite grabbed at Stone Breaker, trying to pull him out of the car with him. Once Hematite was out, Shawn took over, grabbing a firm hold of Stone Breaker and giving him a light toss with only one hand. Stone Breaker rolled a few feet away from them and eventually made an impact with the asphalt beneath him.

Beneath his mask, Mark as Stone Breaker could taste some blood. He lifted his mask just enough to spit it out on the road without revealing his face. As he adjusted it and rolled onto his side, hoping for a moment to recover, he looked up to see Hematite approaching. Hematite's black pants cinched at the ankles, highlighting the shape of his long, muscular legs. Stone Breaker saw Hematite reach for the billy club that gently swung from his belt and detach the clip. Stone Breaker grimaced as the billy club made contact with his arm.

Stone Breaker realized that he made a big mistake in trying to follow Rory home. He waited for the second thwack of a billy club, but it never came. When he looked up, he saw both Hematite and the newcomer staring down at him.

"Bet you weren't expecting him, huh?" Hematite said, as he nodded his head toward the larger fellow.

Stone Breaker couldn't respond. He coughed again. A bit more blood spilled out.

Hematite crouched down, resting his elbows on his knees. He was still holding the billy club.

"What the fuck did I ever do to you?" Hematite asked.

Stone Breaker didn't have an answer ready. He knew that if Hematite uncovered the truth, it would be detrimental to his father's campaign and personal funding. But Stone Breaker knew that wasn't a sufficient answer for two reasons: it wasn't something that Hematite did to him personally, and it would say far too much.

"Go to hell," Stone Breaker said as he coughed again. The second guy kicked him in the stomach. With that, Stone Breaker's coughs became uncontrollable.

"Ease up," Hematite said to his friend. "I'd like to have a heart-to-heart with this asshole here."

Hematite's accomplice scoffed. "Suit yourself. Not my style, but it's your mortal enemy, not mine."

Hematite rolled his eyes. "You know, someone's probably calling the police right about now. What did you think was going to happen tonight?"

Stone Breaker tried to force himself to get up. He slipped on his hands a bit.

CHAPTER FIFTEEN

Shawn got his foot ready again, but Hematite held a hand up to stop him. Stone Breaker noticed that despite being physically stronger, Hematite held the authority over this other super-powered man.

"You can't know the truth," Stone Breaker settled on. "No matter what."

"And why's that? Who will pay the price if I know what they're up to?"

Stone Breaker shook his head. "I'm not a fucking idiot, Hematite. You won't get me to talk so easily."

"Oh, Jesus. You sure you don't want me to just knock him out?" Shawn asked Hematite.

Hematite exhaled through his nose and could feel the tension in his clenched jaw as he faced Stone Breaker.

"You wanna know what happens when the police come?" Stone Breaker laughed, as he realized the reality of the situation. "There's a good chance they're in on it. Do you even know how deep this goes?"

"He's probably full of shit," Shawn chimed in.

"How deep?" Hematite asked.

"They're getting paid." Stone Breaker smirked beneath his mask. "Very well, at that."

Hematite could feel his patience growing thinner by the second. "Who is paying them?"

Stone Breaker kept laughing. "You can't know the truth," he repeated, but this time with more confidence. Most of the police force was aware of the situation, thanks to his father's connections with Chief Daniels. "Money really does buy happiness, don't you think?"

Naomi was surprised to see the call from Rory come through on her work phone. Rory had the number, but only ever called it in the event of an emergency.

"Rory? What's wrong?"

"What are people saying on the scanners? Did you hear anything about Stone Breaker or Hematite by Jefferson's Coffee?"

"Whoa, whoa, slow down. What's happening?"

"I was just followed by Stone Breaker. Hematite got him."

"Police were just dispatched," Naomi said. "They're on their way. I think someone nearby called. Hold on." Naomi paused to listen to what they were saying. "They want Hematite. Someone just said they're tired of him. You said Stone Breaker is there? They haven't even mentioned him on the scanners."

"Fuck! Listen, I don't trust the police. I mean, you already knew that, but I really don't trust them now. Something weird is going on with Stone Breaker, Councilman Stevens, and Chief Daniels. That affair Stevens had with Chief Daniels is probably still ongoing if I had to guess. Plus Kane mentioned to me the other day that we should look into their lobbying records, so I think that he was on to something. Thanks!"

"Rory!"

But all Naomi heard on the other end was silence as Rory hung up. She frowned and turned to her computer, and, in the search bar of her browser, she typed in Councilman Stevens' name.

Rory tossed her phone in the cupholder and, with shaky hands, began driving. Hematite and his friend needed to get out of there, and they needed to get away quickly. Rory made the short drive down the road where they were, maybe only a mile away, and stopped at the pole where the car had crashed into.

She rolled the window down and stuck her head out.

"Hey!" All three faces turned to look at her. "Hematite and … whoever you are! Get in here!"

"And just leave him?" Hematite retorted.

"No way!" The other man agreed.

"It's useless!" Rory said. "The cops won't help you. He's," she pointed at Stone Breaker, "with Daniels and Stevens, and the cops know that!"

"Shit!" Hematite exclaimed. He stood from his spot by Stone Breaker and retracted his billy club. He looked at Shawn and said, "Fuck it. Do your best."

CHAPTER FIFTEEN

Shawn chuckled. He knew Hematite would be furious if he killed Stone Breaker. He opted to give him a light kick to the head to knock him unconscious—or at least light by Jameson's standards. The two of them then ran to Rory's car just as the police lights came into their field of vision. Their sirens were off.

"They're after you," Rory said as the two got into the car. "Come on, we can get out of here before they spot me." She made the first turn she could and felt instant relief once she realized the police weren't following her. They likely stopped to help Stone Breaker.

"Thanks for the getaway car," Hematite said from the passenger seat. "You didn't have to stick around."

"Of course," she said. "We're a team. Friends, even."

Hematite laughed, remembering their conversation from only a few minutes ago. "That's one way to put it."

"Jesus Christ, please make out somewhere else," Shawn said from the backseat. Like Hematite, his voice was also modified, but he used a high-tech face mask to do so.

"Ignore him," Hematite said without hesitation.

"It's fine." Rory glanced at his friend in the rearview mirror. He was wearing a gray shirt with a puffy maroon jacket over it to keep warm. A black scarf wrapped around his neck and kept the black voice-changing mask on over his face. Rory asked him, "So, who are you?"

"I'm Brick Beast, thank you for asking." He tugged at the black-and-red beanie that was covering his hair and his ears. "No one ever does."

"Thank you for your help tonight," Rory said. "I really appreciate it."

"Don't inflate his ego anymore," Hematite warned. Rory couldn't tell if he was being playful or serious.

Shawn laughed from the backseat. "Jealous your girlfriend is giving me attention, Hematite?"

"Can it." Hematite shifted uncomfortably in the passenger seat.

"I'm calling Naomi," Rory said to change the subject. "I didn't call the cops since I don't trust those fuckers. But she checked the scanners for me. They, uh, they said they were looking for you, not Stone Breaker. Like, to arrest you."

She put Naomi on her car's Bluetooth® speaker. Naomi answered after only one ring.

"Are you okay?" Naomi said upon answering. "You scared the shit out of me!"

"I'm sorry, I'm sorry," Rory said. "I'm fine. I have Hematite and Brick Beast in the car, and I'm getting them the hell away from there. Listen, did you hear anything else on the scanners?"

"They just said they picked up 'his' son. I'm not sure who 'his' is. Probably Councilman Stevens. Who's Brick Beast?"

"A friend of Hematite's, I guess."

"I have super strength," Shawn piped in from the backseat. Hematite groaned in annoyance.

"That and a lot of pride," Rory said.

Hematite spoke next. "Naomi Sato, right? You've been helping Rory."

Naomi nodded subconsciously on the other end. She tried to keep her excitement internalized. "Hi. Yeah, I have."

"Listen, Stone Breaker told me tonight that the police are getting paid off. We need to find out who is paying them off. Is that something you can look up?"

"I'm already looking into Councilman Stevens' financial history. Lobbying records have to be public, after all," she said. "I'll let you know what I can find. He's most likely getting paid by someone to keep everything quiet. I'm sure that money is what's going toward the police department, especially given his special history with Chief Daniels."

"Thank you. I think you're on the right track. Keep up the good work."

"Of course," Naomi said. "I'll let Rory know of anything that I come up with, and she can pass it along to you. Sound good?"

"Yes. If there's anything locked down, send it to her too. I know someone who can break into just about anything if it's online."

"Noted," Naomi said. "We'll figure it out. Oh, and by the way, the scanners just mentioned they're bringing 'his son'

CHAPTER FIFTEEN

back to the station. They're headed back. Just avoid the station and you should be clear."

"You're the best, Naomi. I'll catch you later." Once they hung up, Rory asked Hematite, "Where should I take you?"

"Just go home," Hematite said. "We can head out from there. I want to know you're there safe."

"Aw, how sweet," Brick Beast commented from the backseat.

"You okay? For real?" Hematite asked as she pulled into her driveway, speaking in a whisper since he didn't want Shawn to hear. Rory was still surprised by the tenderness in his voice, despite their history. It never sounded like it belonged to him in that outfit.

She nodded. "I am. Thank you."

When she went inside, she locked the door before heading to the window. She peered out of the blinds to see where they would go off to, but they were already gone. Rory couldn't shake the feeling that she knew both of them more than they let on.

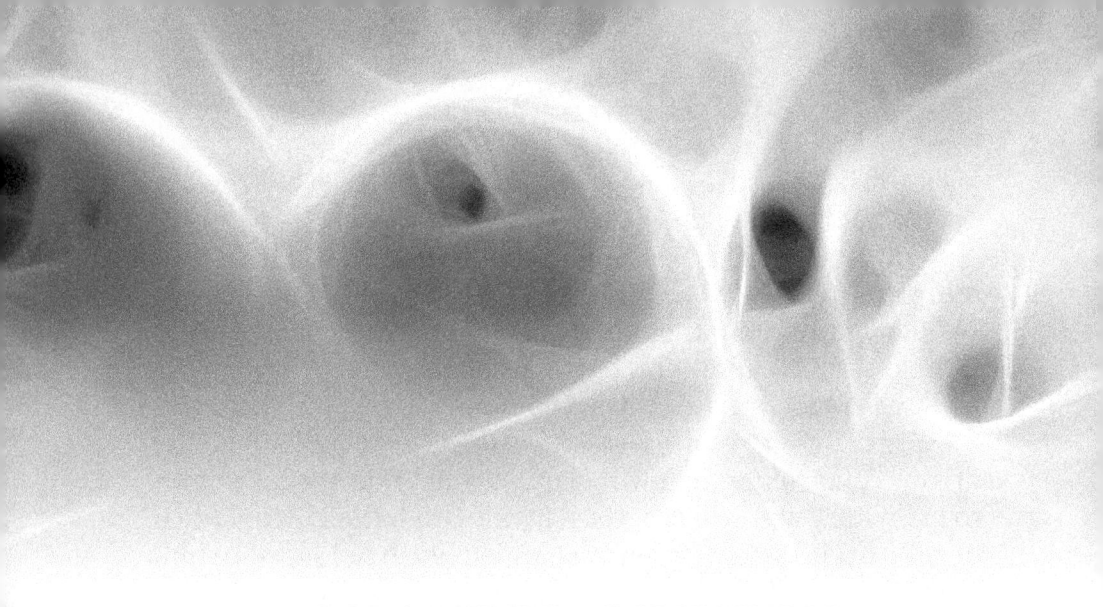

CHAPTER SIXTEEN

Detective McMahon was surprised to see his personal cell phone ringing in the middle of the night. He groaned as he rolled over in bed and reached for his phone, while gently shushing his wife to coax her back to sleep.

"Who the hell is calling you, Jon?"

"I dunno; it better not be work," he said. "Get some rest, honey; you need it." His first instinct was to hang up on them before he even answered, especially since the number showed up as Unknown, but his thumb slipped and he took it. Even though it wasn't on speaker, he still heard the voice loud and clear on the other end.

"Detective, are you there?"

At that, Detective McMahon was wide awake. He'd know that voice anywhere. He leaped out of bed as he answered. "Hematite? What's going on? How did you get my number?"

"Rory Miller gave it to me. Listen closely. There's something going on at your station, and I thought you should know about it. The officers are getting paid off to help Stone Breaker. I understand I'm not exactly everyone's favorite guy with the law, but you don't strike me as the type of person to throw stones from a glass house. Do you understand what I'm saying?"

CHAPTER SIXTEEN

"What?" he asked. "Who is getting paid off?"

"Are you?"

"No, absolutely not. I would never."

"I fear you may be the only one. You have given me no reason to not trust you so far. I hope you don't intend to change that. We coexist well, don't you think?"

"I'd agree, yes," Detective McMahon said. "How do you know this?"

"Councilman Tom Stevens is definitely connected to Stone Breaker, who told us he could get away with whatever he wanted because the police were paid to side with him. Naomi Sato with Channel 10 News confirmed this with the chatter she picked up on the police scanners at the station. We have some loose evidence showing Stone Breaker is Tom's adult son, Mark. The arrest of Mark's friend Douglas Doerr for his activity as Shatterstone also confirms this, as far as I'm concerned."

"You know the only reason they couldn't bust that little twerp out is that I had to convince them to not grant him bail? I had to bust my ass for that. No wonder."

"I hope you're as angry as I am," Hematite said. "What do you say?"

"I've been helping you because I think you're ultimately doing a good thing for this city. I don't like your methods. But I'll be damned before I try to say they don't work. I enjoy coexisting with you, Hematite, and I don't intend to change that. So yes, I'm pretty angry."

"I'm glad you and I are on the same page," Hematite said. "If I hear anything, I'll make you aware if you promise to let me do what I need to do over the next few weeks. Do we have a deal?"

"What do you need to do?" Detective McMahon asked.

"I'm not completely sure yet. But I'm not going to kill anyone, if that's what you're wondering."

"No, I know that's not your style."

Hematite chuckled. "That's one way to put it. Do we have a deal?"

Detective McMahon glanced back at his bedroom, where his wife had fallen back asleep, and nodded. "We do."

Naomi's house had fewer papers scattered about compared to Rory's last few visits, but it still looked like a sea of documents in the living room. There weren't as many newspaper articles this time, but more photos and personal records on the floor.

"Like I said, I've narrowed it down to five people, including Kane," Naomi said; if she had any personal thoughts on the matter, she didn't show it. Naomi was talking strictly business. "I've got their photos all lined up here." She gestured to the coffee table. The five of them were spread out, almost like a row of mugshots, but with social media profile photos.

"It's definitely not this guy," Rory said as she pointed to the first photo. "Hematite has blue eyes, not brown." She looked at the second picture. "And it's not this guy, either." She discarded a photo of a man with brown hair. "His lips are too thin."

Naomi's brows furrowed. "Whoa, whoa, whoa. Hold on. You've seen Hematite close up enough to know? And doesn't he always keep his mouth covered?"

"He usually does. I haven't seen all of his face, but I have seen his mouth and chin."

"When exactly was this? I thought we couldn't unmask him."

"We can't. I... You can't tell anyone." Rory wasn't sure why she was speaking in a whisper, given that she and Naomi were alone in Naomi's home. "This stays between us."

Naomi nodded. "I promise to keep this a secret, but I'd be lying if I said you weren't making me nervous."

Rory exhaled and said, "I may have slept with Hematite a few weeks ago."

Naomi's eyes widened in shock. "You what?!"

"I know, I know!" Rory held her hands up in defense. "On the way back from Carla's birthday dinner, I found him when I was at a red light. He was dead in an alleyway, Naomi. I couldn't just leave him there."

CHAPTER SIXTEEN

"Oh my God," Naomi said. She pinched the bridge of her nose, a habit she picked up from Brad. "I can't believe what I'm hearing."

"I patched him up at my house. He begged me to not take him to the ER. And then everything just sort of happened," Rory explained with a shrug.

"It 'just sort of happened'?" Naomi asked with one eyebrow raised. "So that's how you saw some of his face? Did he take his mask off?"

"Well, no. He pulled part of it up to kiss me, but then asked if he could keep it on, so I let him." Rory realized how it sounded once she said it and grimaced, anticipating Naomi's response.

"Oh my God, Rory! You let him?!"

"He's a fucking vigilante, Naomi; of course I let him!" Rory said. "I didn't want to break his trust or scare him off after everything we've been through!"

"You know what? I'm gonna pretend I don't know this," Naomi said. "Just look at the rest of the lineup and tell me who you think has the closest lips and jawline."

"Fair enough," Rory said. She turned her attention to the remaining photos on Naomi's coffee table. The longer Rory stared at the three photos, the more she couldn't deny it. She lingered over the first two for a moment, really taking in their features to make sure she wasn't mistaken. "Who are these guys, anyway?"

"I had a few different criteria. First, I went off of their age. We know that Hematite started around, what, twelve years ago? But based on what we know, he had to have been a teenager when he started. So, I picked men close to our age. Then, I looked at where they lived and made sure they were in Riverpeak, plus their occupation. If they had a job that keeps them only during the day, then they have the time to live a double life at night. And finally, I tried to see if they'd have a motive. The drug problem on the east side of town isn't exactly small anymore."

Rory then reached for Kane's photo and stared at it. The longer she examined his face, the more she knew that Hematite had to have been Kane. Rory had thought their eyes were identical for a while now, but their lips and jawline were also the same now that she really paid attention.

"Kane insists it's not him, but I just have this gut feeling," Rory said. "I can see it in his eyes, Naomi. These other guys, they look too different. But with Kane … it adds up."

"What are the odds that Stone Breaker has come to the same conclusion?"

Rory frowned. "I don't know. It depends on how much he knows. My guess, though, is that he doesn't, and that's why he's laser-focused on me."

"Can I ask you an honest question without you getting mad at me?"

"Sure."

"I only ask because I know that it's not your style," Naomi cushioned.

"Just spit it out."

"Do you genuinely think that Hematite is Kane? Or are you just hoping that he's Kane after hooking up with a masked vigilante without knowing his name?"

"That's a valid question," Rory said; it was so valid, in fact, that she couldn't even be mad at her friend. "Hematite told me about his history, how it all started as a way for him to protect his sister on the down low since they had a really crappy childhood. Kane is very protective of his sister, Kayla."

"True."

"That and earlier this week, he showed up to watch over my house late at night after I had a mental breakdown at school. Kane comforted me on my lunch break and had to talk me down from it. The same night, I get a text from a random number telling me that somebody told him I needed him there. I've thought for a while Kane has been involved, but now I am positive that he is him."

"Oh, wow," Naomi said, as she ran her hand through her straight black hair. "In that case, then I think you're right."

Their attention was diverted by the sound of the doorbell ringing. They both glanced at the front door and then at each other, unsure of who it could be.

CHAPTER SIXTEEN

"Brad has a key," Naomi said. "It's not him." She reached for her phone and pulled up an app. "Let's check the cameras."

Rory looked over Naomi's shoulder to check the security camera footage from the front of the house. Her heart felt like it stopped entirely as she watched Stone Breaker, wearing his mask, leaving a note at the door before leaving right away. He didn't stay long enough to leave much of a trace beyond the piece of paper he taped to the front door.

"Let's get it," Rory said. She was trying to be brave: she tried to emulate Hematite, wondered how he'd respond to this, and rolled her shoulders back to handle the situation. It didn't change the fact that her heart was now racing at what felt like a million miles an hour. "Come on."

Rory went to the front door before Naomi could even protest. She glanced around to make sure no one was still standing outside before she grabbed the letter and then closed the door again.

"What's it say? Do we even want to know?"

"Yes," Rory said. She unfolded the paper and scanned the typed letters once before reading the note out loud. "It's an invitation."

"What?"

"He wants to meet me downtown," Rory said. "Here, read it."

Naomi grabbed it as Rory processed the words on the page. She wasn't sure if she felt like screaming or throwing up but refrained from both in an attempt to think rationally. The letter read:

Rory Miller,

I am quite tired of playing cat and mouse with you. I'm sure you are too. If you seek answers, I have some—and I'd be willing to provide them on the condition that we learn to coexist peacefully.

If you will let me do my work, then I will tell you anything you want about Hematite. I have the

> *secret to his immortality and may be able to provide you with your own powers too.*
>
> *If you agree, come alone to City Hall on Main Street. I'll be waiting for you next Saturday night at eleven.*
>
> *-SB*

"Provide you with your own powers? What the hell is that supposed to mean?" Naomi asked. "Does he seriously think you'll fall for this?"

"It's obviously a trap, yeah," Rory agreed. "We have about a week to think about it."

"Think about it? No. No, no, no."

Rory nodded as she grabbed the letter. "Yeah. I'll fill Hematite in tomorrow. I want to sleep on it first. We could use this to our advantage."

"Rory, you shouldn't put yourself in danger over this," Naomi said. "You've already toed the line enough."

"And I haven't come this far just to leave an opportunity like this behind. We could sneak up on him. Have Hematite in the wings. You ready to film the whole thing with a news crew. I just gotta work out the logistics."

Naomi nodded, but she seemed hesitant. "Yeah, okay, I can see your point. At least stay here tonight. He might still be outside. You can borrow some of my pajamas."

Rory didn't like that Stone Breaker was still following her every move, but she tried to not think about it too much. She didn't have the energy for another mental breakdown. "Thanks, Naomi."

"In the meantime, though, I'm taking a photo of this," she said, referencing the letter. "I think we know what our 'Breaking at Eleven' story will be next weekend."

CHAPTER SIXTEEN

Rory hoped that a Saturday morning boxing class would ease her worries, but her grip on the steering wheel was so tight that her knuckles were almost white. The drive to her boxing gym wasn't far, but any distance in her paranoid state felt like it was moving in slow motion.

When it came time for drills, Rory hit the punching bag so hard that the rest of her class stopped to look at her. The chain that suspended the bag in the air rattled as the bag swayed back and forth. She became suddenly aware of the thin film of sweat that covered her body and the way her knuckles were trembling beneath her boxing gloves. Her breathing was heavy and labored as she dropped her hands by her sides.

"Miller," her boxing coach called out. "You alright?"

Rory looked at him and then looked around. The class was still looking at her, waiting for an answer.

Rory shook her head, but still said, "I'll be fine." That didn't seem to satisfy her coach, so she added, "It's ... complicated."

When the class ended, she reclined her car's seat back as far as she could. She focused on her breathing, a technique that Marissa taught her, as she looked around her and tried to identify different objects that were white or rectangular. It helped a bit, but her heart rate didn't completely become stable, despite her workout ending.

Rory could feel another good cry impending, so she took out her phone to open up the feelings diary app she downloaded. She answered the little prompts about how she was feeling and what categories were impacting her mood, but she froze when the prompt with a text box appeared.

I often do this when I feel out of control...

Rory stared at the prompt for a few moments as she debated her answer. She looked back, trying to identify her behaviors and come to terms with herself. She remembered Kane once told her she didn't have to save everyone. Now she understood what he meant by that.

Rory simply typed in a superhero emoji, but she customized it to look like herself instead of the standard yellow.

She then switched over to her phone's contacts to pull up Hematite's burner phone. She wasn't sure how quickly he cycled through them, so she hoped the number was still his when she tapped the call button.

Kane spit his toothpaste out as he went to search for his ringing phone. His cell phone was by his side, but the burner was going off in the other room. He quickly rummaged for his voice modifier before he answered just in time for the last ring.

"Rory? Are you okay?"

"Hi," Rory said breathlessly on the other line.

Kane frowned; she didn't sound like her usual peppy self, but meek. He immediately asked, "What's wrong?"

"That obvious, huh?" Rory released a nervous chuckle, and a sob almost came out with it. "I, uh, got a letter from Stone Breaker. He wants to meet me. I think it's a trap. It's pretty obvious actually, but I think we can work with this."

Kane swallowed his anger. The moment she said those words, he felt like he was suffocating. "He what?"

"Yeah, he clearly didn't learn his lesson from the other day." The more she spoke, the more Kane could hear her confidence return, but it didn't stop his scowl. "He gave me a week from today. I think he's planning something."

Kane unclenched his fist to run his hand through his hair as Rory read him the letter. He subconsciously paced through his apartment. "And what are you thinking?"

"I'm thinking we plan our own next steps in the meantime. He gave me a time and place. Naomi said she's going to get a news crew together so they can have cameras and live coverage."

"Live coverage of what?" No matter how hard he tried, he couldn't unclench his jaw. The news of Stone Breaker sending a letter to Rory and trying to negotiate with her had his head spinning with frustration. On the one hand, he knew Rory was right; they'd be foolish to not take advantage of this opportunity, and the still rationally functioning part of his brain knew that. But on the other end, the idea of Rory using herself as bait nearly drove him over the edge.

CHAPTER SIXTEEN

"Whatever happens. Hopefully an arrest," she said. "We'd need to get Detective McMahon involved. I think he's the only one not wrapped up in this whole mess."

Kane nodded. "I wouldn't say I trust him, but we could rely on him, sure."

"That's good enough for me," Rory said. "Can I meet up with you? Maybe at your storage unit?"

Kane swallowed. "Meet me there Monday night. We'll discuss it then. That should give us time to gather anything we might need."

Rory grinned. "Perfect."

Once Kane was off the phone with Rory, he released a loud groan to get the aggravation off his chest. He gave himself a moment to collect his thoughts before he decided, rubbing his temples before plopping on his couch and resting his head in his hands. Kane's biggest fear, the very thing he had been trying to prevent for the last eight years, was coming to fruition.

Kane eventually stood to grab his laptop and started looking for maps of the city council offices. He figured there had to be something available, whether it be a blueprint or a fire escape route. As he got to researching, he grabbed his cell phone and called Elijah.

"Hey man, what's up?" Elijah answered.

"Are you busy?" Kane asked. "I need your help."

"I'm at Jefferson's Coffee," he said. Kane heard Elijah say, "Hey, Aaron? Can you make that two? Sorry, sorry, you're the best. No, keep the change." Elijah then said, "I'll be there in a few. What happened?"

"Stone Breaker made an offer to Rory," Kane said. "She wants to use herself as bait. As much as I want to tell her abso-fucking-lutely not, she's ... she's onto something. I have to trust her." He sighed.

"How much time do we have?" Elijah asked. He then said, "Thanks, Aaron! Okay, I'm on my way."

"A week," Kane said. "I'll fill you in more once you get here."

"Have you told her yet?" Elijah asked. "Does she know you're Hematite? Please tell me she knows."

"I almost don't want to answer that question," Kane said.

Elijah laughed, the kind that came from irony rather than amusement. "You haven't told her a damn thing, have you?"

"I think she's onto me. She asked me at school the other day if I was Hematite. I brushed it off, but I'm not sure she's entirely convinced I was being honest with her."

"I know I don't know Rory quite as well as you and Naomi do," Elijah said, "but I do know her well enough to say that I don't think she'd put her life on the line and re-traumatize herself if she didn't think it was you behind the Hematite getup."

Kane furrowed his brows. "What do you mean?"

"C'mon, dude. Brad, Jameson, and I have bets on when you two will finally get together and on who will crack first. I think I speak for all of us when I say we're pretty tired of your whining about pining for her when we all go out together and you get tipsy."

Kane sighed. "Unbelievable. I'm never drinking with you guys again."

Elijah bore a shit-eating grin, and Kane could hear the playfulness in Elijah's tone as he said, "Oh, please. My bet is on you cracking first, so don't disappoint me. I'll owe Brad twenty bucks if I'm wrong," Elijah added. "No pressure or anything, though."

"Yeah, yeah," Kane said to dismiss the conversation. "You almost here?"

"Pulling up to your complex now. Let's see what we can do."

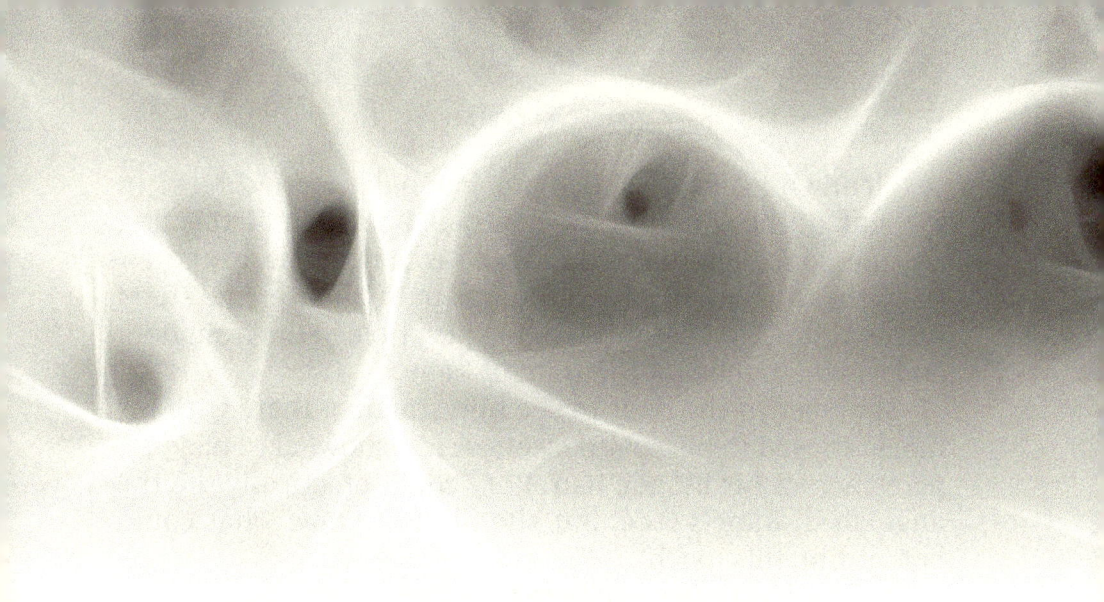

CHAPTER SEVENTEEN

The snow felt soft against Kane's face as he stood outside of Rory's house. He hadn't dressed completely prepared for it but was warm enough. Even if he hadn't, his conviction was burning inside of him enough to make up for it.

Kane stared at Rory's door for a few moments. He wasn't entirely sure what possessed him to act on the bundle of nerves rumbling around his stomach, but he felt like he was going to implode if he continued to hold this in much longer. The light was on downstairs and her car was in the driveway, so he knew she was home as he stood there. Once he knocked, he realized that there was no turning back now. While he waited for her to answer, he ran through how the conversation could go in his head. He wasn't expecting Rory to respond to his protests, but he decided that no matter what happened, this wasn't Hematite speaking. This was simply Kane going into protective big brother-mode like he often did for Kayla.

But Rory wasn't Kayla. As he waited for her to answer, he felt like he was waiting for an eternity. When he exhaled, feeling at war with himself and trying to release some of his internal tension, he could faintly see some of his breath before him.

Meanwhile inside, Rory put her half-cleaned bowl in the sink at the sound of the doorbell. She wasn't expecting anyone, so she approached softly so as to not raise any potential indication about where she was in the house. She stood on her tiptoes to peer through the peephole in the front door and sighed in relief at the sight of Kane.

She opened the door to see him standing there with his hands shoved in his coat pockets. A few snowflakes had peppered across his blonde hair. Rory could practically see the anguish in Kane's face, but she did not know what could bother him this much.

"Hey! What brings you here?"

"I... Can I talk to you?" Kane asked. Rory had never heard him sound so nervous.

Rory nodded. "Of course, Kay. You always can, you know that. Come on in."

Kane was quick to kick his boots off, not wanting to tread snow through her house. He said nothing at first, still trying to pick the right words to speak so he wouldn't reveal himself. He knew she was suspicious, so he had to be even more careful than usual, but his emotions felt like they were going to physically expunge themselves from his body.

Rory kept her eyes on Kane's face, noticing the way his eyes looked. She sensed she was seeing a side of Kane he rarely showed, if ever at all. His vibrant eyes that normally held such life looked like there was an immense sadness behind them.

"Do you want to sit down?" Rory asked.

Kane didn't even answer. He just stood there, looking as anxious as she'd ever seen him.

"Hey, what's going on?" Rory asked gently. "I can tell something's up. Talk to me." She swallowed, took a step to be closer to him, and placed her hand on his shoulder; it forced him to look into her eyes. "I know we haven't been as open with each other as we usually are, and I'm sorry for that. But you can talk to me, Kane. Please do."

Kane just nodded. It was such a slight movement that had she not been focusing on him, she might not have noticed.

CHAPTER SEVENTEEN

"Listen, Rory. I... I've been really worried about you." Although he practiced the conversation a thousand times over in his head, he wasn't sure what was going to come out of his mouth as he continued to speak. "All of this Stone Breaker stuff is getting really out of hand. I know you and Hematite have been working together, and I know he's got your back, but I'm still completely fucking terrified." He closed his eyes for a moment as he said, "I don't know what I would do if I lost you."

"Hey, hey, it'll be alright." Rory took one of his hands in her own to comfort him. "We're so close. Hematite and I have a plan. It'll be fine, Kay."

"And what if it's not fine?" Kane asked. That sadness in his expression was more prevalent than ever, as he opened his eyes again and made eye contact with her. "Then what? You ... you could die. And you wouldn't come back like Hematite does. I love you, Rory, and I'm scared, and I can't just sit here and watch you walk into a death trap!"

Kane realized what he said the moment he said it; that hadn't been a part of his plan.

"What?" Rory asked in almost a whisper, feeling like time had completely stopped. She was both confused and enlightened all at once. Rory had more questions than answers, but it all added up and made sense in her head.

"I love you, Rory," Kane repeated. He couldn't take it back, and there was no use in hiding it anymore. He realized the right moment he was always waiting for would never come. His bright blue eyes never left her dark ones as he said, "I have loved you every single day of my life for the last eight years. It's about damn time I told you."

"I never thought you'd say that," Rory said. She didn't realize it, but she was smiling. When she looked inside herself, she understood in hindsight that she had felt this way all along, no matter how desperately she tried to pretend otherwise for the sake of their friendship. Maybe Naomi had been right about her hoping that he was Hematite for this very reason. Rory felt, for the first time, as if she could finally trust someone in earnest.

Kane let go of Rory's hand so he could kiss her properly, this time as his full self instead of hiding behind a mask. Rory felt completely immersed by Kane the moment his hands cupped her face and his lips were on hers. His calloused fingertips felt rough against her cheeks, but their familiarity brought her comfort. One of Rory's hands fell on Kane's ribs and the other found its way to the back of his head, tangling in his shaggy blonde hair.

Kane moved one of Rory's hands off her face to wrap his arm around her waist and pull her body closer to his. Rory could tell by the way Kane's lips moved with hers and the way his arms held her that he was, in fact, her Hematite.

"I love you so much, Rory," Kane said against her lips between kisses. "I have always loved you."

Now that she knew the truth, both about Kane and herself, Rory knew she could say with confidence, "I love you too, Kane."

Kane wasn't sure how he'd feel if Rory were ever to say those words and now that she had, he was dumbfounded. As he looked at Rory, as if she were the only other person in the world, all of his fears came bubbling back up to the surface.

"It's late," Kane blurted out. He needed to go grab his uniform so he could keep patrol over her home to watch over her, he thought. "I should let you rest."

"Don't go," Rory pleaded. There was no hesitation in her voice. "You're worried about my safety, right? Then stay the night."

Kane froze. He blinked a few times as he stared at her, unsure of if this was really happening. This surprised him more than it did when he was disguised as Hematite. "Rory...?"

Rory smiled at him and nodded.

They both went in for the second kiss. Kane's lips were soft against Rory's, and she immediately noticed how slow and gentle he was, which was unexpected but pleasant. Rory felt as if Kane were acting like she was made of porcelain as they kissed, but the passion from eight years of repressed feelings remained.

CHAPTER SEVENTEEN

It felt different for him now that he wasn't disguised as Hematite, like he was finally able to truly express himself to her. Finally, he thought, he could indulge in his deepest desire. One of Kane's hands softly cupped her chin, and the other ran up her side, from her hip to her ribcage, just beneath her chest. As Kane's hand rested there, the kiss deepened but remained slow and sweet. It was a different type of sweetness than he was used to, but still good.

As Kane deepened the kiss and as his grip on her side tightened, Rory moved the kiss forward by guiding Kane to her bedroom and then slowly lowering him back onto her bed. Kane was surprised that Rory was telling him it was okay to advance. He thought his heart was going to beat out of his chest when Rory brought her lips back to his, only for them to detach to head for his jawline. She kissed and dragged her lips against Kane's skin there and down his neck. Kane's breathing hitched when she kissed a certain spot, so she lingered there for a moment as he unraveled.

Kane enjoyed each sensation, but he was also terrified. He couldn't remember the last time he had ever been in a serious relationship, nor could he remember the last time he hooked up with someone—with the exception, of course, being his romp with her as Hematite. He wanted things to work with Rory, but his fears still lingered. But Rory was different from just anyone, and Kane couldn't help but think that as he pulled his own shirt off and continued to touch her.

What Kane didn't know was that Rory was terrified too, despite her willingness, as Kane's fingers fumbled with her bra clasp and released it. As she continued onward, she worried about what this meant for their friendship. Part of her knew, though, that it would all work out, as she glanced at the faint scars littering his torso, including a fresher one along his stomach in the same spot where she had bandaged Hematite.

Rory trusted Kane with her life, and now she was trusting him with her body. She feared him rejecting her after all of this if it was just his emotions running high. But all at once, it felt right to her, and it was liberating. Both of them felt a sense of intimate trust with the other now that they were vulnerable, literally and metaphorically, and knew each other's secrets.

As Kane worked his way up Rory's body, he lingered at her lips before doing anything else. "The second you want me to stop, I will."

"I don't want you to stop," Rory said.

"You're on birth control, right? I didn't exactly expect this to happen," Kane admitted with a nervous chuckle.

Rory nodded. "Yeah. You're fine, Kay."

Because their first time intimate together happened with him as Hematite, Kane felt like he was experiencing this now for the first time. He wasn't in a rush or worried about hiding anything and thus had every intention of taking his time with Rory. He didn't need to ravage her like a man starved this time but could appreciate the finer details.

Everything about Kane was so undoubtedly familiar to Rory, not just from years of friendship and flirtatious banter, but from her time with Hematite too. Rory tried to silence her thoughts so she could just enjoy the moment, which wasn't difficult with the way Kane seemed to know her body like he was an expert on the subject.

"No more secrets," Rory said against his lips.

Kane just nodded. He knew what she meant, despite the two-fold layers of it. "No more secrets."

That was all the confirmation Rory needed.

When Kane woke up on Sunday morning, he felt disoriented. He had no idea where he was until his eyes adjusted to the light peeking through the blinds. A quick glance around and the feeling of a satin pillowcase beneath his head told him he was in Rory's bedroom.

So, it wasn't a dream, after all, he thought.

Rory was still asleep beside him. Both of them were still naked, her comforter providing a decent amount of warmth despite the early morning chill. Rory stirred in her sleep, so Kane pulled her closer to him and kissed the top of her head.

CHAPTER SEVENTEEN

His heart thumped against his chest when she nuzzled into his body. Kane never thought that this could be his reality.

Kane also thought it couldn't be after this morning. He didn't want to hurt her, and he wagered that trying to brush this off as a one-time thing would hurt her less than potentially getting killed. Before he could get too lost in his own thoughts, Rory woke up. She stretched a bit like a cat in Kane's arms.

"Good morning, pretty lady," Kane said. His voice was hoarse with sleep.

"Good morning, Kay. I can never tell when you're flirting with me for real anymore."

Kane laughed and kissed her forehead. "For real. All the time. I've been too much of a coward to tell you for real, though."

When Rory leaned her head up to kiss Kane on the lips, any thought he had in his mind about telling Rory that they couldn't be like this disappeared. He simply tightened his grip on her body, enjoying the way she felt in his arms and ignored his nagging doubts. Threats on her life aside, Kane was convinced that he wasn't enough for her. But she loved him too, and maybe that was enough after all.

"Is there anything else you'd like to tell me?" Rory asked, a hint of mischief in her voice.

Kane swallowed. He trailed his fingers up and down her spine as he held her. "Like what?"

"Kane, I'm not stupid," Rory said. "I know you're Hematite. I'd bet everything on it." She added with a pout, "And besides, no more secrets, remember?"

Kane couldn't fight her, not here and not now. So, he simply nodded, resigning to the fact that she had him figured out. "What makes you so sure?"

"Your eyes. The way you look at me. The way you kissed me was the same." Just when he thought she was done presenting her evidence, she said, "And the scar on your stomach from when you got stabbed that's still fresh sealed the deal. It's only been about, what, two weeks since then? It's barely faded, Kay. You think I'd forget something like that?"

Kane laughed. "Busted." His smile turned into a frown. "Yep, uh, all my nights of drinking and partying were actually nights I was watching over Riverpeak or a nearby city. If you hate me for lying to you for all these years, then I'd understand," Kane said. "You're well within your right to tell me to go fuck myself."

"Kane, don't be ridiculous." To Kane's surprise, she kissed him again. He had never seen her smile so brightly. "I'm so glad it's you. Not just because I was right, but because it's you."

"I've just been trying to protect you," Kane said. "If I were found out or if anyone were to see you with me, that would put a huge target on your back. But you seemed pretty hellbent on throwing yourself right into the fire anyhow." He gently ran his hand through her hair, letting the loose coils wrap around his index finger. "But know that everything I told you as Hematite... that's all true. And everything I told you last night was true too."

"You're worth the risk to me, Kay. Don't deny yourself what you want because you're scared, okay?"

Kane's heart sunk; Rory suspected, somehow, what he had been thinking earlier. Her words continued to enable his heart to act over his head.

"Stone Breaker is too close for comfort right now. We'll have to keep things kind of on the down low for now, okay? Just in case. Once he's gone, though, fair game."

Rory nodded. "Okay. I can work with that." She shifted her position so her legs straddled Kane's waist. She traced her hands up his well-defined stomach, absorbing the hardness of each muscle and noticing the many scars of varying shapes and sizes across his torso. When her hands reached his chest, she said, "Thank you for saving my life all those years ago, Kane."

He smiled up at her. "I don't need thanks. But I'm glad I was there for you."

"You always have been," Rory said. "Costume or not."

"I think the word you're looking for is uniform."

"It's a fucking costume, Kay. A cool one, but still a costume."

CHAPTER SEVENTEEN

Kane laughed. Rory had never seen him smile more genuinely as he said, "Fair enough." He pulled her body closer to his to kiss her cheek a few times before he kissed her lips. "You have no clue how long I've wanted this," he said it in a whisper, almost as if he was too afraid that speaking the words out loud would jinx it.

"I understand why you hid all this from me, but I still wish you had told me sooner. I get why you didn't, though. To be honest, I probably would have done the same thing, so I can't really be mad at you."

"You're too good for me; I don't deserve this."

"Nonsense."

"How long have you suspected it was me?"

"A while now. You'd been acting weird, you know that? But after that night..." Her voice trailed off and Kane knew what she was referencing. "I was really sure of it. I was getting suspicious, and I had really hoped it was you, which probably is what helped me see it through."

She leaned down to press her lips to Kane's. He met her halfway there. As Rory kissed him, she brushed her fingers through his blonde hair to comb it out of his face. Kane smiled into the kiss and his expression remained when they pulled away. Rory surprised him by turning over onto her back and bringing him with her, so now his head was using her chest as a pillow, with her arms wrapped firmly around him.

"What are you doing?"

"Holding you," she said matter-of-factly. "I can tell you need it right now, so just let me do this, okay? You'll feel better."

Kane nodded. "Can't believe I'm falling for a cheesy line like that one."

She had been right, so he wouldn't deny her this. Hearing and feeling the rise and fall of Rory's chest and her slow, steady heartbeat made him feel more at ease. His hands ran up and down her arms before reaching her sides. Kane let her hold him like this for a few minutes before capturing her face with his hands to pull her in for a final, deep kiss.

"We should probably get up, huh?"

"Unfortunately. Come on, I'll make breakfast."

Kane could tell that Rory's mind was racing as he helped her cook. She was so laser-focused on making the perfect eggs that he could tell she was disassociating a bit. Kane placed his hand on her shoulder and kissed her cheek to help snap her out of it.

As they sat down, Kane said, "You probably have a ton of questions."

Rory sat at the spot right beside him. "That's the understatement of the century."

"Ask away, sweetheart." He nudged her elbow with his own. "While I still feel guilty for my sins."

Rory nearly snorted. "Okay, first up." She sipped her coffee. "Were you ever planning on telling me?"

"Not at first. I wrestled with the idea a lot, though. But I decided a few weeks ago that I'd eventually fess up sooner rather than later; you just beat me to it." He shrugged as he took a bite of his toast. "My anxiety attack last night helped push everything along too."

"I'm sorry that I didn't consider how this might affect you too," Rory said with a nervous chuckle. "Talk about tunnel vision."

"You don't have to apologize. Worked out, didn't it?" He winked before he added, "No, for real though, this has been a big deal for you. I get that." He leaned over from his seat next to her to kiss her temple to show that he meant it. "What else you got? Nothing is off limits."

Rory pondered for a moment before she asked, "How did you find out that you can't die?"

Kane took a long sip of coffee before he answered. "The hard way. My parents actually saw it all happen."

"Oh my God. Shit, I probably shouldn't have asked that."

"No, no, it's fine." Kane waved a hand as he took another sip of coffee. "I told you nothing was off limits. Hm, let's see. I think I was fourteen, fifteen maybe? That's when I started doing all of this, but I didn't know about the whole 'can't be murdered' thing yet. I tried to take on this guy who was selling drugs; my parents just made the stuff from time to time for

CHAPTER SEVENTEEN

the drug ring, and this was their usual dealer. I got my shit rocked, and he stabbed me right in the side."

Kane lifted his shirt up a bit to point to the spot between his ribs. The scar had faded enough over the years that the naked eye could not see it, but now that she knew to look for it, Rory could spot it clearly.

Kane continued, "I was so scared. Never been more scared in my whole life. My parents didn't wanna get busted, and I didn't want Kayla to see anything, since she was still pretty little. So, I ended up just crawling to the back corner of their shed, thinking about all my life choices. No one called for help." Kane frowned at the memory and his lips made a light smacking sound. "I blacked out after bleeding out. Then I was really confused when I woke up about fifteen minutes later. My parents thought it was just a really awful trip and didn't even realize what happened." Kane lightly scoffed. "They left me on my own to figure it out with my doctor. I took myself, and they weren't really any help either, so that's why I go to Dr. Potter now. He's a weird little fucker who probably orders his groceries from Omega Mart, but he gets the job done, at least, and he doesn't ask me any questions that he knows I won't want to answer."

"Jesus, Kane. I'm so sorry."

"I gotta admit, as nervous as I was about telling the truth, it's nice to not feel so alone with it anymore," he said. "It was a lot for one person to carry on top of everything else, ya know?"

"I can only imagine." Rory grabbed his hand. "And don't worry; I'm not mad. Really."

Kane grinned as he chewed his food. "I really thought you were gonna be beyond pissed. Thanks for understanding."

"That's what I'm here for, isn't it? Wait, one more question. So, how are you changing your voice?" Rory asked. "When you're in your costume, that is."

"Oh, easy. Elijah built some tech into a mask for me. It took us a few tries to get it right, but it's pretty cool. It goes under my balaclava and just has a switch. Only thing is that it has a tiny battery so I gotta recharge it every day."

Kane hid it well in the way he spoke, but he was just as terrified now as he was the first time he died. His fear this morning had been that Rory might consider leaving him for knowing the truth, but that intrusive thought had long since passed; her nonchalance simultaneously did and did not shock him. But he knew Stone Breaker could seriously hurt her and succeed at using her as bait. If their plan went wrong, then it could be all over in a flash. His worst fears were unfolding in front of his eyes, and he felt powerless to stop it, but he knew that this could be their only chance to get Stone Breaker right where they wanted him.

He went to express these fears, but he stopped himself because he knew that now was not the time. Instead, he simplified his thoughts and said, "I'm worried about you, Rory."

"Don't be fooled. I'm freaking out too," Rory said. "I'm trying to not think of what could happen if things go wrong. But I trust you, and I trust Naomi."

"Let's get everyone together today. You can call Naomi. I'll call Elijah. He, uh, he's been helping me for a while now."

"Wait, really?"

"When I first started, I offered him protection for secrecy and tech work. He knows now, though," Kane explained. "I filled him in on the letter last night. Let's have everyone meet at the storage unit this morning."

Rory nodded. "Deal."

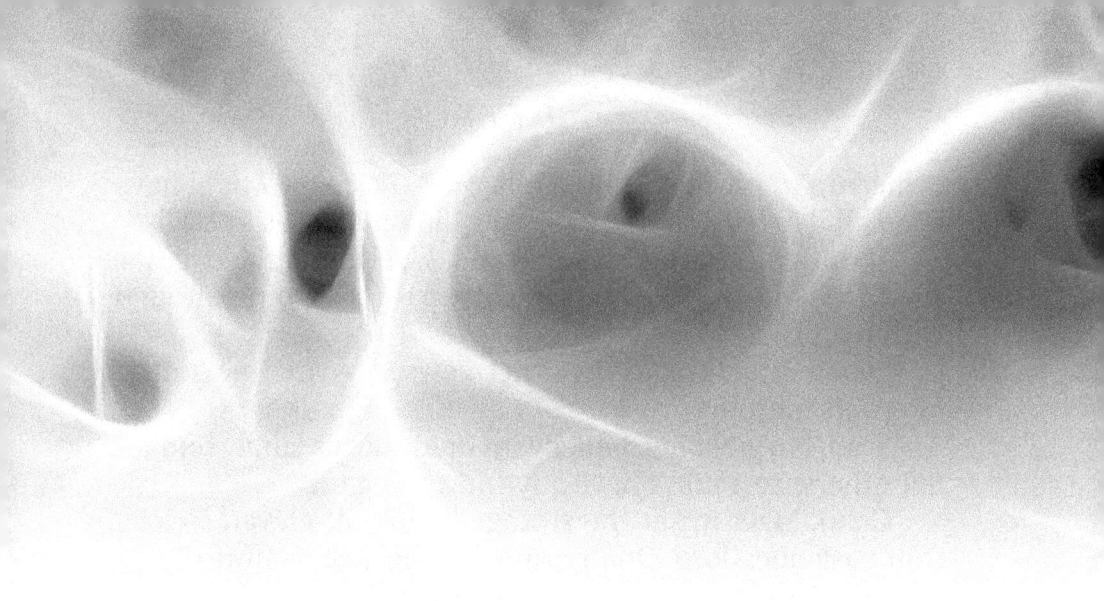

CHAPTER EIGHTEEN

As Rory brewed another pot of coffee downstairs, still on a high from the bliss of the night prior, she set her phone on the counter and put it on speaker. As she waited for Naomi to answer, she grabbed two mugs and hummed to herself. She glanced out the window, noticing that the sky was clear for the day. She welcomed the reprieve from the snow and the way the sun streamed through the window.

"Good morning," Naomi said. "What's up?"

"I have…" Rory pondered the right word, "news. I have a lot of news."

"What kind of news?" Naomi asked. "Hematite news?"

"Yeah. Hematite is here now. Like, right now. He actually has been since last night."

"Did you…?" Naomi sighed. "Again?"

"I mean, yes, but it's not like you're thinking. Just… just hear me out. It's Kane. Kane is Hematite. He told me this morning."

"Rory, Rory, slow down," Naomi said. "What the hell happened?"

"Kane came over last night. He's buggin' out, Naomi. I've never seen Kane so scared in my life. Long story short, he owned up to it when I called him on it. I think it would have been kind of hard to not, given the circumstances, though."

"About damn time," Naomi said. "Well, I'm glad we narrowed that down. So, what's next? Are we still going through with the plan?"

"Even better. This is my other news. Are you free a little later this morning?"

"Yeah, I'm grabbing dinner with Brad and his family tonight, but otherwise, I don't have anything going on."

"Good. Meet me at the storage facility at eleven o'clock. Don't ask questions. Don't bring anyone. Just show up."

"Deal," Naomi said. "I'll see you there. I'm assuming you're bringing Kane?"

"That's correct. We'll get more into it there, okay?"

Meanwhile, Kane was sitting on the edge of Rory's bed, still in nothing but his briefs and a long-sleeved T-shirt. He was grateful that Rory let him borrow her toothbrush, so he didn't have to feel too dirty in his clothes from the night before.

Elijah was quick to answer. "Hey, dude. You're up awfully early for a weekend."

"Yeah, yeah," Kane said. "Sorry if I'm interrupting your family's Shabbat thing."

"You're fine. I could step away. My mom keeps it pretty low-key since it's just us. What's going on?"

"For starters, Rory knows. Don't panic. I told her. I, uh... I told her everything."

"Wait. Everything as in everything?" Elijah laughed. "I'm proud of you, man. What happened?"

"To spare you the gory details, Brad owes you twenty bucks."

"Sweet. I take it that's not all you called to tell me, though."

"You're as sharp as ever. Listen, Rory and I have a plan. Naomi's involved too. We're about to let her in. She's willing to keep helping us. Are you able to meet me at the storage unit in about two hours?"

"Yeah, done deal. I should be out of here by then."

CHAPTER EIGHTEEN

"You sure I'm not interrupting Shabbat?"

"Nah. I think God'll give me a free pass for this. I'll see you later."

As Rory hung up her phone call, Kane announced his presence by wrapping his arms around her waist from behind. He rested his chin on her shoulder.

"Is this okay?" Kane asked, indicating his display of affection.

Rory nodded. "More than okay."

Kane nuzzled his face into her neck before he planted a kiss there. "Good, 'cause I'm not going anywhere."

"I know you're not. But I wouldn't have it any other way."

"I'm kicking myself for not saying anything sooner."

"We've got all the time in the world, Kay," Rory said.

Kane was silent in response. He just nodded and kissed her jaw, feeling unable to get enough of her and like he had to make up for the lost time. He gave himself a moment to soak in the moment before he broke the silence. "Thanks for the coffee." He grabbed his cup. "Naomi's in?"

"She'll be there. Elijah too?"

Kane nodded as he took a sip. He smiled; the coffee was just the way he liked it, a testament to how well she knew him.

"Good. I know Mark is physically weak, but we'll need all the help we can get. Persistent little roach."

"You're really sure it's him, huh?" Kane said. "I think you guys are right, but I never like to be too sure of anything right out the gate."

"We're positive," Rory said. "Though I think there's more than just him waiting behind the curtain."

"One asshole at a time."

Rory brought Kane back to his place before they went to the storage unit so he could get some clean clothes and freshen up. Kane led Rory into his bedroom as he took a quick shower. He swung his closet door open and said, "In case you didn't believe me, feel free to take a look."

Rory did just that as he bathed. The fish-mouthed hoodie from the night she found him on the east side of town was the first thing she saw hanging up. Behind it was a row of black and navy long-sleeved shirts and a few pairs of black tactical utility joggers, all more or less the same pair.

When Kane got out of the shower, he saw Rory still standing in front of the closet. He said nothing at first, wanting to observe her in the trance she seemed to be in. She found the hanger where his cowl was lazily hanging, and her fingers were running slowly over the fabric.

"Do you still have that piece I ripped off for you all those years ago?" Kane asked.

Rory was a bit startled when he broke the silence; she was so focused that she hadn't even noticed the water in the shower stopped running. "I do. I'd never dare get rid of it."

"I remember that night like it was yesterday," Kane said. "Brad told me that Naomi mentioned some guy was creeping you out, so I started keeping a closer eye on you. I was surprised to see you still holding onto that scrap piece when I went to your dorm after changing faster than I ever had in my life."

Rory laughed at the mental image. "This is more than I ever would have imagined."

"I thought about telling you for a long time." Kane stood beside her to grab some clothes. Their shoulders touched as he put on his pants and Rory could smell the subtle sweetness of his body wash. "About this. About how much I liked you. But I kept waiting for the right time. I had every intention of some romantic gesture or something for when I'd tell you I liked you, and I was hoping I could tell you about this just naturally in conversation without springing it on you. But those perfect moments never seemed to come up."

"I both never would have guessed it was you, but always hoped it would be," Rory said. "When Naomi and I started first looking into it, I wasn't sure if I could even trust myself when I thought it could be you."

Kane smiled and kissed her cheek before he put a clean shirt on. "I'm glad I didn't disappoint."

CHAPTER EIGHTEEN

Rory laughed. "You could never."

"Even after all the lying?"

Rory nodded. She could sense that this was the first time Kane truly showed his feelings for her without hiding behind a joke. "I told you, I get it. Kay, I am not walking away from this. I'm not walking away from you."

When Kane held her face with both of his hands and kissed her in response, Rory could tell he put every bit of himself into it. Kane's emotions were still running high from the night before and if he had to be completely honest with himself, he was more frightened than he could vocalize. So instead, he opted to just enjoy the way Rory's lips felt on his own while everything still felt so uncertain.

When they reached the storage unit at 10:45 in the morning, Naomi was already there and still sitting in her car. They parked alongside her, and she got out of the car once they did. They were just waiting on Elijah to break away from his mother's Shabbat brunch to join them.

"I can't believe it," Naomi said. "I won't get too into it until we're in a more private spot, but holy shit, Kane."

Kane made a jazz hands motion. "Surprise!"

It wasn't much longer until Elijah arrived. Once the four of them were together, Kane walked them to the storage unit where he took Rory when she first found him nearly two months ago now. He opened the door with ease and, with an extended arm, let his friends go in first before he closed the door behind them. The storage unit was exactly how Rory remembered it, but Naomi took a moment to look around.

"You've been working out of this?" Naomi asked. Kane nodded. Naomi looked at Elijah. "Have you been here or am I the only new one?"

"I have, but it's been a while," Elijah said. "We usually work out of my office these days."

"Wait, your office? Like, your home office? Does Brad know?" Naomi asked.

"No. You know how heavy of a sleeper he is. So, what's the plan?"

"Right now, it's for me to take Stone Breaker's bait," Rory said. "I figured Kane can follow me in secret, and Naomi can be ready to break the story so that way no one can pay their way out of it."

"Exclusive eyewitness reports," Naomi said with a wink. "No one will ever know it's you, Kane."

"Just the way I like it."

"Why don't we hook you up with a tracker, Rory?" Elijah suggested. "I've got something we can use that gets real specific. Think GPS but on steroids. We'll know exactly where you are in the building. You can just keep it in your pocket so it's inconspicuous."

"I like that idea," Kane said. "That'll make me feel better if we can keep tabs on her in case anything goes wrong." He sat in the folding chair and opened the laptop. "Now all that's left is to figure out how I'm going to get into the building. Can't exactly waltz right in the front door."

"If we're tracking Rory, you can stay outside until we know where she is. Then, you can enter from the closest entrance. Might need to break a window."

Kane grinned at Elijah. "I'm not above property damage."

"What about security cameras?" Rory asked.

"I can jam them," Elijah said. "Easy peasy."

"Whoa, whoa, let's slow down for a second," Naomi interrupted. "This is great and believe me, I am all for this. But I need something from Tom before we start breaking and entering. I don't know if it's possible, but it might be worth a shot to try before Rory gets in there."

"What do you need?" Elijah asked.

"I've been trying to find out who his connection to the drug ring is. I looked into his campaign donors and who is funding his campaign, but nothing struck me as out of the ordinary. Lots of small business owners. I think someone is covering something up, but I don't know who. Elijah, how far are you willing to go?"

"I think I've already broken a few laws and gotten away with it. It's whatever. Are you thinking what I'm thinking?"

CHAPTER EIGHTEEN

"If we could get into Tom's computer, it might uncover this whole thing," Naomi said. "I just don't know how locked down a city government server is going to be. It might be a lot of work for you."

"A lot of work? Please, Naomi. That's kindergarten shit. You'd be surprised at how easy it is to get into government-run servers. I swear, it's like they haven't updated a thing since the nineties. I just need you to do something for me to make this work. You should be able to do this yourself, even during the day."

"What's that?"

"There are ways to figure out passwords or what someone is typing just from their keyboard strokes," Elijah said. "If you can plant something in there to get me a steady audio stream, I could get all the info we need to get in there. I'm sure they have a VPN in case any of the employees have to work from home or while traveling."

"Brilliant!" Naomi said. "I'm sure I can come up with a reason I need some quotes for an interview. I can leave something in there for you."

"I have some audio bugs. They're wireless and should do the trick. Next time you swing by to see Brad, I'll get it to you when he's in the bathroom or something."

They were all interrupted by Kane's burner phone ringing. "Hold on guys," Kane said. "I'm sorry. I gotta take this." He answered with a brief hello.

"Mr. Kelly," Dr. Potter greeted. "Are you alone, my friend?"

Kane rolled his eyes; he'd hardly consider Dr. Potter a friend. "No, but I'm with people I trust. Is that good enough?"

Rory, Elijah, and Naomi all looked at each other, hoping to understand. All they found was mirrored confusion on each other's faces.

Dr. Potter said, "Yes, yes, that'll do. I have some results from the sample you brought me. Now, you know I don't do results for things like this over the phone, but I'm available throughout the day if you'd like to swing by. No one else is due to come in except for your friend Shawn Jameson, though I've been calling him for the last three days now."

"Yeah, he beats to his own drum, that's for sure."

"You're more than welcome to bring the people you trust," Dr. Potter said. "I don't care if you come alone or not."

"Solid. Thanks. I'll be there soon." Kane hung up and then looked at his friends. "That was my doctor. I don't know if he's actually a doctor, but that's a whole other story. He runs that lab on the west side of town. I have to head over there. You don't have to come if you don't want to, but it's okay if you do."

"I'm going," Rory said with no hesitation.

"Me too," Elijah said.

"We're here to help, Kane," Naomi said. "You don't have to do this alone anymore."

"Thanks, guys. I'll explain on the way."

"Should we take one car?" Rory asked. "I'll drive."

"Good idea," Kane agreed.

"So, what's going on?" Naomi asked.

"I broke into my parents' shed a few weeks ago," Kane admitted, "when Kayla was in town. I'm assuming all of you know what I mean by that. Anyway, I grabbed a sample to see if we can find out what the hell it is. My hopes aren't really high because their shed nearly caught on fire after they passed out from the fumes, but I figured it was worth a shot."

Kane spent the car ride filling them in on what they may need to know going into their fight with Stone Breaker. As nervous as he was, part of him felt like a weight was lifted now that the burden wasn't only his to bear. He hated putting that onto others, but he tried to allow himself to enjoy the selfishness of it all.

As they made their way down the winding road to Potter Laboratories, Elijah said, "You know, I've always been curious about what was in here. Kinda looks like Convergence Station."

"Potter's morally questionable at best, but ultimately harmless," Kane said. The moose wasn't there, but a few marmots made an appearance now that the temperatures were slowly rising. "I guess I can't judge."

CHAPTER EIGHTEEN

After they entered the building, Kane led his friends down the familiar stretch of hallway before they reached the lobby, where Dr. Potter was waiting in his white coat.

"Well, Mr. Kelly, I have to admit," Dr. Potter said, "it's a relief to see you have friends. I was getting a tad concerned about your lonely soul."

"Whatever. What do you have for me?"

"Come, I'll show you." Dr. Potter began to walk down a corridor without waiting for them. "Now who do we have here? Miss Sato, I recognize you from Channel 10. I'm delighted to see you without any cameras. And you must be Miss Miller from that Stone Breaker video. Who else do we have?"

"I'm Elijah. I'm the IT support."

"Ah, splendid. A pleasure, Elijah. Well, I'll start with the bad news, per se," Dr. Potter said once they reached one of the testing rooms. The blinding white fluorescent lights and spotless stainless steel were cold and intimidating, giving everyone a slight sense of unease. Rows of test tubes, burners, and various tools that Rory only recognized from the chemistry classrooms at the school lined the walls. "The drug was unfortunately rather burnt off and thus not entirely conclusive, but I did want to test one thing before we call this a wash. The good news is I detected traces of methamphetamines, and I think it may still give us some answers."

"What are we testing?"

"If this reacts to your cells. I want to see what happens. Can you spit in this tube for me? Halfway should suffice."

Kane glanced at his friends as he took the vial. "Sorry, you guys. This might be gross."

Once Dr. Potter had the saliva, he put it in a Petri dish and then added a drop of the liquid that Kane brought. Dr. Potter watched the substances through a microscope and smiled in wonder.

"Well, Mr. Kelly, we have at least one answer. This is definitely the drug that was used to give you your powers in utero. I'd be interested in testing Mr. Jameson's as well."

"Wait, Jameson?" Elijah piped up. "Like, Shawn Jameson?"

"Ah, forgive me," Dr. Potter said with a light chuckle. "Well, I suppose now they know."

"Shawn's been helping me," Kane briefly explained. He looked at Rory and added, "Brick Beast. That's the secret identity he gave himself."

"I honestly should have guessed that it was Jameson with a name like that," Rory replied.

"Your results did look very similar, by the way," Dr. Potter said. "I won't say much else for Mr. Jameson's privacy, but I figured you'd want to know after bringing him here."

"Thanks," Kane said. "Was this all?"

"It was for now. Thank you for coming out, Mr. Kelly and friends," Dr. Potter said. "I'll walk you out."

When they got back in the car, Elijah asked, "Should we get Jameson involved? I kinda hate the guy, but super strength could work to our benefit."

"No," Kane said. "I don't want this to be a huge production."

"Fair enough. Should we at least have him on speed dial?"

"We won't need it, but if it'll make you feel better, sure," Kane settled on. "He's not the most reliable. When he's there, he's often a great help. But it's always a 50/50 shot on if he feels like showing up, and another 50/50 shot on if he'll help because he genuinely cares or because he wants to make a name for himself."

"That sounds like Jameson, yeah," Elijah said.

Rory dropped Naomi and Elijah off at the storage unit before she drove Kane back home. When she pulled up to Kane's apartment, they glanced over at one another. Kane reached for Rory's face and caressed her jaw in his hand. "How are you feeling about all of this?"

"A little scared, but I trust you," she said. "I think this will work."

Kane nodded. "I'm glad at least one of us is hopeful."

"I have to be. I think I'd go insane otherwise. Besides, it's for the greater good."

"Not if it means you get hurt. But I'm proud of you."

CHAPTER EIGHTEEN

Rory smiled. She moved her hand to the back of Kane's neck and brought their faces together, so their foreheads touched. "I couldn't have done this without you."

"Nah." Kane smirked. "I know you've always had this in you. You'd be just fine without me." He ran his thumb slowly along her jaw as he pressed his lips to hers. The feeling sent shockwaves down his spine, and he hoped Rory felt the same as he did. "Just please don't do anything rash."

She kissed Kane's nose. "I won't do anything too stupid without you. Don't worry."

"Good."

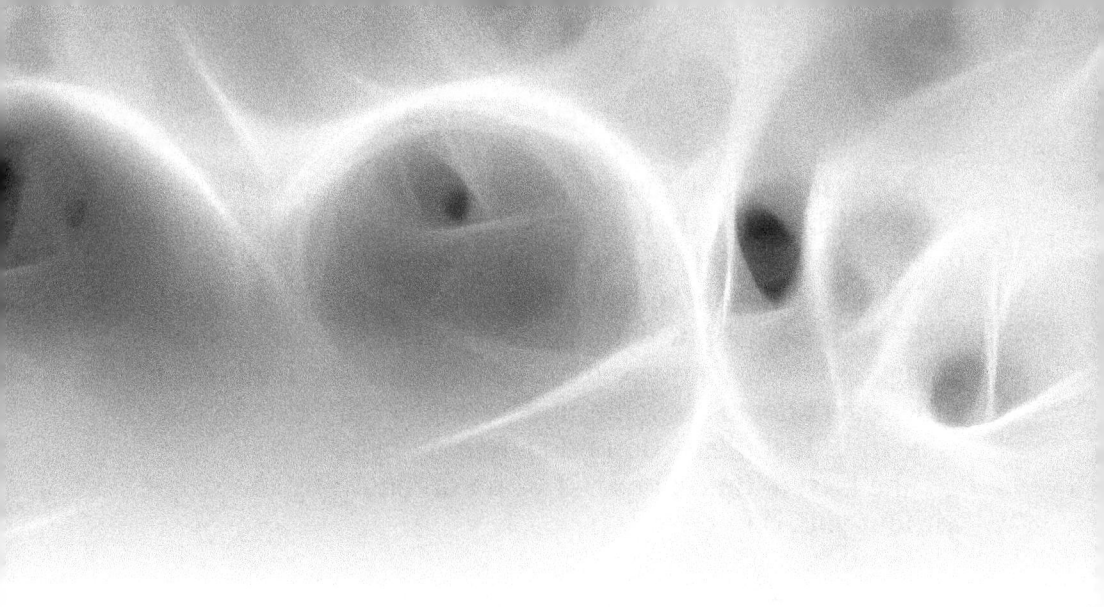

CHAPTER NINETEEN

Rory took a deep breath as she looked up at Riverpeak City Hall on Main Street, the moon shining brightly above it, as if to guide her way. She glanced at her watch, seeing that there were only two minutes until eleven o'clock. She swallowed, unsure whether Stone Breaker would be true to his word and actually show up. As she waited, she hugged her coat closer to herself to generate even a bit more warmth. Even though spring would be there soon, the evening still brought quite the chill. She tried to avoid the voice in her head rattling off everything that might go wrong.

"Rory Miller."

Rory looked up and saw Stone Breaker standing at the top of the city hall steps. He was wearing his 3D-printed mask, but Rory wondered why he even bothered anymore. She decided to not say anything about his identity, wanting to save that for Naomi or Kane in case they needed it.

"Did you think I wouldn't come?" Rory asked as she stepped forward, feeling a fire in her chest that she tried to hide by acting cool and casual. She made her way up the steps. Stone Breaker flinched as she did, clearly on his guard. He crossed his arms over his chest to stabilize himself and hide his fear. Rory added, "You think I don't want to just end this crap?"

CHAPTER NINETEEN

"I wasn't sure if you would," Stone Breaker said. Now that Rory was close to him, she could see the wire of the small microphone. It ran up his shirt and was clipped to the collar; Rory realized that it must be connected to whatever device changed his voice. "Follow me."

Rory just nodded as she followed Stone Breaker. A chill shot up her spine, and she checked over her shoulder every few steps, not wanting to lose her way or be off guard. This was undoubtedly a trap, and she wasn't totally sure what she was walking into. She cracked her knuckles, out of nervous habit, as they walked out and the popping noise from them echoed off of the dark, empty city council hallways. Riverpeak City Hall was small, about a quarter of the size of Denver's, so it made it easy for Rory to see where they'd be going.

As they reached the office labeled with Tom Stevens' name, Stone Breaker held the door open for Rory. "After you."

Rory knew he would make his move now, but she continued to play the part of the unsuspecting victim. The minute Stone Breaker was behind her, she felt him grabbing her hands and tying a rope around her wrists. She shuffled a bit to feign a struggle but had fully expected this to happen.

"I'm surprised you came alone. I doubted you'd have the courage to," Stone Breaker said, "but it's making this all too easy for me." Once her hands were tied, he grabbed her by her shoulders, spun her around, and pushed her backward. Rory stumbled a bit but regained her footing before she could fall; she thanked her boxing classes for that. She glanced behind her and saw that there was a chair there, which was likely where he had been aiming.

"Is there a reason for this?" Rory asked, referencing the ropes around her wrists. "I really don't think this is necessary."

"After what you did to Shatterstone? Oh, it's absolutely necessary," Stone Breaker said. He reached into his pocket and pulled out a handgun. He didn't point it at Rory but simply made her aware of its existence. "Your cooperation is appreciated. Can you sit down for me, Rory?"

It was clear to Rory, even through the mask, that Stone Breaker was serious now. She could feel her heart rate speed up at the sight of the gun, but not wanting to end the operation before it had even started, she took a seat in the chair.

"Thank you."

"Can I ask why you wanted me here if it wasn't for negotiations?"

"You're far too naïve. Haven't you ever seen a superhero movie?" Stone Breaker asked, as he kneeled down by her feet. He pocketed his gun so he could grab the rope with both hands, tying her by her ankles to the legs of the chair. "The superhero always comes and saves the day. I figured you'd have him tailing you right about now. But it looks like you never learn, do you?"

Rory frowned; she knew what he was referencing. "Forgive me for being an optimist, I guess."

"Your optimism has made this easier than I expected," Stone Breaker said, as he grabbed a ring light and shifted it. The sudden addition of a bright light nearly blinded Rory for a moment, the fluoresce of it giving her an instant headache.

"Don't I get to ask you some questions? Wasn't that part of the deal?" Rory asked. "You promised me answers."

"Sure. I suppose I could entertain you while I make sure we have the perfect shot," Stone Breaker said. "What's your first question?"

"You said you know why Hematite can't die. Is that true?" Rory already knew the answer to this question after having gone to Potter Laboratories with Kane, but Stone Breaker didn't know that. She hoped he could give some additional context.

"It's that drug that's popular on the east side of town," Stone Breaker said. "I don't know the exact compounds of it, but it affects women who are pregnant. Gives their babies powers. We're not exactly sure why."

"So why try to cover that up and protect that? Wouldn't that put politicians and leaders in compromising positions if someone like Hematite used their powers for bad?"

"That's where you're playing checkers and we're playing chess," Stone Breaker said. Rory noticed his use of "we" as he spoke. "We're already seeing how we can replicate it in

CHAPTER NINETEEN

living people. Give the people in power even more power, if you know what I'm saying. We're already ahead of the curve."

Rory swallowed at this revelation. "So have you taken it, then?"

Stone Breaker paused; Rory took that as a no.

"You haven't, have you? They won't give it to you."

"You get one last question before I turn the camera on."

"Sure. Why are you doing this?"

"Do you know what it's like to be bullied, Miss Miller? To feel alone?" Stone Breaker said. He paced the office.

Rory tried not to laugh. "Come on, dude. Look at me and take a wild guess."

Stone Breaker seemed to ignore her, which didn't surprise her. "Everyone around me has always been popular. Influential. Powerful. I go to the news thinking I can finally have my voice heard, and what do you know? Nothing. No one cared. It was always Hematite this, Hematite that."

Rory rolled her eyes when his back was turned.

"I'm still surprised Hematite isn't with you now," he said.

"Well, no one else was doing anything about you," Rory said. "And even Hematite can't do everything by himself."

"This is it for you, Miss Miller," Stone Breaker said. He reached into her jacket pocket, pulled out the tracker, and stepped on it. The crushing noise rang loudly in Rory's ears. "Yeah, I noticed this. This will all get paid off. No one will be any the wiser about what happened to you by the time we're finished."

Rory forced herself to stop for a moment and gather her thoughts. She recognized her mind was going back into dark places and internally thanked Marissa for all the help she had received so far.

Rory wasn't safe now. She knew that her grounding exercises wouldn't work here, but she'd be damned if she didn't try to save herself, regardless. She remembered how Marissa told her it wasn't her fault and how she was stronger than she thought.

She tapped into her fight-or-flight, trying to spin some sort of silver lining for herself. Rory hoped she would one day walk away completely healed but realized that she likely would live with this forever in some way, so she might as well try to make the best of it.

Rory said, "I don't let people treat me like this anymore." She wasn't sure where her courage came from, but she trusted Kane would still pull through despite the tracker being broken. She took a moment to take in her surroundings and saw the bug that Naomi had planted earlier in the week. It was still stuck on the bottom of the desk. She grinned.

"And what's that supposed to mean?" Stone Breaker asked.

"Come closer and find out," Rory taunted.

"Oh, no. I like you right where you are, and I like me right where I am," Stone Breaker said. "I'm sure Hematite will see that your little tracker is broken and come running to the rescue. Then I'll have him right where I want him too."

Rory just laughed. "You never learn, do you?"

Rory couldn't see it beneath Stone Breaker's mask, but his brows furrowed. He knew she was now using his own words against him. "What do you mean by that?"

"I swear to God, you are the densest person I've ever met," Rory said. "You think you can get away with all this just because Daddy is rich, and you feel entitled to your power? Do you think you're actually going to win here? Have you learned anything? Haven't you ever seen a superhero movie?"

Stone Breaker's frown deepened. "What the hell are you talking about?"

Rory felt a sense of accomplishment from his response. He was clearly getting riled up now, and she hoped it would buy both her and Kane some time. "You're just a scared little boy. That's why you've got me tied up, isn't it?"

"Watch it or I'll tape your mouth shut," Stone Breaker barked.

"Do you even realize how bad of a look this is for you? White dude in a mask ties up female Riverpeak teacher as a hostage in a government building?"

"You're awfully sure you'll come out of here ahead. Now watch it or else."

Rory grinned again, but wider this time. "Or else what?"

CHAPTER NINETEEN

Stone Breaker stopped to think instead of answering her right away. He took a step back and paced again. He realized she was right: if anyone found her like this, it would immediately be a public relations nightmare for him and his father. "Fuck!" he said it beneath his breath, but his voice-changer made it loud enough for Rory to hear.

The sound of shattering glass was enough to distract Stone Breaker. Both he and Rory looked toward the source of the noise and saw Hematite leap into the office from the now-open window.

"Hope I'm not late to the party," Hematite said.

"You think I didn't think this would happen?" Stone Breaker laughed and pulled the gun back out from his pocket and pointed it at Hematite's chest. "I came prepared for you this time."

But Hematite was not phased. He made quick work of disarming Stone Breaker; *to call it a fight would hardly be accurate*, Rory thought.

"Cute." Hematite moved to where Rory was sitting and, using a pocketknife, cut the rope holding her wrists together. As he cut the ropes holding her ankles to the chair, he handed her the gun. "You know how to use this?"

Rory nodded. "I know enough." She was reminded of the last time he turned over a gun to her all those years ago when he first rescued her.

"Then I'll let you hold on to this." He made eye contact with Rory to ensure she was okay before he turned to Stone Breaker. "That shit won't work on me, Stevens. You should know that by now."

"You know my name," Stone Breaker said softly.

"Yeah, I do. And I warned you, didn't I? You can't just kill me so easily, and you should have just left Rory Miller out of this. Remember?"

"How long have you known?" It was clear in Stone Breaker's voice, based on the way it shook, that he was panicking.

"A while now. You were pretty easy to figure out. You left all sorts of hints in your articles and then some extra digging from some friends of mine just confirmed the whole thing."

Stone Breaker reached behind him for something on his father's desk. He grabbed the letter opener and unsheathed it, revealing the sharp tip, then quickly threw it at Hematite. He dodged just in time, the opener just missing his arm and instead wedging itself into the wall. Stone Breaker then quickly charged at Hematite, pushing him into the wall with his elbow up against his chest.

"Why won't you die?" Stone Breaker shouted in his face, despite knowing the answer. His frustration had effectively taken over, and Rory's earlier goading hadn't helped his mental state.

Hematite shrugged. "I guess it's just not my time."

Hematite laughed at his own joke as he elbowed Stone Breaker to push him off, but then grabbed Stone Breaker's shirt to gain control. Stone Breaker nearly fell as Hematite ripped the 3D-printed mask off of his face. It made a hollow sound as it slid across the floor before eventually joining the pile of broken glass.

Right when Mark stood up, Hematite front-kicked him in the sternum. Mark flew back into the door before falling down to the ground, and Hematite opened the door to shove Mark down the hallway. As he did, he turned to face Rory.

"Get the hell out of here! I'll take it from here!"

Rory glanced at the broken window as Hematite resumed his fistfight with Mark. With Rory getting to safety, Hematite could fight dirty without worrying as much about Rory getting hurt. Hematite swung again at Mark, who continued to stumble backward from the hit.

Mark knew if he were to stand a chance, he needed to think and to think quickly. As he took another blow from Hematite, he glanced around the dark hallway to see where he could get the upper hand. He recognized the secretary's office and quickly tried the door handle. It was locked. Mark cursed under his breath and quickly kicked the door down. The wood shattered beneath his foot as he kicked it a few more times. Once Hematite was closer to him, he weaseled his way through the hole.

CHAPTER NINETEEN

"Where the hell do you think you're going?" Hematite followed Mark into the room and once he was inside, Mark threw a paperweight at the light above. Part of the cheap panel came crashing down, but Hematite moved out of the way just in time to avoid it. He looked at Mark and saw him rummaging for something in a drawer in the secretary's desk.

Mark pocketed something and then grabbed a stapler. He chucked that at Hematite, who held his arm up to block it but still got whacked in the head. Hematite picked it back up and tossed it aside, wanting it out of the way as he continued to approach Mark. He ran toward Mark, ready to punch him again, but Mark grabbed the punch and pulled Hematite toward him. He placed his arm down on a paper cutter, right by the large blade. Had Mark been stronger, it may have worked, but Hematite kicked him off and moved his arm away before Mark could use it.

The two of them exchanged blows as Hematite tried to lure Mark outside. If Naomi was set up, he wanted everyone to see Stone Breaker for who he really was. As they made their way back down the hallway, Hematite kicked Mark in the stomach. Mark reeled back into the wall hard enough to break the glass on where the fire extinguisher was resting. Mark quickly grabbed it, hoping to have a one-up, and threw the tank at Hematite. Kane caught it and tossed it aside; Mark used the distraction to his advantage by approaching Hematite. He swung a punch before Hematite grabbed him, now taking the lead. Hematite regained control for a moment with a few hits, but Mark was picking up on his movements. Hematite glanced behind him, seeing that they were still heading in the general direction that he wanted them to go toward the entrance. Mark kicked Hematite, which brought him up against the wall at the end of the hallway.

Before Hematite could make another move, Mark charged at him. He grabbed the item out of his pocket and held the letter opener he grabbed from the secretary's desk up to Hematite's neck. He had placed it beneath the thick layers of fabric. The blade felt cool against Hematite's skin.

"Got you, you fucking asshole." Mark used his other arm to keep Hematite in place.

Hematite was backed into a corner and knew if Mark bested him, he'd come back in a few minutes. He didn't care about dying, even if a dull blade to the throat would sting like hell. But he worried about Rory and Naomi. He knew Naomi was waiting outside with the news van, and he wasn't sure how far out Rory made it.

"Go ahead." Hematite suspected Mark wouldn't actually slit his throat, which was the only reason he didn't fear calling him on his bluff. "I can't die, anyway. You already know that."

"Unfortunately, the drugs are the only thing keeping me from completely killing you," Mark said, as he pressed the letter opener deeper into Kane's neck. Kane could feel his pulse rapidly against the spot where the blade applied pressure. "I wonder what'll happen if I can bring you to the rest of them, though."

"To who?"

"My father knows all about it," Mark said, as he made eye contact with Hematite. "Why do you think no one in this town ever gets sober? The real guys in charge make sure of that with their wallets. But you'd never guess who runs the show. Just give up."

Before Hematite could respond, Mark sharply gasped. Mark slowly looked down to his right side and saw a large shard of glass sticking out of the side of his abdomen. Hematite glanced at the piece of glass, wondering where it came from. The blood was already quickly soaking Mark's shirt, but the shard sticking there was blocking it from completely releasing. Mark stumbled backward. It was just enough to give Hematite a chance to grab his billy club and whack Mark down, causing him to fall unconscious. Hematite took a second to collect his breath and whacked Mark one last time with the club to be sure that he was down.

Hematite looked up to see Rory standing before him. Rory's breathing was labored, and a thin sheen of sweat coated her face, likely from nerves. Her hand had a strip of blood cutting across it from how tightly she gripped the glass shard before

CHAPTER NINETEEN

plunging it into Mark's side. There were too many thoughts swirling in her brain for her to vocalize. Despite her red palm's sharp pains, she felt more in control than she had in a long time. Even though Stone Breaker had not been her battle to fight, she still felt a vindication that she hadn't known she was longing for over the last eight years.

Hematite said nothing as he quickly took the few steps needed to embrace her. As he did, he buried his face in her hair, holding on to her tightly. "I thought I told you to get out of here," he said.

Rory smirked. Her lips felt dry, and she felt them crack a bit as she smiled at him. "And just leave you here to fend for yourself? Absolutely not."

Kane kissed the top of her head. Rory wasn't sure he'd ever let her go.

"Do you still have the gun? Please tell me you still have the gun."

"I do. Should we give it to Detective McMahon? I already called him for you. I had his business card on me and used the office phone. He should be here any minute now."

"You did the right thing. Bring it to the station with you later, okay? Now let's get the hell out of here."

Rory nodded. "Okay. But we should grab something from Stevens' office first. Elijah might need it and even if he doesn't, I don't think we'll want it there when the cops show up. I spotted it when I was waiting for you in there."

They power-walked back to where Rory had been held. Rory grabbed the bug that was beneath Tom's desk, ripped it off, and pocketed it where her tracker once was. "Elijah should have everything he needs, by the way."

"Perfect. You ready to go?"

Rory nodded. "Yeah, come on."

The two of them snuck out the window that Hematite broke into so they could dodge any reporters waiting out in the building's front. As they moved through the town to walk back to Rory's car and determined the coast was clear, she called Naomi.

"Are you okay?" Naomi immediately asked. "I hear police sirens. They've gotta be close. I think they're on the way. Was that you?"

"Yeah. I called Detective McMahon. We're out of there. Don't worry," Rory said. "It was Mark, after all. He's unmasked. The mask should still be on the floor of his dad's office, in case Detective McMahon asks."

"Roger that. Stay safe, okay?"

"You too. Call us if you need anything."

"Got it. We're live in ten. I'll text you when we're done."

When they reached Rory's car, Hematite said, "Let's go to Elijah's. They won't think to look for you there, and every reporter in town is going to want an interview."

"Good thinking," Rory said. "How do you feel now that this is finally over?"

Hematite shook his head as he got into the passenger seat. "Part of me is relieved that Stone Breaker's taken care of." He frowned as he remembered what Mark had told him. "But I have the feeling that I have a lot more work cut out for me. This is only the beginning."

CHAPTER TWENTY

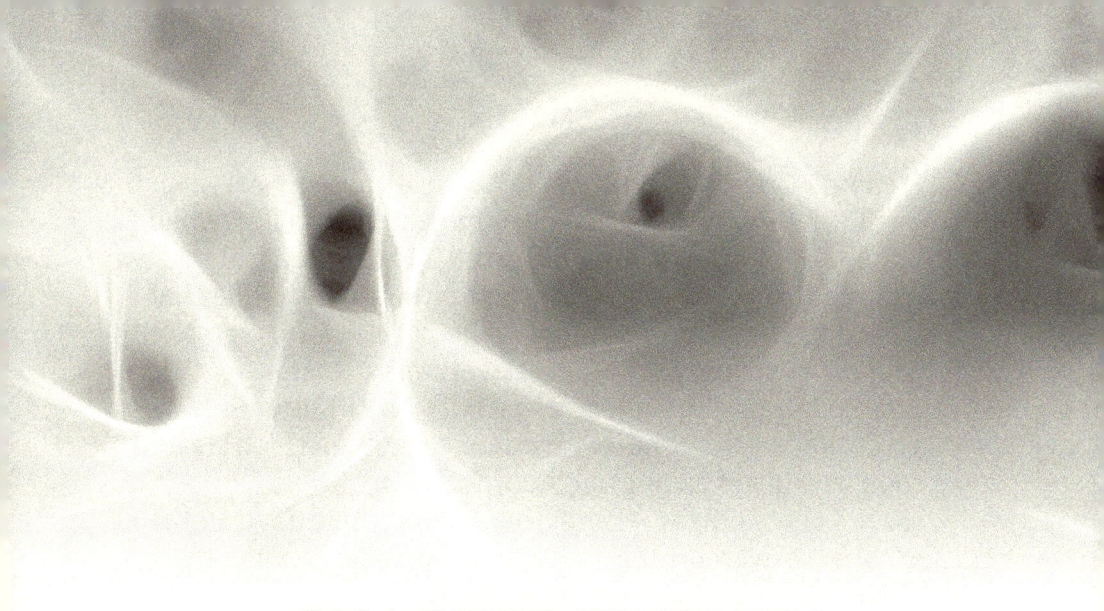

The roads were so dark that Rory felt like her headlights were barely helping, but she didn't dare draw attention to herself with her high beams as she drove to Elijah and Brad's home. Kane still kept his balaclava, cowl, and hood on for an added layer of anonymity, but there was no one else on the road going the same direction, as their car and the streetlights were few and far between. A few news trucks passed by them, heading toward City Hall to report on what had happened.

"You sure you're okay?" Kane asked. He had turned his voice modifier off to preserve the battery. Rory felt at ease hearing his real voice under there, finding comfort in knowing without a doubt that it had been Kane all along.

"I'm sure," Rory said. "I might need an extra appointment with Marissa, but I'm fine." For the first time in a long time, she felt at peace internally. It was so striking to her now, after constantly feeling like she was on pins and needles for all those years. She felt as if a weight had been lifted off her chest that she hadn't even known was there to begin with.

Kane chuckled lightly. "I was really nervous about what might happen if I died."

"What do you mean? I thought you can't be killed."

"I can't," Kane said. "But I wasn't worried about me. I wasn't sure what he might do if he got to me, and you hadn't made it out of there in time." Kane released a long exhale. "I rarely have anyone to live for in a life-or-death situation like that."

She slowed down once she reached the suburbs, grateful for the extra visibility that the streetlamps brought but nervous about being detected, especially with Kane. She was taken out of her thoughts by her phone ringing, which started as soon as she got to her neighborhood.

"Shit," she said. "It's Detective McMahon. I have to take this." She answered him on her car's speaker, connected to the Bluetooth® so Kane could hear too.

"Miss Miller, where the hell did you go?" Detective McMahon asked. "I'm arriving on the scene with a handful of officers I can trust, and the reporter here tells me you're nowhere to be found."

"I was not about to wait around and see if Stone Breaker would wake up," Rory said. "Am I in trouble or under arrest?"

Detective McMahon was silent for a moment. Rory heard him take a deep breath through his nose. "Are you with Hematite right now?"

Rory swallowed. Kane nodded at her, confirming that it was alright to tell the truth. "I am. He's the one who got me out of there safely."

"No, you're not in trouble," Detective McMahon said, remembering his promise to Hematite from a few nights ago. "And I'm not arresting you tonight, Miss Miller. Hematite was the only one to fight with Stone Breaker, right? Right?"

Rory understood what he was getting at. "That's correct, detective."

"I'll get a full statement later but just so I can do my due diligence while I'm here, can you give me a brief rundown of what Stone Breaker did to you?"

"I was tied with rope to a chair. You can see the cut ropes in Tom Stevens' office still."

"We'll have to check tapes too, but knowing Hematite, I will probably have to take your word for this," Detective McMahon said. "Something tells me he had those turned off

CHAPTER TWENTY

like he usually does. You aren't in trouble, Miss Miller. You're a victim. Though I will need you to come down to make your statement, eventually."

Rory faintly heard a reporter—not Naomi, but an unfamiliar voice—asking Detective McMahon if he'd be willing to make a comment.

"We'll call the PIO and let you know when we're going to host a presser. No comment for now... Sorry about that, Miss Miller. If you'd like to wait until the media frenzy dies down, you have my permission to do so. I don't know that my boss will like that, but I can imagine you are very shaken up, especially after being stalked and kidnapped."

"Yeah, definitely. I can swing by later tonight. I will take you up on your offer, though."

"I'll be stuck at the station pretty late. Something like this is gonna require a lot of paperwork, that's for sure. This number is my cell. Just shoot me a text before you come, alright?"

"Thank you, detective." Kane nodded, so Rory said, "Hematite sends his thanks too."

Detective McMahon chuckled. "I appreciate your time. Have a good night, Miss Miller. I look forward to seeing you later."

When they hung up, Rory took a deep breath. She asked Kane, "Can you do me a favor?"

Kane nodded. "Sure. What is it?"

"You don't have to tell her you're Hematite. But can you just text my mom as yourself and let her know that you're with me? And that no matter what she and my dad see on the news over the next couple of days, it's been taken care of? They have been following the story without me really telling them what's going on, and I think they're kind of freaked out."

Kane nodded and grabbed his personal cell phone. "Of course." Kane did so and chuckled to himself when he saw the response from her mom.

"Oh God, what did she say?"

"She said thank you and that if you don't ask me out soon, then she might do so herself. Permission to tell her she doesn't have to worry about that?"

Rory smiled. "Permission granted."

"So, it's not too late for me to ask you on a proper date once and for all?"

She laughed. "I mean, shit, we're both alive. It went as well as either of us could have asked. I think a proper date would be an appropriate means of celebration."

Rory glanced over at him, and she could see his smile reach his eyes.

"I totally fucking freaked when your tracker turned off and Elijah couldn't spot you anymore," Kane said. "Elijah tried to calm me down but, uh, busting through the window, it was. I don't think I've hung up on someone faster. So much for laying out a map of the place to find a discreet entrance."

"I'm okay," Rory assured him. "Your timing actually couldn't have been any better. Mark was rambling about how horrible his life has been."

"Ooh, ouch. That alone had to have been torture."

"Worse than the ropes, that's for sure," Rory said with a laugh. "Seriously, Kay. I'm okay. I, uh, got a little mouthy with him in there. You'd have been proud. Speaking of Elijah, does he know we're on our way to his house?"

"He does. He told me to come here after if we needed. We'll just have to go in through the back, though. I can't exactly hang out on the front steps of someone's house looking like this."

"Fair point."

Rory parked her car in Elijah's driveway on the side furthest from the streetlight to give them some extra cover from the dark. As she looked up at his home, she realized just how intensely she had put her trust in not only Kane and her friends but her own instincts. She wasn't sure if she'd taken the same steps a few months ago, but she was just glad she had now.

"He said the gate to the backyard should be unlocked." Kane tried it and it worked. "Let's go."

Rory followed Kane in before he closed the fence's door and latched it. Rory felt a sense of relief the moment she was on Elijah's property, grateful for the chance to breathe.

CHAPTER TWENTY

They didn't have to wait long for Elijah once they knocked on the back door. Elijah was wearing jeans and a hoodie, having expected their arrival.

"Come on in. Relax," Elijah said. "Let me just double check that all the blinds are closed upstairs in case you need to get up there. You know the drill, Kane."

"Thanks, dude," Kane said, as they came in through Elijah's kitchen. As Elijah moved back upstairs, Kane and Rory took a seat on the couch in his living room. They both released a deep breath, feeling an intense sense of relief, even though they both knew that it would only be temporary. Kane lowered his hood and removed his balaclava now that he was in the privacy of Elijah's house. His cheeks were still flushed from his fight with Mark earlier, but he was otherwise pale from his anxieties.

Kane reached for Rory's hand and gripped it tight. She couldn't tell if he was trying to comfort her or himself. They glanced at one another on the couch. His eyes were wide as he processed the evening's events, and Rory was sure she didn't look much better off than he did.

Rory brushed some of Kane's hair out of his face from where it had fallen out of his ponytail. Her thumb ghosted over a light bruise that had already formed on his forehead.

"You okay?" Only Kane could hear her.

Kane nodded. "Piece of shit threw a stapler at me. I may need your help hiding that with makeup for work. I don't think my hair will totally cover that one."

"I'll grab some in your shade tomorrow morning."

Elijah came back downstairs at that. "Coast is clear, and all the blinds are accounted for. You guys are safe here, and I don't think anyone will think to look here. If they go anywhere, it'll be your place, Rory."

"Thank you, Elijah," Kane said. "I can bring Rory home later. Just want to avoid talking to the media."

Rory nodded. "Seriously, Elijah. Thanks."

"Yeah, no problem. I'm just glad I can help. We've always had each other's backs. That won't change. Here, let me get you some ice for your forehead. That spot looks pretty gnarly."

"Where's Brad?" Kane asked.

"He had to run to his parents' house after work. I don't know when he'll be back," Elijah said from the kitchen. "I can text him, but I don't know if he'll respond. But congrats on finally getting him, you two. Hometown heroes over here!"

"I don't know about that," Kane said with a nervous chuckle, as he leaned back on the couch. He accepted the ice pack from Elijah and used his free hand to hold it up to the forming bruise. His gloves and boxing wraps prevented his hands from feeling the chill. "Sometimes I wonder if there's a better way of going about all of this than just beating the shit out of people. Doesn't feel like there's any heroism there."

"Well, I appreciate you beating the shit out of people when I haven't been able to," Rory said. "I'm sure Kayla does too. And Naomi. And everyone else you've helped."

"Believe me, that thought runs through my head too." Kane squeezed her hand again. "Changes nothing, though."

"Don't beat yourself up, man. Rory's right."

Kane leaned his head against Rory's shoulder, letting his shoulder slouch a bit as he did. "God, I'm fucking tired." Both Elijah and Rory could tell from his tone of voice that he meant both physically and emotionally.

"Let's see if Naomi's up yet," Rory said. "It's only 11:30. Their newscast should still be on. I think they wrap right around midnight."

When they turned on Channel 10, they saw Naomi standing in front of City Hall. Behind her, Stone Breaker was being taken out of the building. The red-and-blue lights from a police car off-camera faintly illuminated Naomi's face.

"Breaking news. Stone Breaker has been caught by the masked vigilante Hematite. Police here on the scene tell me that Stone Breaker's mask was found inside Councilman Tom Stevens' office. They tell me his son Mark was the one behind the mask. Mark is now under arrest on multiple charges, including kidnapping a local woman. Eyewitness reports exclusive to Channel 10 tell me that Stone Breaker brought a Riverpeak High School teacher here to bring out Hematite."

"Thank God," Elijah said.

CHAPTER TWENTY

"I grabbed your bug, by the way," Rory said. "How did that go?"

"Thanks! I got into their server. It took me a few tries, but I have one of my computers set up with their VPN and logged in to Tom's account. I unencrypted the files too." He glanced at Kane. "We can have you gift them to the police tonight if you're taking Rory for her statement. I already made a copy for us to hang on to."

"Good thinking. I'll bring her over later when she's ready. If it comes from me, Detective McMahon won't mind, and chances are he'll let me get away like he usually does. Anything incriminating on there?"

"Oh, yeah," Elijah said with a clap of his hands. "There were so many emails detailing bribes he accepted. Seriously, this dude did not think twice about leaving a digital trail. Typical boomer behavior, I guess." He rolled his eyes with a grin. "Basically, he was being bribed to vote in favor of the guys selling and pushing all these drugs." Elijah paused and blew a raspberry in exasperation. His smile had completely dropped. "I just haven't wanted to say anything to Naomi because it's looking kinda bad for her dad."

"What do you mean?" Rory asked.

"We can't tell her yet," Elijah said. "I'm not totally sure. And regardless, it's looking nasty for Stevens, which is really all I'm concerned about for the time being. But all the dirty drug money is coming from some guys that own franchises of South Main Burgers."

"The restaurant he started?" Rory asked. "I mean, it checks out. He's always lobbied for Stevens. Naomi always tried to convince him otherwise, but her dad never gave in."

"I want to do some more digging first before we say anything to her," Elijah said. "I want to be completely positive. No sense in freaking her out if it's just a coincidence, you know?"

"We have to find out how he's involved," Kane said. "I don't think it's a coincidence. Stone Breaker told me it's not his dad behind all of this, just that he was profiting off it. I don't think he had any direct involvement other than turning a blind eye in exchange for the right price. Plus, Jameson said he saw some suspicious activity by the South Main Burgers in Denver, but he never got with me about if he figured out why."

"Wait, for real?"

"Yeah. He mentioned that all he really got a glimpse of was a ton of traffic in and out of there really late one night. It was well after closing. But you're right in that we shouldn't say anything to her yet, just in case."

"How long has this stuff been going around, anyway?" The more they talked about it and processed it, the more Rory realized how deep this was. "How has this never been on anyone's radar except yours?"

"At least since I was born, and we're all pushing thirty. I'm guessing well before that, though." Kane frowned. "Money's one hell of a drug too, isn't it?"

Rory frowned. "This is so fucked."

"Yeah. What's even more fucked is I think a lot more people are using this here in Riverpeak than we even realize. Dr. Potter ran some extra tests on that sample I gave him. He said even if it wasn't burned to hell, it doesn't look like it's very shelf-stable, which tells me it's probably being delivered only around Denver and some other surrounding cities."

"And if it can't go far, they can't make a profit if they don't have a high local demand," Elijah realized with a sigh.

"There's probably a lot of people who use it, but just aren't addicted," Kane said. "It gets people hyped up. How many people use it to get through a shitty workday, and then the addicted ones get recruited to help them? Just look at my parents, for starters. They've been exploited by those assholes for years."

Rory glanced up and saw a photo of Brad and Naomi from their engagement photoshoot and froze. She remembered her conversation with Naomi a few weeks ago, her words about being suspicious of Noah's death ringing in her head as clear as day.

"Do you think this has anything to do with Noah's death?" Rory asked. Both Elijah and Kane looked at Rory, surprised to hear it. Rory explained, "Naomi told me she wasn't totally sold on her brother's death just being a fire caused by a freak

CHAPTER TWENTY

accident, especially since their dad got out but Noah didn't. She said she wanted to look more into it once the wedding was over and she had the time to, but what if this is why?"

"No way," Elijah said, but not like he entirely believed his own words. "Noah was too good of a guy to be tangled up in all this."

"I think you're on to something, Rory. I know Noah was like an older brother for all of us, Elijah, but think about it. Look at what happened to my parents' shed the other day. They cooked it for too long, passed out from the fumes, and the whole thing nearly went up in flames."

Elijah exhaled. "Shit."

"Especially if it looks like there's a definitive connection to South Main Burgers," Rory said. She shook her head. "Wasn't he working with his dad to help pay off his master's degree?"

"Yeah," Elijah said. "I don't want you two to be right. But Noah's death could be a good place for us to look if we keep going."

They all glanced at the front door as Brad suddenly entered, still in his scrubs from a late work night at the emergency clinic. Brad was a bit of a gentle giant, smaller than Shawn, but still towering above most of his friends. He had been his high school quarterback and was still built like he was, even years later; he had thinned out a bit and his stomach had softened but was still square-framed and wide-shouldered. Since he worked with animals, he kept his dark hair short. Despite his size, he wasn't a threatening guy to look at, the softness in his golden-brown eyes revealing his kindness with nothing more than a quick look.

"Hey, Elijah!"

Brad didn't even notice Rory and Kane at first, going through his usual motions for his after-work routine. It wasn't until the door was locked and his jacket was hung on the coat hanger that he noticed an unmasked Hematite and Rory sitting on the couch.

Brad just stared at them with a blank expression, trying to comprehend what he was seeing before him. As far as Brad was concerned, nothing ever happened in Riverpeak, and his life was a series of routines he was quite fond of. Brad blinked a few times and then rubbed his eyes as if he were imagining things, but Rory and Kane never disappeared from the couch.

"Hey, Brad," Rory said sheepishly to break the silence.

"Hi," he said, clearly feeling lost. "What's…" He pointed at Kane and Rory on the couch and at Elijah standing by them. "What's going on here?"

"I can explain," Kane said. He stood to walk over to his friend, lingering to drop Rory's hand. "Brad, I'm sorry I didn't tell you sooner. But please know that I didn't tell literally anyone until now. Not Elijah, not Rory. It has nothing to do with my trust in you."

Brad scoffed lightly in disbelief. "What, man, are you legitimately Hematite?"

Kane nodded in silence.

Elijah said, "I've been helping him. I didn't know until about two or three months ago, and neither did Rory. She found out after me. A bunch of reporters are desperate for an interview after Stevens' arrest, so I'm letting them hide out here until it's late so they can head home without being bothered. You don't mind, do you?"

"No, of course I don't mind." He sounded like he was in a daze. "Wait, like Councilman Stevens?" Brad asked, the inflection of his voice indicating how truly out of the loop he was. "What happened?"

Kane glanced back at Rory, who spoke up. "His son was Stone Breaker. He kinda kidnapped me tonight." Rory waved her hand toward him in a beckoning motion. "Come on, Naomi's reporting on it now."

Brad looked at the three of them in disbelief. "Wait, for real?"

"Yeah, man," Elijah said.

"Wait, so does Naomi know too?"

"As of a few days ago, yeah," Rory said. "This was the big work project that she told you about. She was sworn to secrecy once we told her it was Kane. I'm sure she'd be apologizing profusely if she were here right now and not on the clock."

CHAPTER TWENTY

"Kane?" Brad asked with a slack jaw. He wanted to hear it from Kane for himself. "This is really for real? You're not joking right now?"

Kane nodded. "Yeah. It's always been me."

Brad ran his fingers through his hair, then over his face. He pinched his nose as he said, "Holy shit, dude."

Hematite & Co. will return to find Noah in
TO BE NORMAL.

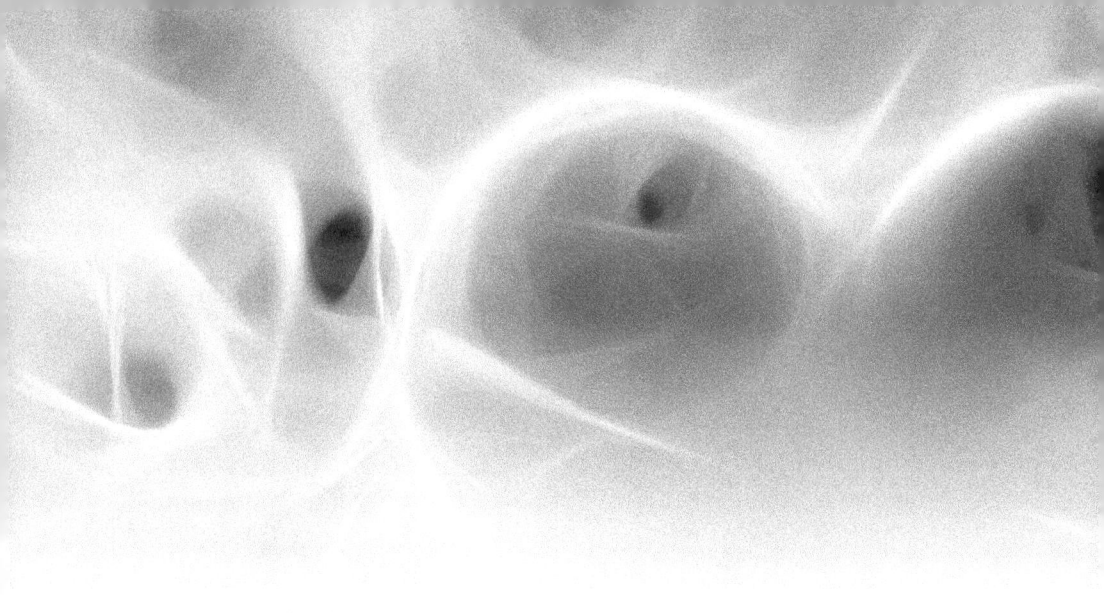

BOOK CLUB QUESTIONS

1. What PTSD symptoms did you see in Rory?

2. Why do you think Kane's power is immortality?

3. Which character did you most relate to and why?

4. How does wealth play a role in the characters' decisions and lives?

5. In what ways is Stone Breaker a foil to Hematite?

6. Kane describes his immortality as a curse when others view it as a blessing. Do you agree or disagree with Kane? Why?

7. Did you agree with Rory's decision to let Hematite keep the mask on while they are intimate? Why or why not?

8. If you were Kane, when would you have told Rory about your secret identity (if at all)?

9. What do you think happened to Naomi's brother, Noah?

10. Which scene(s) stood out to you?

11. What would you do if you were a superhero?

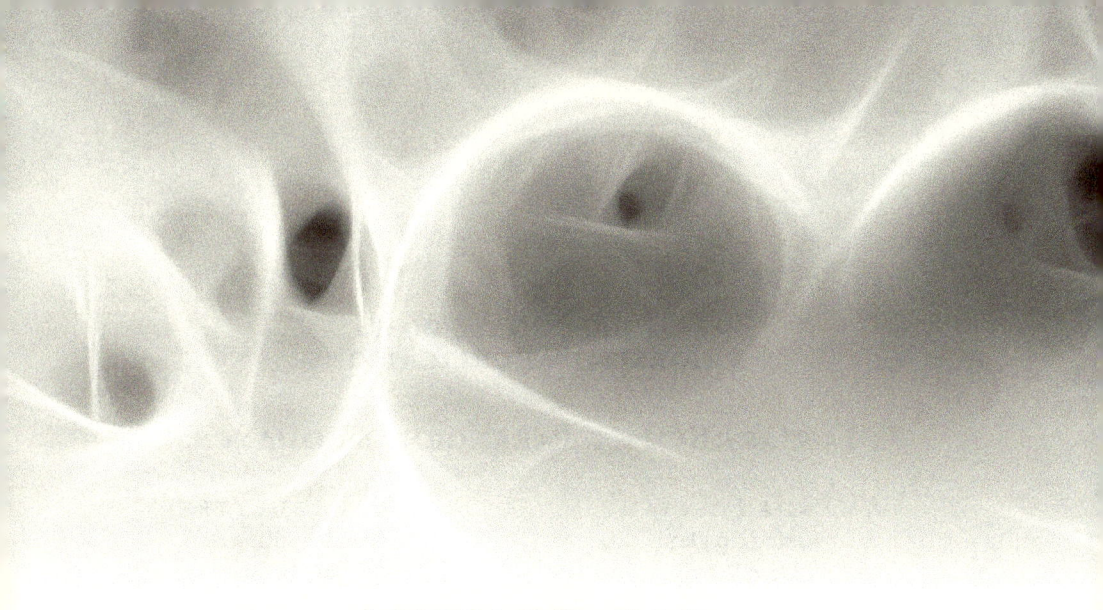

AUTHOR BIO

Jessica Salina is a science-fiction romance author based out of Florida. She's had a lifetime love of sci-fi, fantasy, and superheroes. After getting lost in other worlds growing up, she decided to create her own. When she's not writing, she's often cosplaying from her favorite anime, video games, and Marvel comics with her husband, or finding the next great place to hike. You can find her at jessicasalina.com.

MORE BOOKS FROM 4 HORSEMEN PUBLICATIONS

FANTASY, SCIFI, & PARANORMAL ROMANCE

AMANDA FASCIANO
Waking Up Dead
Dead Vessel

BEAU LAKE
The Beast Beside Me
The Beast Within Me
Taming the Beast: Novella
The Beast After Me
Charming the Beast: Novella
The Beast Like Me
An Eye for Emeralds
Swimming in Sapphires
Pining for Pearls

CHELSEA BURTON DUNN
By Moonlight

DANIELLE ORSINO
Locked Out of Heaven
Thine Eyes of Mercy
From the Ashes
Kingdom Come
Fire, Ice, Acid, & Heart
A Fae is Done

J.M. PAQUETTE
Klauden's Ring
Solyn's Body
The Inbetween
Hannah's Heart
Call Me Forth
Invite Me In
Keep Me Close

JESSICA SALINA
Not My Time

KAIT DISNEY-LEUGERS
Antique Magic

LYRA R. SAENZ
Prelude
Falsetto in the Woods: Novella
Ragtime Swing
Sonata
Song of the Sea
The Devil's Trill
Bercuese
To Heal a Songbird
Ghost March
Nocturne

Paige Lavoie
I'm in Love with Mothman

Robert J. Lewis
Shadow Guardian and the Three Bears

T.S. Simons
Antipodes
The Liminal Space
Ouroboros
Caim
Sessrúmnir
The 45th Parallel

Valerie Willis
Cedric: The Demonic Knight
Romasanta: Father of Werewolves
The Oracle: Keeper of the Gaea's Gate
Artemis: Eye of Gaea
King Incubus: A New Reign

V.C. Willis
The Prince's Priest
The Priest's Assassin
The Assassin's Saint

Discover more at
4HorsemenPublications.com

CPSIA information can be obtained
at www.ICGtesting.com
Printed in the USA
BVHW031541110123
656078BV00011B/41/J

9 781644 507230